THE WILLOW

By Frankee Sullivan

TABLE OF CONTENTS

PROLOGUE

The sky flashed brightly with shades of blue and green as Queen Catrin's carriage drew to a sudden halt in front of an old and tattered chalet just outside Mendacia, the capital of Saleda. The Queen's nose wrinkled in disgust as she breathed in the pungent smells of the slums that she had just arrived in.

Carrying her elegant gown in her hands, careful not to let the fine fabric touch the filth on the ground, she made her way to the door that had been left open. Once she had entered the meager home, she nodded at her advisor, Cormac, who also happened to be her uncle.

The tall and frail man was well-manicured, and his ritzy outfit suggested that he was royalty rather than the hand to the Queen. He held himself in high regard, apparent with how his smile never met his green eyes as he motioned her into the quaint living room.

"I assume you have what we've been searching for," Queen Catrin coldly said as she walked toward the old wooden table inside the cramped living space. A lifeless body of a man with brown hair sat across from her. "Or is there another reason I'm sitting in a peasant's home, with their bodies stinking up the place?"

Cormac disappeared briefly into the adjacent room. When he rejoined the Queen, he proudly held up a beaten and bloodied woman with a swollen belly. Her pale blonde hair matted her face from the tears mixed with blood that streamed from her blue eyes. It was obvious she had just been brutally assaulted by the Queen's men, but the dried blood in between her legs and covering her frock suggested she had also just given birth.

Queen Catrin smiled as her attention shifted from Cormac to the battered woman. "Does she speak?"

He dropped the woman at the feet of the Queen, "She hasn't yet, but I'm sure we can fix that."

The battered woman lifted herself so she was level with the Queen and spat in her face. "I will never tell you where she is," she whispered.

The Queen removed a handkerchief from her gown and wiped the saliva from her cheek before fixing her bright red hair and messing with her lavish crown.

"That is very unfortunate for you," she said, a smile creeping onto her pale face. "Is this your husband?" she asked, pointing to the corpse at the table.

The woman looked away as more tears flowed down her beaten face.

"I'm guessing he kept quiet as well. What a shame," the Queen said as she grabbed the woman's chin and forced her to look into Catrin's hostile gaze. "Tell me where the baby is, and I will make your death quick."

She shook her head. "Never."

Queen Catrin dropped her bloody face and stood. "It can't be far from here. You wouldn't have had the time to plan an escape for it. I made sure of that," she said as she walked around the small room. "But I'm also sure you and your husband were not dumb and likely prepared some sort of hiding place for it."

The woman's arms gave out, and she silently wept on the aged wooden floors.

"Have the guards searched the home?" The Queen asked Cormac.

"Of course they have," he scoffed. "But I wouldn't trust their abilities."

Nodding at her uncle's response, the Queen asked, "How did her husband die?"

"He stabbed one of our guards before they could subdue him. He was stabbed in return." Cormac responded without emotion.

The Queen nodded. "Where was he standing when he stabbed the guard?"

Cormac looked to the guard who stood closest. The armored man nervously pointed towards the bookshelf beside the fireplace.

With the corners of her mouth turning up, she said, "I see." Before moving toward the bookshelf and motioning to two guards to assist her. "See if this shelf pulls out," she ordered.

The woman abruptly lifted her head, and her deep blue eyes widened with fear. "No," she whispered to herself.

The guards began to pull. It took a few attempts, but the shelf started to move.

"Wait!" Cormac shouted. "Instead of pulling both sides, try pulling on the left."

The guards did as they were told, and the shelf slid open like a door. Pleased with themselves, Queen Catrin and Cormac opened the frame all the way until a small child was seen clutching a newborn to her chest.

Without warning, their mother lifted herself to her feet and tackled Queen Catrin back from the children. The beaten woman pulled Catrin's head back with one hand deeply embedded in her red hair. The small child pulled a knife from her pocket, and with the other hand holding her baby sister tightly, she stabbed at the Queen's face, barely skimming her eye. The Queen screamed in agony as blood ran down her face.

Seconds later, the woman's grip went limp, and she toppled onto the ground. A guard had stabbed her in the back. The small child dropped her knife as she stared at her dead mother, who laid on the ground before her.

"That bitch!" Queen Catrin raged and slapped the child across her face and bent down to pick the small knife up from the floor. Just as she was about to stab the little girl, Cormac pulled the knife from her hand. "What do you think you're doing? This little monster tried to kill me! She could have taken my eye if she were stronger!" She roared at her uncle.

Cormac walked past Catrin and peered down at the child, still clutching her newborn sister to her chest. "If they are of the same blood, they may want her as well," he answered his niece. "You must remember why we are here in the first place and ignore your own desires."

The Queen glared down at the small child before she stormed out of the chalet and back to her carriage.

"You're safe," Cormac told the scared child reassuringly. "For now, at least."

CHAPTER 1

19 years later

As I wipe the sleep from my eyes, I can't help but notice that the bed is cold on the other side of me. My older sister, Mia, had fallen asleep beside me just as she had for years. Nightmares sometimes plagued my sleep, and although they didn't happen often, she would always be there to comfort me and hold me. But more often than not, she would be gone by the time I woke up and back before anyone else would notice.

"Finally!" Mia shouted, jolting me into a sitting position. "I was beginning to worry you might have passed on in your sleep," she joked.

I swung my legs over my bed and stretched. "I assumed you'd still be on one of your secret adventures this early in the morning," I told her.

Mia shrugged and made her way over to my side of the bed. "I got you something," she said in a surprisingly sober tone, placing a small velvet pouch in my hand. "I suppose it's a wedding present."

I loosened the ties and discarded the contents when a necklace fell into my palm. My eyes widened at how beautiful the small golden chain was, and I held the pendant up, trying to decipher what it was.

"It's a willow tree," she told me with a sad smile. "I thought maybe you could wear it for the ceremony next week. I remembered how they're your favorite."

Willows had always been my favorite tree. They were known to survive harsh storms and severe weather because of their flexible bark. They could bend to the will of the wind, but they'd very seldom break.

"Mia, this couldn't have been cheap. I can't accept this. You've been saving up to leave Mendacia for years, and this will only set you back."

My sister offered me a smile, but it failed to reach her eyes. "That was when I thought you'd be coming with me. You should know that I'm not going anywhere without you by my side. Remember the promise we made to each other?"

The pain in her voice made my chest tighten, and guilt flowed through my veins, but I nodded my head nevertheless.

"We'll always stick together, and we'll never turn our backs on one another. I meant it before, and I mean it now," Mia stated before continuing, "besides, there are always more jobs to take and more coins to be earned. I'm highly sought after. Aren't you aware?"

She smirked playfully, but I knew her too well to miss the disappointment hidden on her face.

I knew that my sister would never truly be happy inside the gates of this palace. She deserved more than this life, and it hurt to know that I would be the reason she'd never get to leave. I wanted to give her the freedom to choose the life she deserved, but I had no idea how to achieve that without putting both of us in danger. It was hard to find any freedom to give her when I had none myself.

Our parents had died when we were both too young to remember. We were told by the Queen that they were friends of hers, and that is why she decided to take us in. I wouldn't say she raised us, though. The Queen was cold and never showed any affection towards either of us. Instead, she ensured we were fed, elegantly dressed, and educated with what she considered the finest tutors.

Queen Catrin betrothed me to her only son, Prince Seth, on my fourteenth birthday. I would have happily accepted a handwritten note as a gift, but I took the betrothal as a sign that she must have had some sort of sentiment for me. After all, if she disliked me, I do not think she'd wish for me to be her daughter-in-law.

I was often confused by her actions and the reasoning behind them, but I accepted them without question. I was genuinely grateful that she had chosen me and *not* Mia. I would have never wished my future for my sister. She had always deserved much more.

Despite being sisters, Mia and I could not be more different. She was four years older than me and had always been the strong one who was constantly sure of herself and never missed an opportunity to right a wrong. Even her looks radiated strength. Her hazel eyes burned with authority and she often wore her long brown hair tightly tied back, as if she was always ready for a battle. She had paid a seamstress to make leather trousers for her despite the expensive gowns we were expected to wear. They accentuated her long legs, which carried her with both power and grace, which made it hard for everyone in the palace to miss, especially the Queen. Mia was seen as a troublemaker and was long given up on by everyone in the palace, especially the Queen. She didn't mind, though. In fact, I think she found joy in the mortified looks she received as she trotted down the marble halls that she never called home. I would have been too intimidated to even look in her direction if she were not my sister.

I, on the other hand, was the exact opposite. I almost always wore my light blonde hair down and braided back to keep it out of my face. My eyes were deep blue, a great contrast to Mia's. I was also much shorter than her and had curves instead of her athletic build. The seamstresses often said I was lucky to have them, but I wished I looked more like Mia on many occasions. I craved her strength, both mentally and physically. The men in the palace made it abundantly clear on many occasions that they enjoyed my curves; it always made me feel uncomfortable like I was nothing but prey to them. I did not want their lingering eyes on my body.

The biggest difference between my sister and I was my submissiveness. Mia looked forward to a fight, but I on the other hand, I'd do anything to avoid conflict. Early on, I found that life would be much easier if I bent to Queen Catrin and her uncle Cormac's will. They both had violent tendencies that I would do my best to avoid. I had spent years molding myself into precisely what they had wanted: meek and agreeable, traits a good wife must have. If, for any reason, I acted in a way that was seen as unfit, I was punished harshly. And if Mia found out, she would always be close to my aid, followed by an even harsher punishment for herself. That was much worse, I learned. Despite my sister's strong demeanor and courage, it pained me to see her get hurt more than it pained me to get hurt myself. I would take lashings without complaint every time if it meant the Queen would spare her, and more times than not, unbeknownst to my sister, I would. I had become extremely efficient at covering any signs of my abuse so that my sister remained ignorant and wouldn't get involved.

Mia's defiant and strong personality often irritated and angered Cormac and the Queen. Because of this, she was never included when they would summon me. She didn't mind. She would rather sneak out to explore the towns outside the palace grounds. I'd never receive too many details of her adventures, but I would always ask nonetheless. I loved hearing about life outside of the palace. Of course, anything had to be better than dinners and events with the Queen, Cormac, and the Prince.

When it came to my upcoming marriage, I had really tried to be taken with Seth. I was to be his wife and eventually his Queen, after all. Even though I hated the way he had begun to treat the staff in the palace, my sister, or even me on occasion, I forced myself to look past his flaws. I knew that he was my future, whether I had chosen him or not, and I wanted to look forward to marriage with him. I wanted to love him and for him to love me back, just as we had as children.

There was a time when the three of us had all been the best of friends. Seth was two years younger than Mia and two years older than me, and there weren't a lot of kids around our age that lived within the gates of the palace. Despite the Queen's disapproval, we truly loved each other. Then, when I had become betrothed to him, everything changed. He was no longer my childhood friend who I had played and danced with for years, but a distant and sullen version of himself. When he wasn't acting like a spoiled brat, he was making crude comments to me or any other unmarried lady around the palace. While some enjoyed his lewd attention, it only made me miss the old version of him more. I did my best to ignore how he had changed, and it helped that he was truly good-looking. All of the women in the Kingdom thought so. Well, *except* for Mia. It became a habit for me to try and tune out his actions and words and to just pretend that he was the happy-go-lucky Seth I had loved years ago.

His well-kept blonde hair often fell in front of his mischievous green eyes, giving him a boyish charm when he wasn't terrorizing those surrounding him. Seth was lean and very athletic. I often admired his sword fighting technique as he practiced in the courtyard during the afternoons. Mostly because I would try and memorize his form and style in the hopes that he'd finally let me pick up a sword and learn beside him someday. The other reason I had taken up watching him was that during these sessions, he seemed like his old self. As if he had forgotten anything and everything that had caused him to become the ugly version of his former self, and it gave me hope that perhaps he could remain that way for some time afterward, but he never would.

Mia's voice pulled me from my thoughts, "If my sister is to become a Princess, then I will take my rightful place at the royal table," she joked. "But if you were to change your mind, I know this man who lives in town, and he has an entire room dedicated to different explosives. He showed me once because I refused to believe him! We could blow this place up and be out of the capital before they even knew what had happened. We could find a small corner of Lorus to live in and they'd never find us."

I turned to look at my sister, who now stood by the small window looking out at the courtyard. "Mia!" I yelled, trying my hardest not to laugh at her outlandish confession. "First of all, I am very concerned with who you spend your time with while you're sneaking out into town. Second of all, I have no choice. Short of burning down the palace, there aren't a whole lot of options for my future at this point. The Queen has made that very clear."

She rolled her eyes. "Don't you find it a little odd that she betrothed her only son to someone whom she can barely stand to be in the same room with?"

I shrugged and lifted myself from the bed. "Nothing that woman does has ever made sense to me. Why would I start trying to figure her out now?"

Mia chuckled. "Jokes aside, you know that I can get you out of this, right?" She asked me, looking deeply into my blue eyes. "I know this place like the back of my hand. I've been sneaking out of here since I was thirteen. I could get you out without them even realizing it."

I held my sister's hand and smirked at the difference in our skin tones. She always had the perfect olive glow while I was so pale that I almost matched the white sheets on my bed due to barely ever spending any time out of the palace and in the sun. "While I don't doubt your smuggling skills, you know we can't do that. The Queen would happily host a manhunt for the both of us, and who knows if she'd even ask for us to be taken alive. She's done worse before. We'd just become two more missing people in Saleda."

A silence fell between us as we both stared at one another in agreement. Queen Catrin was known for being cruel and strict. The Kingdom of Saleda had become a dark place ever since she acquired the throne. She wasn't royal by birth but by marriage. When the King died unexpectedly, she became the sole ruler. Within a month, she had tripled the taxes of her people, and crime-filled the streets as people became desperate with hunger. Because of this, she forced strict laws and curfews within the city. If anyone were caught breaking her laws, they would be given a harsh and public punishment. In the years of her reign, thousands had gone missing, and it was unknown if their disappearance was related to her strict punishments or if they had found some way to flee Saleda. I had always hoped it was the latter.

There were public flagellations in the townsquare on the same day every week. Saledians were forced to watch their peers endure pain and humiliation for crimes as small as stealing a loaf of bread, but that wasn't even the worst punishment. If anyone were caught speaking out against her or her rulings, they would be hanged for all to see, and their body would be left to rot as a warning to others.

This was why I refused my sister's help in escaping my betrothal. She was the only family I had, and the fear of losing her occupied my thoughts constantly as she continued to engage in her risky behaviors. Once Seth became King and I his Queen, it would be possible for me not only to protect her but to protect all of Saleda from Catrin's cruelty. I had hoped, at least.

A deep sadness filled her hazel eyes as she looked at me before finally pulling me into a tight embrace. "I will never stop protecting you, even if it means certain death," she whispered.

My heart warmed from her words, regardless of the pain I had endured due to her actions, unbeknownst to her. "I know. That's why I have to marry Seth. There has to be some sort of safety when you acquire a title. Right?"

Mia wrinkled her nose before tossing her satchel over her shoulder and walking toward the door. "I guess we'll find out," she muttered. "Anyway, I'm meeting someone at the market in town. I'll be back this evening. Give your sweet beau all my love, okay?" She said sarcastically, prompting me to laugh.

CHAPTER 2

My conversation with Mia replayed in my mind as I quickly got dressed for the day. Queen Catrin had always sparked fear in me. The image of her scarred eye would sometimes visit me in my nightmares, and even during the day, I constantly felt her focus on me even when I walked through the corridors. She rarely said a word, just stared. Cormac was no different. Although he would usually stand in her shadow, his gaze was as cold as ice and made me squirm more than hers did. She was cold and calculated, and she'd wait until the most opportune time to execute her will.

When I was around 14, I was chasing Mia playfully in the courtyard. She had taken a ribbon from the braid in my hair, and I was trying to get it back from her. The Queen had warned me not to run. She had told me it was unladylike, but I was still a child, so I didn't listen. I had run straight into the hard chest of someone I'd seen around the palace but didn't know by name at the time. I was mesmerized by the handsome stranger's green eyes. They were identical to Seth's, but they were warmer somehow, almost inviting, and I was immediately lost in them. The stranger laughed and helped steady me with his hands on my shoulders. No words had been exchanged, but I often thought of him after that. I learned soon after that the handsome stranger was the late King's bastard son, Florian. I had hoped and prayed that no one, besides Mia and him, had seen the incident. After my betrothal, it was forbidden for me to even look in the direction of any other male, let alone touch them. And even though it was not my intention, nor did I even realize who he was, I knew that if the Queen found out, she would punish me.

Weeks had passed without mention of my run-in with Florian, and I thought I had gotten away with it. But one day, I was called into the Queen's chambers, where I was stripped naked and branded with a large royal crest on the side of my lower abdomen. She told me that if I ever thought of 'flirting' with Florian or any other man again, I should remember that I was her property and honor my betrothal to her son.

Just as I was finishing up getting dressed there was a knock on my door. "Come in!" I shouted, smoothing down the ugly dress I was forced to wear. It was an off-the-shoulder white dress with a daringly low neckline and embarrassingly thin fabric. The Queen had permitted Seth to pick and choose everything in my wardrobe. His style was almost profane, but I wouldn't dare refuse to wear any of it.

Seth walked into my room and slowly looked me up and down, which made me shift uncomfortably. "I love that dress on you," he said as he walked closer to me. "But I'd love it even more on the floor." I forced an awkward laugh while internally rolling my eyes at the familiar vulgarity of his words. "Cormac sent me to retrieve you. My mother would like to speak to you."

Dread took over me, and I tried my hardest not to let it show on my face as I nodded. "What do you think she wants to speak to me about?" I asked, following him out into the long corridor that led to the other side of the palace where the Queen's chambers were located.

Seth shrugged. "If I had to guess, she will most likely want to go over things for the wedding next week." I nodded my head again as I continued to follow beside him. "Speaking of which, how are you feeling about everything?"

I lifted my head to look up at him. I couldn't remember the last time Seth had ever asked me how I was feeling, and I couldn't help but wonder if this was some sort of test. "I feel excited," I lied with a sweet smile. "I've been looking forward to our marriage ever since we became betrothed."

His green eyes searched my own for any traces of deceit. "I wouldn't blame you if you were nervous, you know. Our circumstances are slightly less than ideal, and I am well aware of that."

My eyes narrowed as I stared back at him. His openness reminded me of a time when we could talk for hours without the fear of angering him, but I refused to let myself be vulnerable. I was no stranger to what may happen if I said the wrong thing.

"What do you mean?" I asked innocently.

Seth stopped and turned to face me. "Siv, I know things haven't been the same since we were children. I loved you then, and I love you now," he quietly admitted, placing his hands on my shoulders. "But I would be a fool to believe the same goes for you. I know you do not like who I've become in these last couple of years, let alone love me."

I was startled by not only the self-awareness that I wasn't aware he had but also his honesty. "I-"

Seth cut me off before I could say anything. "It's okay if you don't. In fact, that was the entire point. Honestly, I'm surprised you haven't thought of a way to get out of this marriage yet. But I have to warn you about something." He looked around us, making sure we were alone before he continued, "My mother didn't betroth you to me because she thought you'd make a good Queen or wife."

My brows drew together out of confusion as I peered back at him. "I don't understand."

"Look, I know next to nothing about why my mother does the things she does. She tells me next to nothing, but I've been overhearing things." He looked around once again. "I don't ever hear much, but there's something about you that makes you valuable to them. I don't know what it is, but I know that as long as you're an asset to her, you're safe. But that safety can go away in an instant if you're more trouble than you're worth to her."

Confusion clouded my mind. Nothing about what he had just said made any sense to me.

"What is that supposed to mean?" I asked him, trying to keep my anger at bay. I was well aware of the Queen's tendencies, and I didn't need to be reminded of the danger she posed to me and everyone in this Kingdom.

Seth began walking once again. "It means to do whatever she asks of you and to not ask any questions," he said, cutting any emotion out of his voice. "I meant what I said earlier when I told you I loved you, but I can't keep protecting you from her." I bit my tongue and nodded my head instead. It was laughable that he thought he had protected me. I subconsciously rubbed my abdomen where the Queen had branded me years ago. That and all of the other scars she had given me were the only reminders I needed when it came to his mother's cruelty. Where was his protection then?

We had arrived at the doors of the Queen's chambers when Seth stopped and turned to look at me. "Remember what I said," he told me before awkwardly kissing my cheek and walking away, leaving me alone and at the mercy of his mother.

I took a deep breath and balled my shaky hand in a fist to knock on her door. "Enter!" A male voice called from inside.

As I opened the heavy door, I saw Queen Catrin sitting at her desk, and I swiftly curtsied before standing once again. "Good morning, Your Majesty."

The scar next to her cold, pale blue eyes twitched as she looked at me with a look of disgust. "Sit," she ordered, pointing to a chair on the other side of her desk. Her eyes lowered to the golden necklace Mia had just gifted me. "What a lovely necklace. Is it a willow tree?" She asked with venom in her voice.

I nodded. "Yes, my sister gave it to me," I answered.

The Queen scowled, and once I was seated, she slid a small piece of paper over to me.

"What is this?" I asked her while I nervously took it in my hands.

The Queen laughed shrilly. "I was hoping you could tell me," she answered. "One of my spies intercepted this letter, and I'm beginning to believe you're not the sweet little Siv you made yourself out to be."

Panic and fear filled my chest as I digested her words. My mind raced to think of anything I may have said or done to anger her, but I came up short. I lifted the small letter with shaky hands, and my brows furrowed with even more confusion.

All have been prepared and ready for the ceremony. Once the willow has been retrieved, the plan will be carried out. Assemble your team and be ready to finish what we have started.

I shifted my focus from the paper back to the Queen. "Am I supposed to know what this means?" I asked her nervously.

Her nostrils flared as she looked at me across from her desk. "I have given you everything you have ever needed, and this is how you repay me! Have you forgotten who you are? You were nothing when I took you in as a baby! I let you sit at my table and eat my food. I welcomed you into my family, and I even promised you to my son, but this is how you treat me. What have you been plotting?"

Tears began to fill my eyes, and my breathing became erratic. "Queen Catrin, you-you must believe me. I have no idea what this means! I-I don't know who wrote this, and I don't know who it was meant for. I haven't been plotting anything!" I pleaded.

She swiftly rose, knocking her chair over and walked over to the chair I was sitting in. She ripped the golden chain from my neck and threw it to the ground. Looking back at me, she hissed, "you must think I'm a fool!"

"No," I answered in between sobs.

Her cold fingers lifted my chin up to meet her eyes. "You know what? I think I actually believe you, Siv. I don't think you're capable of something like this. You're too weak and too simple-minded to lead. Let alone create a rebellion."

My eyes widened, and my shoulders sagged in relief. I was well aware of the insults she had just thrown at me, but the slight hope that I may leave this room without enduring one of her punishments was enough to have me completely ignore her verbal abuse.

"No, it had to have been that feral sister of yours," she said with a wicked smile.

Whatever sense of relief I had in that moment faded, and my heart dropped. To rebel was to die. If the Queen even remotely thought that Mia was capable of this, she was in danger, and she would surely die for treason against the crown. All she had ever done was protect me, and here I was, feeding her to the wolves.

"No," I said with fake confidence. "Mia had nothing to do with this."

Queen Catrin lifted an eyebrow, making her scar twitch once more as her pale blue eyes examined me. "Then who did?"

I took another deep breath and straightened my spine. Wiping the tears from my face with the back of my hand, I held the Queen's cruel gaze. "I lied. It *was* me. The letter was meant for me."

I had no time to prepare for the swift blow to the side of my face. The throbbing pain made me disoriented, and I hadn't realized that I had fallen from the chair until I attempted to lift myself up from the marble floor, but before I had the chance, a boot kicked me in the ribs, forcing me back onto the ground. As I tried to regain my composure, my eyes focused on the once pristine marble below me that was now splattered with drops of my blood.

Hazy and confused, I looked up from the ground to see that it was one of the Queen's guards who had inflicted my pain. The humor of the situation hadn't been lost on me despite the agony my body was in. The Queen couldn't even hand out her own punishments. She never had. Every lashing I had received was given by a guard or Cormac.

A pained laugh escaped my mouth, surprising me and forcing a bloody cough to follow.

"Is your treachery funny to you?" Queen Catrin asked, looking down at me beside her guard.

I shook my head. "No," I croaked. "It's just ironic how you're so quick to hand out punishments, and yet you're never the one to bestow them."

My boldness had also surprised her as anger transformed her face. "I am a Queen. To touch such filth as yourself or any other peasant in this Kingdom would be an insult to my title," she answered before stooping to the ground and smirking at my helplessness. "Do not forget the only reason you will not find yourself at the end of a rope is because of my mercy." She stood and motioned to the guard to continue with my punishment before she left her chambers.

The world seemed to spin around me as the guard landed blow after blow on my helpless body. A sharp, throbbing pain took hold of me, so much so that all I wanted to do was vomit and hope the pain would come out with it. I had hoped it would stop soon, and surely, there would be an end to it. Ten seconds passed, then twenty, then thirty, but the guards' assault seemed to never end.

As I lay on the floor, accepting every punch, every blow, and every kick, it seemed like the pain had been there forever. In a way, I was getting used to it, but at the same time, the fact that it might last a little while longer was terrifying. But finally, I was no longer able or perhaps simply unwilling to deal with any more agony that day. Ready to block out both the pain and the world, I closed my eyes and let the darkness swallow me and my broken body whole.

CHAPTER 3

It was difficult to focus between the moments of sharp discomfort and the voices surrounding me as I slowly regained consciousness. My head felt heavier and heavier as each pulse of throbbing pain pounded my senses over and over again. Cold shivers shot through my body and I could feel both my hands and legs trembling. I tried my best to block out the excruciating aches, to find some form of meditative trance in order to cope with the agonizing sensations, but all I could do was moan and wreathe underneath the soft sheets of my bed.

"Hey, it's okay. You're going to be okay," a male voice whispered at my side.

I attempted to open my eyes, but my vision was restricted to my left eye since my right was swollen shut. The man kneeling beside me looked familiar but my head was too hazy to figure out how I knew him or where I recognized him from. "W-wha-" I tried to speak, but my throat was too dry and too sore for anything to come out besides hoarse croaks.

"Don't try to speak, just listen," he told me.

I nodded and tried my hardest to place where I knew him from. It wasn't like I had been acquainted with many men over the years. His piercing green eyes were identical to Seth's, the only difference being their shape, and I thought perhaps that was why I recognized him. He ran his fingers through his short brown hair, messing it up slightly. He smiled warmly, and I couldn't help but fixate on the dimple that formed on his cheek as he looked down at me.

"I know you're probably scared and have no idea what's going on. I will have answers for you; I can promise you that. But I need you to be brave, and I need you to get through these next few days, okay?" He took a small glass bottle from his pocket and uncorked it. "This will accelerate your healing, but it's going to make you sleep for a long time. When you wake up, I need you to keep quiet about this and go along with whatever they make you do." He gently placed the bottle to my lips and poured its contents into my mouth. I gag at the horrid taste, which made him chuckle.

A guard from outside my room entered and glanced at the man beside me. "You need to leave now," he tells him. "My shift is up in a few minutes, and the next guard is a loyalist."

The familiar man nodded before turning back to me. "Mia is safe. The Queen is looking for her, but I promise you she is safe," he told me before bending down and kissing my forehead tenderly. I gasped at his forwardness and the novelty of being touched with such gentleness, but he didn't seem to notice.

"I will see you soon, and when I do, everything will be different." With that, he slid the empty glass bottle back into his pocket and discreetly exited my room.

I had so many questions, but my sister's safety made me content with the wave of exhaustion that began to overtake my senses. The excruciating throbs that were overwhelming only minutes ago had become dull aches, and my body no longer felt cold and shaky. It was as if the contents of that small bottle had covered my battered body in a blanket of warmth and comfort. I was more than okay with it as I became consumed with a deep sleep once again.

The soft caress of a hand on my cheek pulled me from my dreamless slumber. As I opened both eyes, I waited for an agonizing throbbing to follow, but I was both surprised and delighted when all I felt was a bit tender and sore. One glance at my arms and hands told me that even though my pain had subsided, the physical marks of my beating were still very much apparent. However, my delight was cut short when I realized the hand on my cheek belonged to Seth.

I looked him over, noticing the purplish bruise underneath his eye but chose to ignore the sympathy that started to rise for him. He had no doubt been injured by the orders of his own mother, but I couldn't afford to feel bad for him when I was fighting for my own life not long before now. "Why're you here?" I asked him with nothing but hostility.

His gentle expression morphed into both surprise and sadness. "I-I've been here every day. I wanted to make sure you didn't wake up alone."

I rolled my eyes and turned my body away from him. "I would have rather woken up alone than next to you," I snapped at him. "You can go now."

I heard him shift in his seat. "You have no right to be upset with me. I didn't do this to you, Siv. If anything, you did this to yourself. What were you thinking? Why would you say you were a part of some sort of treasonous plan?" The softness in his tone had disappeared, and the harshness in his voice reminded me that he was no longer the Seth that had been my best friend growing up but instead the Prince I was being forced to marry. "When will you stop taking the beatings that are meant for your sister," he said under his breath.

I turned back around to face him. "How do you know that I wasn't a part of it? You know nothing about me! You stopped being my friend a long time ago. We're nothing but strangers who are required to marry one another."

Seth didn't do well to hide the shock on his face as he processed my words, and I couldn't blame him. This was the first time I had ever raised my voice at him or expressed the hurt he had caused me.

He loudly swallowed before he responded, "Siv, I know it may seem like I've distanced myself from you, but everything I have ever done has been to protect you from-"

I interrupted him and laughed loudly. "Protect me?" I pointed to my bruised and swollen face. "You've done a swell job, Seth. Truly."

He looked away from me, and silence filled the space between us before he finally stood from his chair. And without a word, he picked me up from my bed and began carrying me out of my room and down the long corridor.

"What're you doing?" I asked him, trying to wiggle my way out of his grip, stopping when the deep throbs echoing throughout my body became too much.

Seth looked down at me, and his pained expression began to fill my chest with dread. I knew that whatever was about to come was not going to be good for me. "I have to do this," he answered. "If I don't, someone will do something worse to you."

My heart began to beat faster, and a cold sweat started to cover my pale skin. "What does that mean? What do you have to do?" I asked him, losing the hostility and confidence in my voice.

He didn't answer me but instead stopped in front of a door that I had never used before and opened it. The small room looked to have been some sort of storage closet at some point, but it was now empty except for a stool and a bucket.

He gently sat me down on the stool before kneeling in front of me. "You don't deserve any of this. I want you to know that I know that," he told me, tears brimming his green eyes. "If I could go back, I'd get you and Mia to run far away from here with me. We'd leave all of this behind. My mother, my great-uncle, this kingdom, everything." He paused, looking at me with pure guilt as he retrieved a small blade from his pocket. "But we're here now, and there's no escaping them or our duties."

"What're you going to do with that?" I asked him as I eyed the blade in his hands.

He looked down at the blade and back to me. "Siv, I would never hurt you."

"If you don't plan to hurt me, what are you going to do with the knife?" I asked him.

Seth ran his hands through my hair as a tear fell from his green eyes. "My mother believes a lesson needs to be learned. I tried to tell her you've been punished enough. I tried to help you, but this is what happens when you speak out against her." Seth pointed to his bruised eye. "I know you already hate me, and you'll hate me even more after this, but I couldn't bear anyone laying their hands on you again." He shifted the knife back and forth, cutting through the first fistful of blonde hair.

Before I could comprehend what he'd done, I saw the locks of blonde fall to the floor, and when he had finally finished lacerating what used to be my long hair, he carried me back to my room. Once he gently placed me down, I limped over and sat at my vanity, looking into the mirror. I counted as I held my breath and then counted again as I inhaled and exhaled. I didn't recognize the bruised and beaten reflection that stared back at me, especially now that my hair had been butchered. I ran my hands through the short, uneven strands.

Seth unevenly inhaled as he stood behind me. "I didn't want to do it, but it was me cutting your hair or my mother ordering a scalding brand to be put to your face," he said before placing his hand on my shoulder and dropping a muddled-up piece of fabric in my lap. "My mother ordered for you to wear this."

I grimaced as I lifted the material, only to realize it was the gown I had been wearing when Queen Catrin's guard had given me my never-ending and barbaric beating. The previously white fabric had been soaked in my blood and now appeared almost entirely a dark shade of crimson.

"I'm sorry," he repeated as he looked down at me with remorse.

"Why?" I asked, reminding myself to breathe and stay calm. "Why does she want me to wear this?"

"I don't know why my mother does any of the things she does," he whispered. "But I do know that if you try to defy her, she will only come down harder on you. I don't want to see you get hurt again, so please, just do what she says."

I knew it was meaningless to try and plead with him so I did my best to stand up, ignoring the dull aches. Seth turned his body away from me in an attempt to offer me some sort of modesty, which angered me even further.

"No," I uttered suddenly, surprising both him and myself. "You don't get to turn away from me when it's convenient for you. You will see every mark, bruise, cut, and brand your mother has given me."

Seth reluctantly turned back around, and for a split second, he flinched but quickly regained composure so as not to let me see. "I know it probably means nothing to you, but I am sorry," he said quietly. His eyes widened for a moment, and he dug his hand into one of his trouser pockets. "I almost forgot. One of the guards picked this up from my mother's chambers. He said it was yours."

I eagerly grabbed the golden chain from his hand after throwing the stained gown over my head and unclasped it, putting it around my neck. Seth stepped closer to help, but I swatted his hand away. I was thankful he had given me back my necklace, but I couldn't forget what he had just done to me or what he had allowed his mother to do to me. "Don't touch me," I told him. "You don't have to act like you're my friend. We haven't been friends in a long time, Seth. We don't have to pretend this marriage is something either of us wants."

I heard Seth take a deep breath. "If only you knew," he said under his breath.

Ignoring his comment, I finished putting the necklace on, and he motioned for me to follow him. While I was happy he was letting me walk on my own instead of carrying me; I had an uneasy feeling about where he may be leading me.

"Where are we going?" I asked him.

Seth's head dropped, and he avoided my eyes as he answered, "Siv, our wedding has been moved up. We're getting married this evening."

My body froze, but he kept walking for a moment until he noticed I had fallen far behind him. "W-why?" I asked him when he had gotten close enough to hear me.

Seth exhaled loudly. "She doesn't want to take any chances. A surprise wedding would make it harder for any planned uprisings."

Although his answer made sense, I couldn't wrap my head around the fact that I was to become Seth's wife so soon, let alone the fact that I was filthy, wounded, and my hair had been unevenly chopped off. Furthermore, I had always assumed the ceremony would still occur in the great hall, as that is where every other marriage ceremony in the palace is held, but Seth had been leading me in the opposite direction of the hall. We were headed toward the courtyard, which overlooked the capital, Mendacia. I could see crowds filling the streets, much like they would if there were a public flogging ordered by Queen Catrin.

My hands began to sweat, and my heart sped up. "Why aren't we going to the great hall?" I asked him.

Seth still avoided my eyes and began walking again. "Mother wants our wedding to be an open event for all to see. Your false confession about the letter has made her believe that your allegiance lies with the townspeople of the capital, and I'm sure this is her way of punishing you for that," he answered without emotion.

It had all started to make sense to me. My beaten appearance, uneven haircut, torn and bloodied gown. Catrin wanted to parade me in front of the entire city like this. It was her ploy to ensure that the people of Saleda would see me as weak and broken. I wouldn't be surprised if this is what she had planned all along.

After a moment of silence, Seth looked back at me. "If you wouldn't have covered for Mia, neither of us would be here right now."

A deep anger woke within me from his words. "She would have done the same for me. You know that," I snapped. "She's not like you. She doesn't just say she'll protect and care for me; she actually does."

Seth stopped and turned toward me, slightly bending so that he was eye-to-eye with me. "Mia is the one who you should be upset with, not me! If it weren't for her galavanting around town and inciting violence among the people, you would have never been beaten and punished. We would have had a grand wedding inside the palace like we deserved and everything would have been fine. But no, she has never been able to conduct herself like a lady. Her insolence is the reason for all of your suffering. It always has been. Nothing will ever change with her. So instead of blaming me for all of this, perhaps you should open your eyes and realize who is really behind all of your suffering, Siv!" he yelled, glaring down at me for a moment more before continuing to the courtyard.

His outburst left me with nothing more to say. I couldn't be sure that my sister was behind the plans of treason against the crown. She had never mentioned being connected to a rebellion or a coup, but I wasn't sure if she would tell me even if she was. All I knew was that Mia would have never intentionally put me in harm's way, but nevertheless, here I was.

The weight of my situation had finally dawned on me, and nothing but fear and anxiousness was left in the wake of my anger. Tears began to fill my eyes, and I couldn't do anything to stop the sobs that began after that.

Seth stopped once more and looked back at me. His face, which had just been twisted with rage, softened, and he closed the gap between us, caressing both of my wet cheeks with his large palms. "Siv, I'm sorry. I shouldn't have said any of that," he sighed. "Look, I'm not going to lie to you and tell you that everything is going to be okay tonight. We both know it's not, but we just have to get through it together. After the ceremony, we'll go back to my chambers, and no one will hurt you. It will just be you and me."

Though his words were meant to be comforting, the idea of being alone with him made me sob even harder. I had always known this day would come. I had always known what my duty to this Kingdom would entail, but I never thought it would be like this. The realization that my body would no longer be my own hit me hard, but at the same time, I realized it never had been anyway. I had endured years of abuse by the orders of the Queen. I had been beaten, whipped, branded, and scarred. Yet the idea of my body being freely given away to Seth scared me more than any of that ever had. I didn't want this, but there was nothing that could be done, and that was maddening.

CHAPTER 4

As Seth's betrothed, I had to attend a few weddings of the Royal court with him. I was forbidden to speak to anyone unless I was spoken to first, and rarely anyone ever did. But I enjoyed watching others have fun. I remember the beautiful decorations, the echoes of laughter, the low hums of music being performed, and the general happiness of the crowds attending. I would observe how freely the other women acted as they spoke and danced with one another, and then I would daydream about what it would be like to have that freedom. I treasured those moments of make-believe.

An open carriage had finally arrived as I was trying to mentally prepare myself to be publicly humiliated. Seth gently lifted me into the seat after I failed at lifting myself in, and when the carriage arrived at the Town Square, it was nothing like those other ceremonies. There was no laughter, music, or decorations. Just a simple wooden platform with torches so all could witness my humiliation. The crowds of people did not buzz with excitement or joy. Instead, they looked uncomfortable. Many even showed looks of outrage. The silence was deafening.

Seth exited the carriage first before he held his hand out for me. Knowing that I would need the help, I reluctantly took it. As soon as I was in view, I could hear audible gasps. My stomach curled in on itself, and I wanted nothing more than to hide, but there was nowhere to go as we climbed the steps to the wooden platform. My eyes followed the old blood stains from the weekly lashings, and I counted the seconds in between the breaths I took, trying my best to avoid a meltdown in front of everyone. I was embarrassed enough by my own appearance, and the last thing I wanted to do was make it even worse for myself. I forced myself to stand tall while nervously holding the thin fabric of my stained gown in my fisted hands. The silence soon gave way to whispers that grew louder until they were no longer whispers but shouts.

"This is a disgrace!"

"How could they do this?"

"Unforgivable!"

I glanced in Seth's direction. He looked genuinely saddened by the reaction from the people and I watched as he searched for his mother. This may not have been the reaction he thought he would receive, but I was well aware that the Queen knew exactly what she was doing. People may give me looks of sympathy, pity, or maybe even outrage, but that just fed into the narrative that I was weak and helpless. She wanted them to see me as a victim because victims could not be leaders.

As if the mere thought of the Queen summoned her into existence, she emerged and was followed closely by her uncle and advisor, Cormac.

"Mother, the people do not seem pleased," Seth whispered in an attempt to get her to stop all of this. "Perhaps we should go back to the palace and have a private ceremony."

The Queen laughed loudly, "You stupid boy. Did you think they would be? Charming the crowd was not tonight's goal. So stop looking like a lost child and stand tall like the King you will be," she said harshly. "If you're capable of such a thing," she quickly added.

Queen Catrin stayed near the back of the platform, and Cormac ushered Seth and me toward the front. Cormac stood before the public, and silence once again filled the air.

"As you all know, you have been ushered here tonight to witness the union between Prince Seth and Lady Siv-" Before he could finish, a voice erupted in the background.

We stand with you, Queen Siv!

My eyes grew wide, and I turned to look at Queen Catrin. For the first time tonight, she looked bothered. The corners of my mouth turned upward. After everything I had been through, the look of anger and bewilderment on her face had brought me some joy. Her ploy to humiliate me was already starting to crumble.

Cormac struggled to regain the crowd's attention as whispers filled the air once more. "As I was saying, the union between Prince Seth and-" He looked down at me and visibly flinched at my bloodied and bruised appearance. "-Lady Siv is a grand celebration that the Queen thought everyone should be witness to."

Unable to listen to Cormac any longer, my eyes began to scan the crowd again. Almost immediately, I spotted my sister deep within the mass of strangers. Tears began to swell in my eyes, but I quickly wiped them away. I wanted to hug her so badly. To pull any comfort from her that I could, but she was there, and I was here. I felt the wall that I had built up to shield my emotions begin to crumble, so I shut my eyes tightly and started counting my breaths once again.

I reminded myself that the Queen could not see her, or she would be taken back to the palace, and who knew what would happen to her there. I had to keep it together. I had to keep every bit of hopelessness, rage, and dread locked deep within myself. So, I forced myself to look straight forward into Seth's green eyes and swallowed the bile that had risen from my stomach. Cormac's voice was all but a deep hum in my head, and the ceremony continued as I willfully left my body. It was easier to completely disassociate than to come to terms with my predicament.

At some point, Seth grabbed a ring from his pocket and began to slide it onto my finger, but before he got the chance, a rock flew from the crowd and hit Cormac right in the middle of his forehead. We all stood there in disbelief for a moment while a thin red line of blood began to fall down his sunken face.

Almost instinctively, I looked toward Mia in the crowd. She was already staring back at me with fire in her hazel eyes. "All hail, Queen Siv!" She yelled loudly.

The focus of the crowd now fell on her, and my chest seized in panic. She would definitely be captured by the Queen now. There would be no stopping it. Why would she do that?

Mia's eyes never left me, and she placed her hand over her heart. Without thinking, I mirrored her hand and placed my own over my heart. This was our goodbye to one another because I knew she'd be put to death for this. Perhaps I would be, too. I knew there'd be no going back.

I heard the Queen barking orders behind me, and Seth was staring at me like he was unsure of what to do. But I stayed standing there with my hand over my heart.

Disbelief swallowed me whole when movement from the crowd stole my attention from my sister. The strangers in the crowd had also begun placing their hands over their hearts. A tear escaped my eyes once more. Then, unexpectedly, someone shouted, "Now!" The crowd suddenly started charging the platform.

Without warning, I was pulled off the platform and into the hard chest of the man I had seen in my chambers, the man who had given me the healing elixir and kissed my forehead. "Try not to panic! I need you to have your head," he shouted above the roar of our surroundings as we ripped through the tide of the crowds ambushing the platform.

Together, we ran out of the street and down an alleyway; the echoes of the crowd disappeared the further we went. Finally, he stopped in front of a large and decaying door and unlocked it with a key he had pulled from his pocket. With the door opened a pungent smell of ale lingered in the air. I realized that we were inside of a pub. I glanced around as he rushed around the bar. I had never been in a pub before, but this was exactly what I would have pictured one to look like. The walls were made up of exposed brick, and candlelight had cast shadows over the random stools and tabletops that littered the aged wooden floor.

I watched as he grabbed a torch from the wall before hurriedly walking towards another door on the opposite side of the room and glanced back at me impatiently. His deep green eyes squinted with confusion and urgency. "Would you rather wait here for someone in the Queen's Guard to deliver you back to the palace, or do you want to follow me?" He asked urgently.

I reluctantly walked towards him. "Where are we going?" I asked as I was pulled through the doorway and into a small stairwell, the only source of light coming from the torch he held.

"So you can speak!" He exclaimed, shutting the door behind him and locking it.

"What's going on? Where are you taking me?" I asked once more.

He squeezed beside me and continued walking down the stone steps until we reached the bottom. "We are taking back the Kingdom," he answered gruffly. "It has been in the works for a while, but we weren't aware that your, uh, *wedding* would be tonight. So we had to improvise," he said as he put his hand on my shoulder, filling me with an unfamiliar warmth. "We are saving you, Siv. Along with everyone else in Mendacia and eventually the entire Kingdom of Saleda."

"We?" I asked, confused.

He pulled me back toward him. "We'll have time to discuss all of this later, but right now, we need to focus on getting you to safety."

Safety.

That word alone pulled me out of my shock and directed my thoughts toward Mia. "What about my sister? I can't go anywhere without Mia!" I yelled as I yanked my shoulder from his grip. "She was in the crowd tonight. She's still out there!"

He stilled for a moment, and then he began laughing.

I pushed his chest with both hands. "It's not funny! She's not safe. The Queen was already looking for her before-"

The man immediately cut me off and placed his hands on my shoulders, causing my cheeks to flush at the novelty of another man's gentle touch. "Siv, I know who your sister is. We all do. Who do you think is behind all of this? Your sister and I have been working together for years now. We knew something had to change, and we are delivering the change tonight," he told me confidently as he let go of my shoulders and walked over to a small table in the corner of the dark cellar we had ended up in.

I watched him, taking in his familiar features. It finally dawned on me who this man was. Although his brown hair was cut shorter and he had filled out quite a bit, he was the same man I had run into all those years ago. He had unknowingly been the cause of the brand I carried on my abdomen. He was Seth's older illegitimate brother. "You're Florian," I said, more to myself than him.

The man laughed quietly, his dimple appearing and his green eyes creasing. "Are you just now connecting the dots?" He asked me. "Yes, I'm the King's bastard son. Your beau's half-brother," he answered playfully.

I cringed. "Seth's not my beau. Our betrothal was forced upon me," I told him sternly. "So, are you the one who sent that letter that got intercepted by the Queen? Is this all because of you? Am I the willow?" I asked him.

His smile dropped, and guilt overtook his features. "Yes and no. Your sister is the architect of this rebellion, Siv. But that letter was never supposed to find its way to the palace and when we found out what had happened, you had already been punished for it. I've never seen your sister so distraught after she had found out. She blames herself." Florian's hands ran through his short hair before he looked back at me. "And yeah, willow was just the alias we made for you at first, but it's kind of become a symbol for the rebellion as a whole," he answered before gently grabbing my necklace and rubbing the pendant between his fingers. "Why did you take ownership of the letter?"

I shrugged. "Mia's life would have been at risk if the Queen thought she was a part of some sort of treasonous act like that. I knew I would be punished harshly, but I also knew she would never kill me, no matter how much she would like to. Seth told me that for whatever reason, I'm an asset to her."

Florian nodded as if he already knew what I had divulged to him. "What you did was brave but stupid. When I snuck into your chambers, you looked like you had been teetering on the edge of death, and that cannot happen again. We need you alive."

"Why?"

Florian's green eyes burned with determination. "I don't have time to explain everything to you quite yet, but we have plans for you. Plans that require you to be among the living."

Although nothing he had said made any sense, I nodded. I wasn't sure I had the strength or energy to learn just what those plans consisted of, so I was content with letting it go for the moment. But there were questions that still needed answering. "How do you know my sister?" I asked him.

Florian smirked. "The night of your 14th birthday, I was still living at the palace."

"I know," I said, without thinking and immediately blushing. I reminded my-self that he didn't need to know about my massive crush on him after running into him in the courtyard.

His smile grew even wider. "I see Catrin wasn't the only one who had her eyes on me." Florian winked. "As I was saying, the night of your 14th birthday, I was sneaking out of the palace when I came across Mia.

"I remember that night. The Queen had thrown an elaborate party for me but forbade Mia from attending, even though she was the only family I had. That was the night she announced my betrothal to Prince Seth," I told him.

"I know," he said flatly, looking at me with deep emotion embedded in his green eyes. "Your sister had been following me for a while, and I had no idea. She finally made herself known and asked if I could teach her how to leave the palace gates without alerting the guards. I was immediately charmed by Mia. Here I was, almost 20 years old, being outsmarted by a mere teenager," he told me, shaking his head with a faint grin. "I agreed and showed her the tunnel entry from the servant's corridor."

"There's tunnels in the palace?" I asked, completely surprised. "That's how she could always sneak in and out without anyone noticing," I said to myself, smiling at my sister's cleverness.

He nodded. "Yes, they lead all over Mendacia. That's how we'll escape the capital. They were constructed hundreds of years ago during the Great War, and the best part is that Catrin, Cormac, and Seth have no idea. They were never meant to rule, so they don't even know their way around the palace, let alone the country." He paused. "Anyways, Mia and I became good friends after that night. I introduced her to the friends I had within Mendacia and, eventually, the friends I had outside of the capital as well. Mia quickly became a leader, and we had start-ed a rebellion before either of us knew it."

A smirk escaped me. That sounded like my sister.

"Without her, I would be just another bastard in the Kingdom of Saleda. She ignited the fire within me. I owe her my life for that." He handed me a leather bag. "When she knew we would have to act tonight, she told me to give you this."

I took the bag from him and spread its contents on the table. There were a couple of pairs of Mia's trousers and tunics, a scarf, undergarments, socks, boots, and a letter in her handwriting. I ripped it open and immediately started reading.

Dear Sivvy,

If you're reading this, my plan worked, and you're currently safe. I will meet up with you shortly, but I need you to find safety first. I know you will try and fight us on this, but please don't.

We have been planning tonight's events for almost five years now. Do you remember the night of your 14th birthday? I remember it like it was yesterday. That was the night I met Florian. That was also the night that we unknowingly began the hidden rebellion. I trust that he will divulge that story to you. Unfortunately, it is too risky to be written at this time.

Furthermore, I ask that you forgive me. No words will even begin to express how sorry I am that I could not have liberated you from that swine sooner. You will always be my sister first. If I had the chance to retrieve you sooner, I would've.

So now, I will remind you of who you are. You are the name and face of the hidden rebellion. You hold the power of an entire nation in your hands. You are our Queen, and you will bow to no one. We will fight for you, and in return, you will lead us to greatness. We will be reunited soon, but until then, hold down the fort.

Love, Mia

P.S. Do you still have a crush on Florian? He's a significant step up from the garbage that goes by the name of Seth.

CHAPTER 5

I swiftly folded the letter and shoved it back in the bag before Florian could get a chance to read my sister's last parting sentences, hoping that he had not already read her words prior to giving them to me. I laughed at her untimely and inappropriate humor, but then the gravity of the rest of her words fell on me. I sat down on one of the chairs adjacent to the table and buried my face in my hands.

"I'm not sure how much she told you, but I'm aware that even the shortest version would be hard to swallow," Florian said as he sat next to me and placed his hand on my bare back.

His touch startled me, and I shied away by reflex.

"I'm sorry," he said as he pulled his hand back.

I glanced back at him, avoiding eye contact. "It's okay. I'm just not used to anyone touching me." I paused. "Not without pain, I guess."

Florian flinched for a brief moment before he looked away. "I may not know the extent of Catrin's actions towards you, but I do know that my brother and his mother are monsters," he said bluntly. "I give you my word. They will pay for their actions towards you and this Kingdom."

I pulled my eyes from the floor and stared at him. His jaw flared with anger, and his fists were clenched. "Why is everyone calling me a Queen?" I asked him. "I have no title. I didn't marry Seth, and I have no claim to the throne."

He turned back to me, and his face softened. "We don't have enough time to explain everything, but I will tell you that you have more claim than anyone else in this Kingdom and that includes Catrin. That throne, that *crown* belongs to you." Florian stood and began walking toward the stairs that led up to the pub. "There's a clean pot of water to bathe yourself in and towels." He pointed to the opposite corner of the room. "Clean up and get dressed. I'm waiting for a signal that the tunnels have been cleared and it's safe for us to travel, but we have a long journey ahead of us," he told me before climbing the stairs and leaving me alone.

The cellar's jagged stone walls were lit by the torch that now hung on the wall by the stairwell. The back wall was consumed by large shelves which harbored books, dishes, utensils, and several other random items. Although slightly chaotic, there was a charm to the dark and damp room. Oddly enough, I found comfort in the disarray. It was the exact opposite of the preciseness that I was used to in the palace, and I wasn't sure when I would feel this sense of safety or ease again. So, I allowed myself to indulge in the feeling while I could.

There was a small mirror above the chest where the pot of water and towels sat. I began to undress and used the smaller towel to rinse my body. Wincing from all the minor scrapes and cuts covering me, I tried to finish up quickly. As I moved the damp towel to my head, I glanced in the mirror. I no longer recognized the face that stared back, but I was eerily okay with that. I washed the blood from my bruised face and rinsed off the dirt and debris from my body. Although I looked far from attractive, I smiled at my reflection. This was the first time I wasn't worried about my appearance. I wasn't worried that the Prince or the Queen would deem my appearance unworthy and force me to change or restyle my hair. I used a straight razor that I had found in a shaving kit on the shelves and shaved what was left of my blonde hair before tying the scarf around my head and changing into the trousers and tunic Mia had packed for me.

Shortly after I was dressed, I heard Florian's heavy steps coming down the stairwell. When he looked at me, his gaze lingered. "What?" I asked him with a defensive tone. "I figured a shaved head was better than that uneven mess your brother left me with."

He quickly dropped his eyes and shook his head. "It's not that," he said. "I've just never seen you in anything other than those foul dresses my brother would pick out for you. You- you look different."

I scoffed. "I'm fully aware of how I look."

Florian shook his head again, chuckling. "That's not what I meant. You looked good then, even in those, but something's different now. You look-" He paused, seemingly stuck. "You look like you're coming into your own if that makes sense."

"Not really, no."

"I'm horrible at this," Florian told me. "I'm trying to say that I think you're beautiful."

Florian's words had left me flustered. "Oh, uh, thank you," I said as I clutched the leather bag to my chest.

I was not accustomed to the kind of compliment he had just given me. How could he think I was beautiful as I was dressed in a mix of Mia's trousers and men's tunics, which were both too long and too big for me. On top of that, I was battered and bruised, with barely any hair. It made no sense to me. I was well-versed when it came to the type of compliments given to me inside the palace walls. Those were calculated and always came with a price, but this was seemingly genuine.

"You must be exhausted after the day you've had," he said, interrupting my thoughts. "Go ahead and rest. I'll wake you up when it's time to go."

I pushed my confusion aside and decided he was right. The adrenaline that had been surging through my veins only moments ago had subsided, and my body felt as though it would give out at any moment. So I made myself comfortable in the chair by the table in the corner of the cellar. Before too long, my eyes had grown heavy, and I had fallen asleep.

I was woken up by someone tapping on my shoulder, and I jumped from the chair.

"Whoa! Sorry, I didn't mean to scare you," Florian said, stepping back with his palms up. "I got the signal. You ready?"

I glanced over my surroundings, remembering the events that had led to me being in the cellar underneath the pub with the man I had fawned over as a child. "Yes," I told him as I stretched my arms over my head and watched him press the stones on the wall next to the shelves as if they were buttons. "What are you doing?" I asked.

He smirked but remained concentrated on whatever it was he was doing. "You didn't think this was just some random cellar of a pub, did you?" All of a sudden, the shelf extended out from the wall. Florian pulled on the frame, which opened as if it were a door. Dust floated in the air as I covered my mouth in shock.

Florian held out his hand, motioning for me to enter the dark tunnel, but I hesitated. All I had ever known was the palace, and the idea of traveling through a dark and damp tunnel made me uneasy. "I promise to keep you safe. Nothing will happen to you if I'm by your side," Florian said, extending his hand.

I took his hand reluctantly, "You're making a lot of promises tonight."

"And I intend to keep all of them," he told me with a look of certainty.

I followed Florian through the dark stone tunnels, unsure of where we were going or how long it would take to get there. So many questions occupied my mind, but I didn't allow myself to interrupt the quiet Florian had left me with. A skill that had been well-developed throughout years of abuse by the Queen and her son.

After walking for about half an hour, Florian broke the silence. "Do we need to take a break?" He asked, looking over at me.

I nodded, gratefully accepting a moment to breathe. My body was still exhausted and my muscles and bones still ached. Every step took immense effort.

We both sat against the stone wall of the tunnel and shared a few sips of the water from a pouch he had brought. "How much do you know about the Kingdom of Saleda before Catrin came into power?" He asked.

Embarrassed, I looked down. "I wasn't allowed to go to school, and my tutor taught me almost nothing about the history of Saleda," I told him.

Florian laughed, but his smile did not reach his eyes. "I don't think it would have mattered if you did go to school," he said, shaking his head. "Catrin has erased any history she is not a part of. Unless you're older, most know nothing about life before Catrin's reign." He helped me back up, and we started walking again. I had to focus on keeping up with his long strides, and my body yelled at me with every movement. "My father's family had ruled for hundreds of years. He married my mother, Queen Rose, and they ruled Saleda for almost ten years before her death," he said with grief deeply embedded in his voice.

My brows furrowed in confusion. "Your mother was Queen?"

Florian smiled briefly before nodding. "I was the only son of King Dramond and Queen Rose. I held the title of Prince before my mother was murdered and my father married Catrin." He explained. "A year after she became Queen, Seth was born. Not long after that, my father mysteriously died in the same manner my mother had. After Catrin was the sole ruler, she stripped me of my title and proclaimed that I was a bastard."

I couldn't help but shudder. "So you are the rightful King of Saleda?" I asked quietly, and Florian nodded.

"That is until you were born," he told me with pride in his voice. "Now, the throne belongs to no one but you."

A line appeared between my brows as I tried to understand. "Mia and I were born with no titles. How can I have more claim to the throne than you? That makes no sense."

Florian chuckled before shrugging. "All in due time, Siv."

I shook my head in frustration. I wanted to argue that he should explain everything to me, but I also knew that I had no leverage in this situation. I was at the mercy of Florian and although I had developed childish feelings for him years ago, the reality was that I didn't know this man. If my time living in the palace had taught me anything, it was to never take safety for granted. I wasn't sure of his temperament, and the last thing I needed was to anger or annoy him while he was leading me to safety, so I kept my mouth shut as I followed him.

After about an hour of traveling through the dark and cold tunnels, we arrived at a stairwell. Florian looked back at me and gave me a reassuring smile before he led the way up. When we reached the top, there was a large latch. "I feel the need to warn you. This place is much different than what you are used to. So stay close, Siv."

Florian pushed the latch open and pulled himself up and out of the tunnel. He glanced back down at me, reaching for my hand. He pulled me up quickly as if I weighed nothing, which was far from the truth. I squinted as soon as the sun's brightness fell on my face. I must have slept longer than I thought if there was already daylight. It took a few minutes for my eyes to adjust, but the sounds of livestock and people shouting were the first thing I noticed when I was pulled up. I was both amazed and startled by my new surroundings. The tunnels had led us up right into the middle of some sort of marketplace. There were booths on either side of us, selling spices, produce, meat, fish, materials, and much more. I watched, bewildered. I had never seen anything like this before.

"Is this what the markets are like back in the capital?" I asked Florian.

He grabbed my hand and led me through the crowded street. "I think they used to be. Now, if anyone steps out of line or raises their voice, the guards could accuse them of making a disturbance, and lashings are given," he told me. "Suffice to say, the markets are a lot quieter nowadays."

I wanted to be shocked, but I wasn't. The guards acted in the same manner inside the gates of the palace. The scars on my back were evidence enough.

"What is this place called?" I asked him.

"We are inside the city of Kantar," he answered as he guided me through the boisterous crowd of people. I had never heard of such a place, but then again, my tutor did not teach much about any city outside of the Capital of Saleda, Mendacia.

We finally reached the end of the market, and the crowds began to disperse. "Where are we going?" I asked.

Florian pulled me forward so I could walk beside him rather than behind him. "I have a place here."

"You live here?" I asked, surprised.

"No, well, yes, kind of. I've been back and forth between Mendacia and Kantar for the last couple of years." Florian explained. "We'll lay low here for a few days until it's safe enough for you to be in the capital."

It occurred to me that still, no part of the plan had been explained to me. "When will you tell me what's going on? We walked almost the entire way here without saying a word, and you told me you'd explain when it was safe. We're safe now, aren't we?"

"I prefer to speak when we're not out in the middle of the street where anyone could listen to us," he said stiffly.

Panic began to creep into my chest. I truly did not know this man, and I began to think about how he could have easily forged that letter from my sister, and he could be taking me who knows where to do and who knows what. The haunting thought that I could be walking into a situation far worse than the one I was just in forced me to a halt. "Florian, I have no idea what kind of man you are or what your intentions may be. I am walking blind, and I am not okay with that. If you don't share even the smallest bit of information with me, then I will make this a lot harder for you," I told him with a raised voice.

Florian rubbed his brow and looked down at me, frustrated. "Siv right now is not the time to grow a backbone. We need to--"

My eyebrows rose and I refused to let him speak any longer as I stared back at him defiantly. "I'm done being quiet. I'm sorry if I picked an inconvenient time for you, but I have been through too much in the last couple of days to let you kidnap me and lead me to an unknown location without asking any questions. I've kept my mouth shut and followed you this far, but you owe it to me to tell me something, anything!" I screamed.

Florian swiftly pulled me into an empty alleyway and covered my mouth with his hand. "I get it! Okay? I get it," he said in a hushed tone. "I'm sorry. I will admit that was harsh," he said, easing his hand. "It's just if the wrong person were to hear us, the entire rebellion could fail, and I-I just can't think about that. I can't think about what would happen to you or us if we failed. I'm just trying to keep you safe, and I can't do that if you're announcing to everyone in the street that you've just been kidnapped."

My mouth fell open. I wasn't expecting him to apologize. In my experience, men barely ever did that. I also couldn't deny that he had a point. My defiance would lead to nothing but more issues, so I accepted that he was my best option at the moment. "Okay," is all I could think to say.

CHAPTER 6

I followed Florian in silence down a long and meandrous path leading us to a small cottage outside of the town. It was made of pale gray stone and had a roof that consisted of hay and rope. A few horses stood behind a wooden fence on one side of the path and a large well on the other. I could see the appeal of this place. Despite how loud it was in town, it was quiet here. It wasn't the kind of quiet that would usually cause me unease in the palace, but a peaceful calm.

"This is where you live?" I asked Florian.

He smiled at me. "I wouldn't say I live here. This is not my home. The capital is. But yeah, this is where I spend quite a bit of time," he answered.

Before I could respond, two massive men walked out of the house and started heading toward us. I would have hidden behind Florian if it weren't for their warm smiles. Florian wasn't a small man by any means, but these men were taller than him by at least half a foot. Furthermore, it was their sheer mass that had me baffled. They were huge. Their muscles looked as if they had been doing manual labor since they were children.

"Welcome back!" One of the men exclaimed, swallowing Florian into a tight hug. He had light brown hair that was slightly lighter than Florians. It reminded me of the chestnuts I had snacked on back at the palace and it fell just below his ears. I couldn't help but chuckle at how uncomfortable Florian looked in the large man's arms. "You must be Siv," he said, letting go of Florian and extending his hand.

I smiled until I noticed his eyes. They were mostly brown but had such a strange hue of red that I had trouble looking away. "Yeah, um, hi," I said, shaking his hand and looking away after realizing that I was staring at him.

He laughed at my awkwardness. "I'm Marco," he said, letting go of my hand and pointing to the other large man who had stopped short of us. "And that strange beast is my cousin, Jude."

I looked behind Marco to see Jude staring at me intensely. It was almost as if he was caught in a trance, and I found myself being pulled into it as well. He shared the same strange eyes as his cousin, a deep brown with a red hue, and they blazed with curiosity. His long black hair was tied into a bun, revealing his handsome face, and I quickly noticed that he had a scar that ran from his forehead down to his chin. I squinted, trying to think of what could have caused it, before catching myself and looking away.

"Jude?" Marco hollered at him when he failed to blink.

The man shook his head, willing himself to blink and made his way over to us. He smiled slightly, revealing a perfect white smile that made me look down at my feet, hiding my blush. "It's nice to meet you, Siv." When I looked back up, my eyes landed on his scar again, and I quickly diverted my eyes down. "It's okay to look. I know it's huge," he said, pointing to the scar.

I smiled at Jude and tried to hide my embarrassment as I shook his hand a little too eagerly. The moment my skin made contact with him, goosebumps covered my body, causing me to jolt slightly. When our handshake seemed to linger a little too long, Florian shifted uncomfortably. "Let's get you inside. We have a lot to talk about," Florian said, ushering me into the quaint home and away from Jude.

The cottage's interior was the definition of cozy and comforting. The stone walls were bare except for a few watercolor paintings and herbs hanging next to the kitchen window. There was a small fireplace with a black pot hanging over the flames, cooking some sort of stew that smelled amazing. A wooden table with four chairs stood in the middle of the main room on top of a faded woven rug. I felt at ease, even though I was a stranger there. Though I'm sure it had something to do with the fact that I was no longer within reach of Catrin, I knew that the coziness of the cottage helped.

Marco and Jude left to tend to their horses out by the stable while Florian ushered me to the table. "You're probably pretty hungry," Florian said, breaking the silence.

I sat down at the table and tried to remember the last time I had eaten or drunk anything. "I'm pretty thirsty, too," I told him.

Florian joined me at the table with a glass of water and a loaf of bread. "I was in the pub with Mia and some other members of the rebellion when we heard word of your assault in the palace," he told me, almost whispering. I cringed, looking down at the bruises on my arms. He noticed and pulled my arm from my lap to the table, where he held my hand. "There are a few guards whose loyalties lied outside of Catrin's reign. They would keep me informed of anything worth knowing, including your safety. Mia knew she couldn't step foot inside the palace or her head would be on a stake, so she sent me to our healer, where I obtained the healing elixir that I gave you." Florian paused again, and when he looked up, his warm green eyes had tears swelling in them. "Your face was so swollen, and your body looked completely broken. How you're on your feet is still a mystery to me."

I nodded, taken back by what seemed like genuine concern on his face. "That elixir really worked some magic on me," I teased uncomfortably, trying to make light of the grim conversation.

He grinned slightly. "You could say that." Florian's face became serious once again. "You have no idea how important you are to all of us. To me, to the rebellion, even to Catrin."

I laughed sarcastically. "I *must* be very important to Catrin. So important that she almost killed me."

Florian glanced sternly at me. "You yield more power than you know. Everyone knows it, including her. She may hate you, but she needs you."

"Florian, I don't yield any power. I'm not special. I'm lowborn. The only thing I had going in my favor was being betrothed to the Prince, and I didn't even want that. I have no claim to anything." I buried my face into my hands. "I'm sorry, but I think you all need to put your faith into someone with a little more- I don't know, experience? I'm not cut out for any of this. Whatever plans you have for me, I don't think I'm capable of them. I don't want you to be disappointed when you realize I'm not whoever you're counting on me being."

Florian smirked as he shook his head. "You have no idea what you're capable of, Siv. You're exactly who we need you to be. Catrin has kept you extremely sheltered for a reason. She didn't want you to realize what and who you are."

He scooted his chair closer to me. "There are things in this world that-" Florian sighed again. "I'm not very good at this. Mia was supposed to be the one to explain all of this. Not me."

"Well then, where is she?" I demanded.

Florian stared at me for a brief moment before speaking, "our original plan was to have her with us when we left Saleda, but everything just- everything got messed up after what Catrin did to you. So we had to improvise, and Mia needed to lead everyone that was left with the aftermath. She refused to leave them all behind, but she didn't trust anyone else with you. So here we are," he explained.

I slid my hands underneath my thighs and breathed in nervously. "Can I ask you something?"

Florian nodded. "You don't have to ask permission, Siv."

I paused before looking back up at him. "Were you and Mia... you know. Were you together?" I cringed as soon as the question left my lips. I knew there were much more important questions that needed to be asked, but I couldn't concentrate without knowing more about their relationship. They sounded like they were close, but Mia hadn't ever mentioned anything about him. It was hard not to feel like my sister had kept her personal life from me for all these years.

Florian stared back at me with surprise before laughing loudly. "No, no, no, no." He told me, still laughing.

I felt my cheeks burn. "It's just- the way you speak about her. You guys just sound close, is all." I tried to explain.

Florian finally stopped laughing. "No, your sister and I never have and will never be together. Although we are very close, and there is love between us, it's more like a sibling-type love." His eyes narrowed. "Wait, do you not-" Shaking his head, he mumbled, "nevermind."

After realizing he wasn't going to continue with his question, I nodded, feeling slightly better about the fact that my sister hadn't kept a relationship from me, regardless of her keeping an entire rebellion and planned coup from me.

Almost as if he could sense how I was feeling, Florian said, "You understand why she couldn't tell you about everything, right?" I shrugged. "She wanted to tell you everything, but we were trying to protect you. The less you knew about us, the safer you'd be. Or so we thought."

I didn't have a chance to ask any more questions before Jude and Marco's voices filled the cottage as they came in from the stable. "Siv, do you like Stew?" Marco asked, looking in between Florian and me.

"Umm, I don't think we ever had stew at the palace," I answered him. "But it smells amazing and I'm pretty hungry still."

Marco quickly grabbed a spoon and bowl from the kitchen and filled it before placing it in front of me on the table. "It's a new recipe that I'm trying. I made it in anticipation of your arrival," he said excitedly, staring at me expectantly.

I tried a bite, and my eyes widened. The savory flavor filled my mouth, and warmth filled my belly as I swallowed. "Marco, this is amazing!" I told him truthfully. "Have you always been such a good cook?"

Jude chuckled. "Absolutely not," he said, sitting beside me. "There were a few rough years of him experimenting before he refined his skill."

Marco shrugged, filling bowls for Jude, Florian, and himself.

My appetite took over, and I spent most of the dinner silently eating while listening to Jude, Marco, and Florian talk. Their familiarity and kinship with one another made me yearn for my own sister. My heart deeply ached as I thought of her and what she could be doing at that very moment. I wanted to be assured that she was safe and that I would see her soon, but I knew assurance would never come. The rebellion wanted a war, and even in my naivety, I knew there was no certainty in war.

"Are you okay?" Florian's voice pulled me from my thoughts.

I nodded. "Yes, I'm fine. It's just been a long day, and I'm exhausted. I'm going to turn in for the night. Where will I be staying?"

Jude stood first, pointing to the back room I was in before dinner. "You're the guest of honor. You will be taking the main bedroom," he said with a proud smile.

Florian stood and pulled my chair out, making me laugh. I allowed myself to take a moment to look him over briefly. His brown hair was a mess after our journey and a loose strand had fallen and caressed his cheekbone. He was wearing a loose-fitting linen shirt that was so thin I could see the silhouette of his sculpted figure underneath. The trousers he had on were a lot more form-fitting, but they required some serious mending. It was hard to believe that this disheveled man was the rightful King of Saleda, but for whatever reason, I believed it. In the short amount of time I spent with him, I had grown to trust Florian more than I had ever trusted a man before.

"I expect answers tomorrow," I told him but looked at all three men. "From all of you."

Each man nodded, and Jude led me to my room. I turned back to say good night to the two other men and I couldn't help but notice Florian looked slightly disappointed. "Thank you again for all the hospitality you've shown me," I said to them, and I meant it.

Jude opened the door to the bedroom where I'd be staying, and I couldn't help but smile at the inviting room. There was a small circular window across from the comfy bed which overlooked a neverending meadow. The sun was just starting to set, lighting up the walls with an orange hue. "It's beautiful," I whispered more to myself than Jude.

"Really?" Jude asked me. "You think so?"

His voice reminded me that I wasn't alone, and my cheeks instantly reddened. There was something about him that made me feel both comfortable and timid. I had just met the man, and yet I wanted nothing more than to know everything about him. "You sound surprised," I said, hiding my face from him.

He chuckled. "I would have thought someone who grew up inside the palace of Mendacia would find this place a little too small or simple for their taste."

I turned to him and furrowed my brows. "I may have grown up in the palace, but it was never lost on me that I didn't belong there," I told him. "Marble floors and golden frames with elaborate paintings of nothing important has never been my style. Your home is soft and warm, and I feel more comfortable here than I ever have there."

Jude smiled and shook his head. "You're not what I expected."

I set my leather bag down on the desk that was across from the bed. "And what were you expecting?"

His smile dropped and I couldn't help but notice his red-hued eyes had traveled to my lips. He straightened his back and quickly reverted his gaze back to my eyes. "I should let you rest now," he said, ignoring my question. "My room is the door to the left of yours. If you need anything, don't hesitate to come get me." And with that, he left me alone in the beautiful, quaint bedroom.

I was surprised by the feeling of emptiness in his absence but shook it off. I realized that Mia hadn't packed any night clothes in my bag, but I didn't want to sleep in my dirty clothing. So I shed my trousers and tunic before sliding open the door to a small closet. Men's clothing was folded neatly on the shelves, and I helped myself. I couldn't help but savor the masculine scent of the soft tunic as I slid it over myself and collapsed against the soft cotton sheets.

CHAPTER 7

Cold, long fingers caressed my cheek, waking me from my slumber. I stretched my arms above my head before slowly opening my eyes. I hastily sat upright when my focus landed on Cormac, a sickening grin forming on his sullen face.

"No, no, no," I began to cry, shaking my head. "How are you here?"

Cormac began laughing, the coldness of his voice sending chills down my back. "We will always find you, child."

I screamed and tried to get away from him, but my limbs refused to move. "Please," I begged. "Please, just let me go." Sobs began to escape me as I realized this was it for me. I would never be able to escape them.

He placed one of his cold fingers against my lips. "Shhhh, you're safe," Cormac told me. "For now, at least."

I writhed and squirmed against his grasp, sobbing uncontrollably. My mind raced as I thought of all the things the Queen would have done to me once I was taken back to the palace. I began to remember the agony from the last beating she ordered, and my sobs became so loud that I almost didn't hear the familiar voice calling to me.

"Siv, you're okay!" The voice yelled. "Wake up! You're safe, Siv. Please, wake up!"

Finally, I was jolted awake. Confusion and haziness clouded my senses, and it took me a moment to realize I was laying in someone's lap with their massive arms cradling me. Panic was still seizing in my chest, and I quickly pushed myself out of their grasp, backing myself into the corner of the room and pulling my knees to my chest.

"Get away from me!" I cried, still shaking.

"Siv, it's me. It's Jude. You're okay. You were having a nightmare."

I wiped the tears from my eyes and allowed my eyes to adjust to the darkness that now covered the small bedroom I had fallen asleep in. "Jude?"

He slowly stood from the bed and made his way over to me. "Yeah, it's me," he said, his voice soothing me and warming the coldness that had seeped into my bones.

The embarrassment of my situation struck me suddenly, and I buried my face into my knees as I sat in the corner of the room. "I'm sorry," I mumbled. "I woke you up, didn't I?

Jude sat beside me and wrapped his arm around me. "I'm happy you did. You shouldn't have to go through something like that by yourself," he told me. "I have them too, you know."

My head sprung up. "You get nightmares?"

Jude chuckled. "Why does that surprise you?"

I looked him over. "I guess it's just hard to believe that someone like you could have something that scares them so much that it haunts them in their sleep." Jude shrugged. "This may be too personal, and you don't have to answer, but what are your nightmares about?"

His face hardened, and I could feel his arm stiffen around me slightly. "I'll tell you if you tell me what yours are about," he answered before turning to me and offering a comforting smile.

I thought about it for a moment before answering, "It sounds silly, but they mostly consist of Catrin and Cormac. Every now and then, a guard will make an appearance, but for the most part, it's just them." I shivered as I remembered their cold smiles and cruel words. "Sometimes I'm receiving punishments from them. Other times, they just verbally assault me. The most recurring nightmare is me finally feeling what it's like to be free of them and then them finding me, telling me that I'm safe with them, but I know that I'm not. I have this feeling of impending doom in every single one. I wake up with it and it takes hours to finally feel okay again."

Jude pulled me closer, gently making circles on my arm with his thumb, but said nothing. After a moment of comfortable silence between us, I looked up at him. "Your turn," I whispered.

His thumb suddenly stopped moving against my shoulder, and he inhaled loudly before speaking, "What do you know of the great war?" He asked me.

"I've heard Florian mention it, but before that, I had never heard of it. I was tutored inside of the palace, and according to him, they taught me next to nothing," I laughed awkwardly, slightly embarrassed by what I began to realize was my lack of education.

Jude nodded. "About a century ago, a war was waged upon my people, The Krigs, by the Vaegarian Dynasty. They saw us as a threat because we wouldn't stand for." Jude paused, rubbing his eyes. "They were doing things that we didn't agree with, and they didn't like how vocal we were about it. Our people had never gotten along, and this was just the final nail in the coffin. Although we could out-fight and out-strategize them any day, they caught us off guard and ambushed us. It didn't help that they had technology far more advanced than any of our weapons. Within a night, more than half of my people were slaughtered, and whoever was left was forced to abandon their homes and seek refuge in Saleda. A lot of us ended up here in Kantar."

My heart ached for him. I could hear the pain in his voice, and it killed me to know that his home and his people had been ripped from him before he was even born. "I'm so sorry," I whispered, resting my head on his chest.

"My people thought Kantar was safe, it wasn't home, but it was a refuge for their families and children, and it was for years, but that safety didn't last after Catrin had become the sole ruler of Saleda. She ordered all and any Krigsman in Saleda to be slaughtered. She believed my race was impure, that we were savages, and we were soiling Saleda's soil by living here." I could feel Jude's heart begin to beat faster as he continued, "Most people knew her claims were outlandish, but there were some who sought her favor and gave us away. I was only ten when someone ratted my family out. My aunt took Marco into the next town over to pick up some material she wanted to use to make a dress for my mother's birthday, and when they came back, blood covered our home. My brother Quinn was fourteen, and my sister Libby was sixteen when they were killed. My mother and father died trying to protect us. This scar was from that night; they assumed I was dead too, but I was barely clinging on to life by the time my aunt and Marco had discovered us."

I couldn't help but wince at his words. My parents had died when I was just a baby, but I still felt their absence deeply. I couldn't imagine the pain that came with not only losing your family at ten but seeing their murdered bodies litter the floor of your home. I had just met this man, but I wanted to ease his suffering. I hated that he carried that with him.

"Marco's father and his older brother had died that night in their own home. His mom and us were all that was left of our family, and we had to go into hiding for several years. That's actually how we met Florian. He had been hiding from Catrin as well. She saw him as a threat once he came of age to claim the throne and she had been trying to kill him, so he had to lay low," Jude slightly smiled as he spoke of Florian, but his face quickly turned serious again. "Our last straw was when my aunt was found in one of the markets, and we never saw her again. After that, we decided we wouldn't hide any longer. I came back here to my family's cottage and fixed it up. We've been living here ever since."

My forehead creased in shock. "This was your family home?"

He nodded. "I know it seems eerie to live in the home your family was murdered in, but I don't see it like that," he told me. "I have so many good memories of them here. Those memories are worth more to me than anything. Catrin's taken enough from me. I wouldn't let her take this place, too."

I smiled against his chest. I admired him so much for how he had overcome all the tragedy forced upon him. "Thank you for sharing this with me," I told him.

Jude smirked. "You're the only person I've ever told any of that too. Florian doesn't even know the details," He squeezed my waist with his hand, sending sparks throughout my body.

I pulled away from his grasp to look at him. "Jude, there's something so familiar about you," I whispered. "Why does it feel like I've known you for longer than a day?"

"You'll find that there are many things in this world that are unexplainable, and perhaps this is one of them," he answered. "You should go back to sleep now, or you'll be sleeping all day tomorrow. If you want answers, you have to be awake to ask them," he teased, grabbing my hand and leading me back to the bed.

After I was underneath the comfortable quilt, Jude turned to leave, but I grabbed his arm. "Um, my sister, she, uh, she used to stay with me until I'd fall back to sleep. Can you-"

"I'll stay with you," he said before I had a chance to finish my sentence, walking around to the other side of the bed. "Nice shirt, by the way," he quietly teased.

I couldn't hide the smile on my face as he sat on top of the quilt and rested his back against the headboard. A dreamless sleep grabbed hold of me quicker than it ever had before.

Several days had passed and I was beginning to form an attachment to Florian and Marco, but especially Jude. The comradery that they had was quickly shared with me as well, and it was hard not to feel like I had known them for much longer than I had. Jude and Florian would often butt heads, but Marco almost always served as the comic relief, and I had a hard time holding in my laughter at most of his witty replies to the men. I still missed my sister dearly, but the friendship I had found with them had made me feel more at home than I ever had before.

Despite constantly seeking answers to my questions, the men had dodged the subject each time. Subconsciously, I was okay with that. I wasn't quite ready to deal with the real world and the problems that came with it. Instead, I was content with pretending as if everything was okay. It made it easy to enjoy myself as well as the company I surrounded myself with.

Jude had been sleeping in a cot in the corner of my room that he had obviously built for himself, as it somehow fit his burly body. I had told him that my nightmares didn't come every night. In fact, I rarely got them anymore, but he insisted on staying with me just in case. He had told me that he didn't like the idea of me tossing and turning in torment while he slept in another room, so I let him. I would be lying if I said I didn't thoroughly enjoy his company in my bedroom, even if he refused to sleep in the same bed for fear of being disrespectful toward me.

A week after I had arrived at the cottage, a woman's laughter from the kitchen forced my eyes from my slumber. The unfamiliar sound had me throwing the blankets off in a hurry, but not before I noticed Jude's absence. I pushed aside the disappointment I felt, reminding myself that I had only known the man for a brief time. I felt silly for how strong my feelings were for him, but I also couldn't deny them.

Another high-pitched laugh pulled me from my thoughts of Jude. Logically, I knew the laughter did not belong to Mia, but I was hoping she might also be here. I swung open the door and ignored the leftover aches in my body as I jogged towards the kitchen.

"Mia?" I called before stopping in my tracks. My sister was not here, but a woman I had never seen stood before me.

"You must be this new Queen of Saleda I've heard about." The unfamiliar woman said, extending her hand to me. "I'm Nabilla, but my friends call me Billy."

The sheer beauty of the woman had me speechless. Billy towered over me, about the same height as Florian but shorter than Marco and Jude. Her black hair was in braids, and her dark skin made her eyes even more prominent. They had the same red hue to them as Marco and Jude's.

I offered her a shy smile and shook her hand. "I'm Siv, " I told her. "I'm sorry. I thought that maybe my sister was here."

Billy shifted her gaze over to Florian, then back at me. "No, Mia isn't here."

"You know Mia?" I asked her.

Billy smiled brightly. "Oh, I know her very well."

Marco laughed loudly from the kitchen, and Jude punched him in the arm. "Ouch!" Marco yelled before punching him back.

Billy rolled her eyes, "Mia and I are—we're good friends," she said before giving Marco an intense glare.

I couldn't help but feel slightly envious that my sister had friends other than me, especially a good friend. I only had her, but she seemed to have plenty of people she surrounded herself with, and before now, I had never heard of them. I shook off the sting of jealousy and smiled back at Billy. "Well, it's nice to meet you. Are you related to Jude and Marco?" I asked her, but she started to shake her head and furrowed her eyebrows, seemingly confused by my question. "You have the same eyes as them. Before yesterday, I'd never seen anyone else with that unique red color blended in."

Understanding dawned on her face and she briefly looked at the men before answering, "In a way, I guess. I'm half-Krig."

I nodded and gave a small smile, trying to hide my gut-wrenching disappointment from my sister's prolonged absence. I knew I should be proud that she was managing to overpower the Queen's army and lead an entire rebellion, but I selfishly wished she was with me instead. I was starting to notice how dependent I had been on her, and although I wasn't proud of it, I still yearned for her comfort. We had never been apart for this long, and her absence was beginning to wear on me.

Florian's hand on my shoulder brought me back to reality. "Are you all right?" He asked with a worried look.

I gave him a reassuring smile. "I just miss Mia and can't help but feel guilty that she's over there fighting while I'm here doing nothing," I told him.

Florian shook his head and led me to a worn chair in front of the fireplace in the corner of the living room. "Keep your head up. We'll be back in the capital before too long."

I nodded reluctantly and watched the flames dance in the fireplace. I decided that instead of wallowing in my own misery, I would make good use of this time away from Mia. I still knew next to nothing about why I was so valuable to both Catrin and the rebellion. There were still so many unanswered questions, and I deserved to know everything. Especially if I were a key part of what I knew was about to be a war.

CHAPTER 8

I made my way to the table and sat. "So, who's going to fill me in? I told you I wanted answers and I have still received nothing from any of you. I can't keep pretending that there's not a war being fought back in the capital while I'm here and my sister is there." I announced, looking at each and every body in the room.

Jude was the first to take a seat next to me. Florian quickly found his way to the seat on the other side of me and I couldn't help but notice the two men stare at one another for a brief moment before returning their attention to me. I could feel a tension between them, but I decided against asking about it. I needed this time to be about the information I've been asking for, not their dramatics.

Marco plopped down across from me and Billy wasn't too far behind him. Silence filled the space between us before Billy finally spoke up, rolling her eyes. "You're not going to believe anything we're about to tell you. Nothing we say is a joke or a lie. You need to trust us, and eventually, you will have proof of everything," she proclaimed, never breaking eye contact with me. "Catrin kept you extremely sheltered, and she tried to erase any evidence of your importance throughout Saleda. She created an environment that prohibited you from reaching your full potential or even knowing who you truly are. She instilled doubt and insecurity deep inside of you."

The embarrassment of my lack of confidence being announced in front of everyone at the table made my cheeks redden and my body stiff. "That's not-"

Billy raised her hand, effectively silencing me. "This will take time and a lot of hard work to undo. But when you finally do, you will realize who you are and who you're meant to be," she grabbed my hand across the table and held it softly. "By telling you this, I'm not trying to belittle you. I'm trying to empower you. For you cannot begin to improve yourself by hiding within the depths of your doubt." With my cheeks still on fire and red, I simply nodded, accepting her words as advice rather than an insult.

Florian picked up where Billy had left off. "There's an ancient prophecy that has been spread and taught for thousands of years. This prophecy spoke of your birth and your rise to power. Until you reach the throne, people will suffer, and people will die."

A long and tense silence came over the table before Marco chuckled and looked around the table before turning back to me. "No pressure, though," he joked, succeeding in easing the grimness of the conversation.

I snickered at Marco but still recognized the absurdity of what Florian had just told me. How could they have possibly thought that I was who the prophecy spoke of if the prophecy was even real in the first place. "There had to be a mix-up, and somehow you got the wrong person. My birth was nothing special. Catrin told me I was born in rags. Why would a prophecy be written about someone like me?"

Jude shook his head. "Great people don't have to be born into royalty or riches to become great, Siv."

"Besides, it would be kind of hard to miss the only person born during the year of barrenness," Marco chimed in. "You may have been born in rags, but every person alive heard of your arrival into this world. Your birth brought an entire Kingdom hope. It was celebrated continuously until-" Florian coughed loudly, cutting Marco off.

My brows snapped together. "The year of barrenness?"

Marco looked around as if he were perplexed that I had never heard of such a thing.

Jude placed his hand on my thigh and came to my aid. "Do you really think Catrin would have had her learn about the year of barrenness if she didn't even let her learn the cities outside of Mendacia?"

Marco shrugged before looking back at me. "There was an entire year where there were no children born. People started to become nervous that this meant the end of times, but when you were born, it was proof of the prophecy which told of a new Queen that would free her people of hunger and torment." He pointed at me. "That's you. You were born in the year of barrenness, and you're the Queen who will save Saleda."

I tried to come to terms with what I had been told, but my mind refused to believe it. None of this made sense to me. For as long as I can remember, all I had ever wanted was to find peace but being a Queen would never bring me that. Fear and anxiety occupied my thoughts almost every second of every day, and the thought of having to live that way forever was daunting. I didn't want this responsibility. I didn't want people to depend on me.

I cleared my throat before looking back at everyone at the table. "What if I don't want this?"

They all looked at one another for a moment before returning their attention to me, and Billy stood. "Siv, I know this is a lot to take in, but you can't deny your destiny. One way or another, it will always find you."

Her words sent chills down my back. *It will always find you.* Similar words were spoken to me in my nightmares, and that was all the confirmation I needed. I couldn't be who they needed me to be. I didn't want to be. I'd given enough. Why must they ask for more?

I stood from the table as well and looked at each face staring back at me before I stormed out of the cottage and found solace by the large dead tree overlooking the meadow. I sat against the back of the tree, out of sight from the cottage. I hadn't let myself mourn the life that I had once had. All of a sudden, tears brimmed my eyes, and I let myself cry silently.

It wasn't that I missed my old life back at the palace. I was miserable there. But I'd be lying if I said I didn't miss the certainty that life held. There was no mystery surrounding my future. I knew exactly what was to come, regardless if I liked it or not. But now, I had absolutely no idea what was to come. They expected too much from me, and the pressure of their expectations sat heavily on my shoulders. I didn't know how to be the Queen they needed me to be. I was raised to be the exact opposite of a leader. Obedient, submissive, and to never forget my place. I hugged my knees tightly to my chest and let my head drop as I cried. It wasn't until I heard a few twigs snap that I looked up to see Florian standing over me.

"Are you okay?" He asked me.

I chuckled. "What do you think?"

Florian nodded and sat beside me. "Dumb question," he told me, looking straight ahead. "Siv, I know this whole situation is overwhelming and I'm sorry that we had to spring it on you like this, but fate would have never chosen you if you weren't worthy of the throne."

I shook my head. "Florian, you don't understand," I cried. "I'm not cut out for this! I have always been the one who needed saving. I've never been the one to save anyone else. Let alone an entire Kingdom!"

"That's not true."

I looked up from my knees and peered back at him. "How is it not?"

"You saved your sister when you covered for her with that letter," he reminded me. "You didn't hesitate either. You knew you'd be punished, and you still took the blame for something you had no part in. Something tells me it wasn't the first time you'd done something like that either."

I shook my head. "That's different."

"How is that different?"

I shrugged. "I would die for my sister. I love her. Her safety is more important than my own."

Florian chuckled. "There it is."

"There what is?"

"That right there is why you were chosen for this," he told me. "Do you love your Kingdom?"

I thought for a moment. I wasn't sure how to answer him. The only time I was allowed to leave the gates of the palace was for the weekly lashings and the occasion hanging. The only parts of my Kingdom that I had ever seen were horrid, ugly, and sickening. I saw people whose clothes hung loose over their emaciated bodies, children crying as they watched their loved ones be tormented in the town square, and guards beating anyone who looked at them wrong.

I came to the conclusion that I didn't love the Kingdom. Not how it was anyway. In fact, I hated it. Catrin had made a sport out of torturing her people, and I had become so accustomed to her cruelty that I never realized that it didn't have to be that way. It was possible to make Saleda the safe haven it had once been before Catrin soiled it with her cruelty and selfishness.

I looked back at Florian. "I never knew the Kingdom before Catrin's rule, and I'm not sure I even know it now, but I'd like to. I'd like to love it but I don't think I can with how things are," I told him truthfully.

"Billy says that there's barely any of Catrin's soldiers left in town after our army ambushed them. She thinks it's safe enough to have you return," he said, looking at me with a serious expression. "We'll have to lay low, of course, but perhaps this is your chance to get to know your people outside of Catrin's shadow."

I wiped my tears away and couldn't stop the smile that spread across my face. "When do we leave?"

Florian looked back to the cottage. "We'll leave first thing in the morning, so enjoy the rest of your time here. Who knows when we'll get another chance to enjoy peace like this," he uttered.

I nodded. "Thank you, Florian."

He chuckled, clasping my hand and kissing my knuckles. "I'm not so sure you'll thank me when you realize what we'll be walking into. War isn't pretty, Siv." He lifted himself from the ground and began walking back to the cottage, leaving me alone with my thoughts.

I was well aware that war wasn't pretty. I may have never seen the blood and sacrifice on the battlefield, but I had sacrificed plenty and bled even more during my time in the palace. I had been fighting a war my entire life. What Florian didn't understand was that underneath the elaborate gowns I wore were wounds, bruises, and scars. I may not have realized it until that moment, but I had been a soldier my entire life.

"Come eat, Siv!" Florian yelled back at me, motioning for me to follow him, and I did.

CHAPTER 9

During breakfast, I learned that Billy's parents had also died when she was young by Catrin's orders. Marco's mother had taken her in as well, so they were all more like siblings than friends. I watched how they interacted with one another and admired how Billy was not treated any differently because she was a woman. It was a foreign concept, but one that I enjoyed. Up until recently, I had never seen women be friends with men. Seth's friends never acknowledged me besides the crude comment here and there, and the other women who lived in the palace only kept female company besides their spouses.

When I finished my meal, I excused myself and decided to take a walk around Jude's property. I knew I wouldn't be here for much longer. Although I was eager to be back in the capital with Mia, I knew I would miss the calm that this place had provided me with. Not only that, but it was beautiful. Not in an elaborate or ornamental way, like in the palace where I had grown up, but naturally and serenely.

An old wooden fence separated the pasture from the grown-out grass surrounding the small cottage. Beside the stable and beyond the fence, all you could see were green hills until the horizon. I had been sitting on top of the fence for a while, enjoying the stillness around me. I knew there would only be chaos as soon as we were back in Mendacia, so I tried to embrace it while I could.

That was until I heard two familiar voices shouting at each other. I hopped off the fence and ran toward the cottage to see what was going on, and that was when I saw Jude and Florian face to face with one another. I didn't hear what Jude had said before Florian punched him in the side of the face, but it was hard to miss the tension between the two.

Words failed me as I tried to run to Jude, but Marco forcefully pulled me aside. "That wouldn't be smart," he said, pulling me in between him and an unamused Billy. "Jude may be a softy for you, but he's still a Krig. It's best that neither of them know you're here to see this." Both men were too immersed in their brawl to even notice the three of us watching them.

Furrowing my brows, I asked, "am I supposed to know what that means?"

Marco chuckled, which irritated me further. "I keep forgetting that you were withheld a proper education," he teased.

I was about to give him a snarky reply when I heard Jude's fist make contact with Florian's face and the crunch of the bones from his nose that quickly followed. My focus quickly shifted back to the scene that was playing out before me.

Florian was now on the ground, holding his bloody nose with a fierce look on his face, and Jude held an expression I had never witnessed from him before. I was used to his soft smile and intense stares, but not the look of pure rage that he had at that moment. Suddenly, his charming demeanor disappeared. If I hadn't known him, I would have been frightened.

"You know you won't win this fight, Florian," Jude growled, wiping blood from his brow with the back of his hand. "I was born for this."

Florian chuckled and stood from the ground. "One of these days, you'll be forced to shed that cockiness of yours. Perhaps today will be the day," he responded.

I turned to Billy. "What are they even fighting about?" I asked her.

Her eyes shifted to Marco for a moment before she answered, "it's not our place to disclose their disputes. You'll have to ask them."

"Florian, brother, you know this is out of my control. Why must you fight me on something I cannot change?" Jude asked as Florian paced in front of him.

Florian smirked and shook his head, still pacing. "Just because you claim she is your Erosa doesn't mean she is. Why would I believe that some Krig myth is true just because you say it is? I won't step down just because you tell me to. You forget who has a claim on these lands. You may have a title within your people, but not here in Saleda."

His words seemed to have set something off within Jude. Before I knew it, he had Florian's throat between his hands, and Marco jumped from beside me, trying his best to pull Jude off of Florian, but he wouldn't budge. Finally, Billy helped Marco, and Jude's grip loosened enough for Florian to escape. His knees gave out on him, and he fell to the floor, coughing on all fours. I stood there with my mouth wide open. I couldn't comprehend what had just happened. The speed of his movements didn't seem possible.

"She's not *yours*, Jude," Florian coughed. "She's not yours, and you don't get to stake a claim on her. She's coming with me."

Jude lunged for him once more, but Marco and Billy held him back. When he turned to go inside the cottage, he finally saw me, and the look of wrath on his face immediately softened, and he looked as if he were embarrassed. He opened his mouth to say something but quickly shut it and walked past me without muttering a word.

I turned to follow him, but Billy gripped my shoulder, keeping me in place. "Give him a second to calm down," she whispered in my ear. Overwhelmed by what I had just witnessed, I nodded and walked toward the barren willow tree I had sat against the day prior and clasped the necklace around my neck as I thought of Mia.

I had been lost in my thoughts for a while by the time I felt the heat from Jude's body taking a seat next to me. My eyes glanced over his face, which had just begun to bruise. "Are you going to explain what that was about?" I asked him.

Jude didn't look at me; his gaze was fixed on the meadow in front of us. "There's something I need to talk to you about, but I'm not sure this is the time," he answered, followed by a long silence. "This place will miss you," Jude finally said. "I will, too," he added.

I turned to him. "You're not coming with us?"

Jude shook his head, looking straight ahead still. "No. I need to travel west to build our numbers if the rebellion is to have a future," he told me.

My brows furrowed in confusion. "Why? Billy made it sound as if we were doing just fine with the numbers we had now."

"We honestly shouldn't be winning this easily, and I'm worried that Catrin has something up her sleeve. Florian disagrees with me and believes that we're capable of destroying her with the numbers we have now, but I have serious doubts," he said. "I don't agree with you going with him, either. I don't think it's safe. But unfortunately, he has ranked over me when it comes to Saleda. So there's not much for me to do besides recruiting others and preparing to back the rebellion if things go badly."

I sighed loudly. "How long will that take? When will I see you again?" I asked him, afraid of his answer.

"I'm not sure. There's a large Krig population in the west, and I have no doubt they'll join me, but they'll have to prepare, and I'm not sure how long that will take." Jude finally looked down at me, and his red-hued eyes were full of emotion. "I don't know when we'll see each other again."

I felt my heart drop, and I couldn't understand why the thought of being distanced from Jude hurt me so much. I knew I had just met him, but it felt like I had known him for much longer. My body ached for him as if he were the only sustenance that I needed in order to stay alive. I felt embarrassed at how strong my feelings were for Jude, but they grew every time we spoke.

I stared at him for a moment. I took in his beauty and tried to memorize every detail of the scar that ran from his forehead to his chin, every strand of his black hair that he always seemed to tie back, and every muscle his thin tunic outlined. Jude wasn't handsome in a conventional way. He had many flaws, but they didn't take away from his looks. They added to them.

It wasn't his appearance that attracted me to him, though. It was how he had been through things that would have made most people hard and cold, but he wasn't. He was kind and warm. He had every reason to look for revenge, but instead, he had sought peace in this cottage. The same cottage where one of his many tragedies had occurred. Jude was everything I had ever wanted to be, and in the short time I had known him, I had fallen for him. It was hard not to see that now. I knew I'd miss him and was afraid I would never see him again.

"Can I come with you?" I asked him hesitantly, my cheeks reddening at my vulnerability.

Jude's eyes stayed on me for a moment as if he couldn't believe that I had asked him that, but then he looked down to the green grass and shook his head. "I can't take you with me, Siv."

I scrunched my eyebrows. "Why not?"

"You're not mine to take."

I rested my head on his shoulder. "I could be."

Jude finally shifted his gaze from the meadow to me. "It's not that easy, Siv." His hand eased over my shoulders, and he pulled me into him. "My presence alone puts you in even more danger than you already are. You still don't know so many things about this world, and it would be selfish of me to claim you before you could comprehend what that would mean. I won't do that to you."

I lifted my head and looked up at his mesmerizing eyes. "Then explain it to me! Explain whatever it is that I don't know, Jude," I pleaded.

"You'll learn everything in due time, Siv," he answered. "This world isn't something that can be explained within a conversation. Some things you have to see and experience for yourself. You've been sheltered and kept from this life for too long to be able to handle everything within a day."

I could no longer look him in the eyes. Jude claimed to want me with him but when I offered to go, I was denied. I felt both rejected and humbled by his words. I knew I was ignorant of the reality of this world, but I was trying to learn. I was trying to adjust, but it was hard to do when I was only receiving breadcrumbs of information at a time.

Jude hugged me tighter into his chest, seemingly aware of the dismissal I felt. "I pray to

Rheis and Stes that our fates will collide once again," he muttered. "But until then, I can't be selfish when it comes to you, Siv. You're the people's chosen Queen, not just my own." He stood up, offering me a hand and pulling me up.

Ignoring his comment about his foreign gods, I stretched on my tippy toes while simultaneously pulling down on Jude's tunic. Surprising myself, I pressed my lips against his and enclosed my arms around his neck. Jude hesitated for a moment. It was as if he was fighting a war in his head about his next move, but then he pulled me up and wrapped one arm underneath me while using his other arm to guide my legs around his waist. We stayed like that for a while, enveloped in one another's embrace, lips pressed against each other. I didn't want to let go of him. I didn't want him to leave, so I tightened my grip. I felt Jude smile against my lips, and he pulled away before he gently kissed my cheek. He finally set me down on the fence beside the willow tree and stood in front of me, his hands still wrapped around my waist.

We stood like that for several minutes before I noticed the bruises on his face had completely faded. I pulled away from his grip on me and gasped when the green leaves of the once-barren tree behind Jude swayed in the wind. Jumping from the fence, I peered down at the different colors splattered across the overgrown grass. Wildflowers that hadn't existed only moments before seemed to be dancing in the breeze.

The warm, tingly feelings that had resided in my chest from Jude's touch instantly disappeared as I began to panic. I had to be losing my mind. My breathing became fast and erratic, and before I could begin to calm myself down, my vision became blurry, and within seconds, everything was black.

CHAPTER 10

My entire body felt heavy as I began to gain consciousness back. I forced my eyes open and blinked slowly up at Jude. His uniquely colored eyes were consumed with concern and awe, and he was trying to say something to me. It wasn't until my hearing slowly began to return that I realized it had gone in the first place.

"Can you hear me?" Jude asked. "Siv, can you hear me?"

I slowly nodded.

"How do you feel? Are you okay?" Jude straddled my waist, careful not to put any weight on me, and held my face with both hands.

My cheeks quickly reddened when I realized his position, and I couldn't help but let an embarrassingly immature giggle escape my lips.

Jude's thick brows furrowed in confusion. "Why is she laughing?"

"Probably because you're straddling her," Billy answered.

I forced my head to turn in the direction of her voice and became even more embarrassed when I noticed that Billy, Marco, and Florian all stood at my side, staring with wide eyes and looks of both anger and distress.

It was my turn to be thoroughly confused. "What is going on?" I asked them. There was a brief moment of silence as they each glanced at each other in unison.

"I feel like we should be asking you that," Marco said before his attention turned to Jude who still straddled me, and I couldn't help but notice that my cheeks still burned bright red.

"Jude, maybe you should help her sit up," Billy said, noticing my blush.

He glanced down at his knees on each side of me before swinging his leg around and placing his hand underneath my back, helping me to sit. "Do you remember anything?" He asked me.

I thought back for a moment. I remembered kissing him, and I remember how, for the first time, I felt what it is to be truly at peace. At that moment, I felt no fear, anxiety, pressure, or sorrow. Jude's touch had eased my soul but then everything went black. I must have passed out.

I felt my cheeks burn, and I nibbled on my bottom lip before answering, "I think I fainted."

Marco, whose eyes still remained on Jude, turned to Billy. "What do we do?" He asked her. "She's a lot stronger than I thought she'd be at this stage. This tree has been dead since we were kids, and she brought it back without even trying."

My brows lifted in surprise and bewilderment. What did he mean by giving the tree life? I shifted my focus from him and glanced up at the blossoming branches above me. I pulled back and forced myself up, standing in front of the vast and alive willow. I closed my eyes tightly before opening them again, and low and behold, the blooming tree still stood there. I shook my head in disbelief. I knew this tree was barren when I sat down, but now it was full of life and stunning. Then I turned to Jude, and although his scar was still prominent, his bruising had been completely healed.

"How?" I asked, staring at limbs moving subtly from the gentle wind and gripping the necklace that hung from my neck. The irony of the willow on the pendant and the beaming willow in front of me was too much to fathom.

My question remained unanswered as they all looked at one another, seemingly as baffled as I was and then Billy broke the prolonged silence. "It's begun."

I swiftly turned back to face her. "What's begun?" I asked her.

Billy still didn't acknowledge me as she stared angrily at Jude. "Do you understand what you've done? We warned you, Jude. They'll know her power has emerged. She's now in more danger than she was in the first place," Billy pulled her braids back in a tie. "You need to leave before you cause her to draw even more attention to herself. The rest of us need to leave tonight," she said.

"I'm not going anywhere until I've been told what's happening," I told her bluntly.

She shook her head, looking at me with nothing but seriousness. "We will, but right now, your safety is our priority. If that means knocking you out to get your cooperation, I will do so without a hint of guilt," she urged. "If we were to lose you, not only would our entire cause be for nothing, but everyone inside and outside Saleda would suffer for it. So put your curiosity aside for the moment and think about your Kingdom and the lives that depend on you."

I tried to respond, but Jude placed his hand on my shoulder, forcing me to pause. "It's for the best, Siv," he told me before silently following Marco and Billy back to the cottage.

I turned to Florian, who stood beside me. I hadn't noticed the look of pure anguish on his face until then. His green eyes bore into me, but he remained silent until he finally told me to go inside and pack my things.

I didn't argue with him. I could tell something about our current situation had troubled him and although I wasn't sure which part, I couldn't help but feel blameworthy. So I nodded and silently walked back to my room in the cottage.

My feet came to a halt when I saw Jude sitting on the bed. The gloomy expression clouding his features told me that this was goodbye. I took a seat next to him, my eyes focusing on my feet dangling off the edge. "So this is it then?" I asked him.

Jude nodded, silently handing me an envelope with a red wax seal. "I can't be there with you when you finally understand everything, but I wanted you to hear some things from me," he told me. "You'll know when to open it, but try to wait until then."

Despite the confusion from his words, I accepted the letter and finally looked up from my feet to his face. "I feel like this is my fault, and I don't even know what *this* is," I admitted. "I don't understand why everyone is angry."

Jude chuckled, but his eyes remained sullen. "They're not angry. They're afraid." He took my hand and kissed my knuckles. "And it's my fault, not yours. I knew the risks of that kiss. I knew what we were to one another, and I still went through with it," he muttered, barely loud enough for me to hear.

"What are we to one another?" I asked.

His jaw clenched, and he shook his head. "You're my other half, Siv. Rheis and Stes believed me to be worthy of you, but I'm not so sure."

Nothing about what he had just said made sense to me, but I knew there wasn't enough time to ask questions, so instead, I rested my head against him. "You're worthy," I whispered, prompting him to tighten his grip on my hand.

After Jude had said his final goodbye and left me with nothing but a kiss on my forehead, I packed the few things Mia had given me in my leather pouch and met Billy, Marco, and Florian in the main room of the cottage. The air was thick with emotion, and no words were spoken as we made our way down the rural path leading back to town.

Marco seemed to have had enough of the tension-filled silence and wrapped an arm around me as we walked. "When we had heard the news of your birth, my mother made Jude, Billy, and I the closest thing we'd ever had to a feast. She had spent everything we had on a boar, sweet bread, fruits, and even pudding," he told me with a smile spreading across his tanned face. "She said Rheis and Stes had blessed us with your birth, and to not celebrate would be an insult to them. So we ate until our bellies were so full, the buttons on our pants had to be undone."

I heard Billy chuckle from in front of us. "You say we, but I don't think anyone, but you ever got the chance to taste that pudding before you had your fill," she chimed in, making Marco laugh even louder.

"Can you blame me? I was almost a teenager, and I had never tasted such a divine thing in my life. It was your fault for not getting to it fast enough," Marco retorted.

I couldn't help but join in their laughter as the two of them bantered back and forth. It was a welcomed distraction from the somberness that had consumed me only hours before. Their relationship reminded me so much of Mia and I's and although I was saddened by Jude's absence, I was relieved at the idea of finally seeing my sister again.

When Billy and Marco finally stopped arguing about the pudding, I decided to try my luck with yet another question in the hopes that this one may be answered without the threat of being knocked out. "Who or what is Rheis and Stes?"

Marco chuckled. "Seriously?" He asked, seemingly shocked by my ignorance once again. "Is there anything you do know?"

I rolled my eyes. "I'm sure my knowledge of grammar and math could beat yours any day," I answered with confidence.

"And I'm sure you'll be using those skills quite often during this war," he answered sarcastically before continuing, "Rheis and Stes are the primary gods of the Krigsmen."

Billy turned back to me. "Rheis is the god of war and battle strategy. He is called upon and prayed to during times of hardship when courage, strength, and knowledge are needed. Stes is the god of love and harmony. We pray to her when our hearts are broken, and it feels impossible to continue on. She blesses us with happiness, peace, and companionship. Together, they are the gods of life."

Marco pulled me closer to him and whispered in my ear, "It is Rheis and Stes who decide our destinies, fates, and soulmates or *Erosa's* in our native language."

"Soulmates?" I asked, curious if I had heard him correctly.

Billy turned around and gave Marco a look of warning. "Watch what you say, Marco. She must discover things in due course. You know what could happen if too much is revealed too quickly," she warned.

Marco rolled his eyes. "I'm not revealing anything, Nabilla. Relax. I'm only teaching her the history of our gods," he told her before turning his attention back to me. "It is said that Rheis and Stes were once of the same mind and body; they were simply the god of life. They were called Umnas, and they held the perfect balance that was needed in order to watch over the Krigsmen. But Eti, the god of death, was jealous of the praise and worship that Umnas had received from their people. So when Umnas was sleeping, Eti split them in half."

"You see, Eti thought that in doing so, Umnas would die, and he'd become both the god of life and death and thus have complete power and control as well as all the praise from the people," Billy interjected. "But the opposite had happened. Umnas had become two halves instead of one, Rheis and Stes. The love and understanding between the two of them gave them more power than they had when they were Umnas. So they realized that perhaps their people, the Krigs, deserved to feel such love as their own, and they blessed them with soulmates, their other halves," Marco continued. "For centuries, Krigs searched for their Erosa and their lives would become complete when they would finally find them. It was like all of a sudden, everything made sense and their urge to fight or wage war soon depleted, which angered Eti even more. Fewer and fewer prayers were being said to him because fewer people were dying in battles or wars."

Billy turned back towards us once again. "So Eti cursed the Krigs and made it so they could no longer recognize their Erosa. We were doomed to live our entire lives without knowing the peace or happiness that came with finding our other half. We no longer had that sense of being complete, which made us irritable and quick to anger, fueling wars once again."

Marco grinned down at me. "For the last five hundred or so years, we had begun to believe that true soulmates were just a myth. That the stories that had been carried down for centuries were nothing but wives' tales. That was until you came along."

Billy stopped walking and turned around. "Marco!" She yelled. "Your words will get us all killed!"

I had finally started to put everything together. During their fight, Florian had said that Jude claimed I was his Erosa. "Marco, look at me," I ordered, and he complied without hesitation. "Am I Jude's soulmate?" I asked him, his eyes wandering back to Billy, who glared at him, warning him to keep his mouth shut. "Yes or no, Marco?" I asked again.

A long stretch of silence came over us as Marco tried his best to come up with a way to both answer me and oblige Billy, but Florian had enough. "Siv, it doesn't matter. Krig mythology differs depending on who you ask. The tales of Umnis, Eti, Rheis, and Stes are children's bedtime stories. None of this is going to help our cause, so let's drop it and keep walking. The sooner we get to the safe house in Mendacia, the better," he barked before continuing down the path into the town of Kantar.

Billy's lips drew back in a snarl, and she ran up behind Florian, swinging him around to face her. "I will not stand for your disrespect of my people's beliefs!" She roared. "Regardless of your feelings for Siv and your disputes with Jude, you will not call my gods children's stories. We have endured enough prejudice and abuse at the hands of your step-mother. I will not tolerate it from you, too."

Florian balled his fists and leaned into Billy, closing any space that had been between them. "Well, I will not stand for you and Marco filling up Siv's head with nonsense. How will any of this help us?"

Billy didn't waste a second before she tackled him to the ground, and Marco pushed me behind him. He looked genuinely amused as they brawled with one another. "You're not going to get them off each other?" I asked him, horrified.

Marco chuckled. "He had it coming, did he not?" He asked, never taking his eyes off of Billy, who had Florian fighting for his life. "You don't get to attack our gods without retribution. To ignore comments like that would be an insult to them."

I winced as I watched Billy pull his brown hair back and utter something in his ear. "Why would he say such a thing, then?" I asked him.

Marco shrugged. "It has nothing to do with our gods. Florian has always seeked physical pain when he's hurting on the inside. It helps him cope, I think." Marco finally lifted Billy off of a bloody Florian. "He's had enough, Billy," he told her before offering Florian his hand. "Next time, just insult her girlfriend or something. Leave our beliefs out of it, okay?"

Florian accepted Marco's hand and mumbled an apology before taking his worn tunic off and using it as a towel to clean his face. I kept my distance from him after that. It didn't matter that Jude and Billy had already forgiven him; his actions seemed rash and callous. I was beginning to think he had a habit of saying deeply hurtful things when he was upset. It reminded me a lot of his half-brother, my ex-betrothed Seth. He had acted similarly for most of his life. If his mother had hurt him, he'd insult me. It was a vicious cycle that I had been forced to be a part of, and I hated being reminded of it.

CHAPTER 11

For the rest of the walk through town, the three of them engaged in conversations that I had no interest in. But, even if I did I think I would have still stayed quiet. I was too caught up in watching the people of Kantar go about their daily lives, completely blind to the war that we were currently marching toward. I'm not sure if it was the shortening of the distance between me and the capital or if I had only just realized the danger I was heading into. Regardless, I was becoming nervous. I still had next to no information on who I was or what I was expected to do. But I was also still coming to terms with the fact that Jude may be my soulmate, and I had just watched him leave. The uncertainty of whether or not I'd even see him again was creeping up on me.

Fear, anxiety, loneliness, and despair filled the cavities of my heart as we finally entered the tunnels and began our descent into the bowels of Mendacia. Florian lit the torch and led the way, avoiding eye contact with me every time he'd look back. He was seemingly as embarrassed of his earlier actions as I was disappointed.

After some time, Billy gently grabbed my wrist, gaining my attention. "When we arrive at the safe house from here, several members of the rebellion will be waiting to meet you. I'm telling this to you now so that you don't become overwhelmed. You need to make sure to keep control over your emotions from here on out. We still don't know much about your abilities, and an outburst from you could cost lives if we're not careful," she said, matter of factly. "We'll be able to know more if we gain access to Catrin's personal library. I'm almost certain she has access to sacred texts concerning your prophecy."

"How would we gain access?" I asked her, knowing Catrin has several guards with her and surrounding her chambers at all times. It would be nearly impossible to get inside without being noticed.

Billy laughed out loud, gaining a loud and sarcastic shushing from Marco. "I forget how innocent you are sometimes, truly," she said in between laughs. "We're not going to sneak in, Siv. We're going to take possession of it. How did you think we'd take over Mendacia without acquiring the palace?" I blushed with embarrassment as she and Marco laughed. Even Florian chuckled from up front.

"Don't get flustered. Your pureness could be exactly what this country needs; don't be ashamed of it," Florian shouted back to me without turning around.

Billy and Marco nodded in agreement. "The last thing these people need is another depraved Queen," Marco chimed in.

Suddenly, it occurred to me that Marco, Billy, and even Jude may have a leader of their own since they didn't consider themselves citizens of Saleda. "Do Krigs have their own King and Queen?" I asked Marco and Billy. An unpredicted silence filled the tunnel the moment the words had left my lips. "Did I say something wrong?" I finally asked when no one had answered me.

"No," Billy rushed to answer. "It's just, we don't usually talk about our leadership out loud with non-krigs," she explained. "After years of being hunted down, we tend to be pretty careful about where we say things and who we say them to."

"Oh, of course. I-I shouldn't have asked," I told her while I did my best to ignore the slight hurt her words had caused me. I understood why they would be cautious, but I had just assumed that they trusted me. I also knew that I didn't have a right to be hurt by the methods of how they and their family had survived.

Marco turned around and offered a sheepish smile. "Not King and Queen, though. Chief and Chieftess," he revealed, making me feel slightly better about our relationship.

"We're close. Keep your voices down from here, just to be safe. We don't want any lingering guards above us to figure out that there are tunnels running underneath the capital. If Catrin finds out about them, we're done for." Florian announced from the front.

When we had finally come upon the large door to the cellar, Florian knocked three times. There was a period of time when nothing had happened, and I started to worry that no one would let us in, but then the door creaked open, and a man with red hair smiled widely.

"Welcome back," he said, shaking Florian's hand and patting him on the back.

The cellar looked the exact same as it had on the night of my rescue. The only difference was that it was filled with members of the rebellion this time. I scanned the room as their eyes quickly shifted focus to Florian and me making our way down the stairs.

Once I stepped out of the tunnels and into the cellar, the red-headed man knelt in front of me. "It's an honor to have you in our presence, Queen Siv."

As the rest of the room realized who I was, they all began kneeling. I shifted closer to Marco, feeling uncomfortable but as I looked over at him as well as Billy and Florian, I realized that they were kneeling as well. I pulled Marco up beside me. "What's going on?" I asked in a hushed tone.

Marco gave me a lop-sided grin. "They're showing respect to their Queen," he answered.

I looked back to the kneeling bodies before me and cleared my throat. "Kneeling is not necessary," I told them. "The honor is truly mine. I owe each and every one of you my life," I said, meaning every word.

The man with the red hair was the first to return to his feet. "My name is Luis," he said, extending his hand.

As I went to shake his hand, something made me hesitate for a moment, but I shook it off and returned his smile. "Luis, it's nice to meet you. Call me Siv."

His face lit up as he nodded. "Come meet everyone."

Luis introduced me to every single person inside the cellar. There had to have been at least thirty people, and I tried my best to remember all of their names and their jobs within the rebellion. I'd be lying if I said it wasn't a little overwhelming, but I felt like meeting all of them and speaking to them was the least I could do after all they had sacrificed for me and Saleda. One of the women I had met, Sara, had four children she had sent to live with family members in the next town over so that she could stay and fight. A man named Ishaan had lost both of his brothers in the battle the night of the coup but refused to give up the fight.

These people had suffered so much by Catrin's hands. Every doubt and every ounce of insecurity I had felt on the way here had vanished. What remained was the hunger for justice. They all deserved a Queen who would fight for them, and I knew that I would do everything in my power to be that for them.

I heard the sound of the heavy door to the cellar opening but what grabbed my attention was the voice that followed. "Where is she?"

I turned around so quickly that I almost fell over. The sight of Mia standing at the top of the stairwell paralyzed me. I had to convince myself that this was, indeed, not a dream. She stood there and paused, just as I had. Her long brown hair had been braided back into a high ponytail, and black ash was smeared across her eyes, making her look even more intimidating than she usually did. She was not wearing the unfitted gowns Catrin forced her to wear on palace grounds, but a leather bodice with chained sleeves and matching leather trousers. She did not look like the Mia I had known my entire life, but she somehow looked more like herself than she ever had. This was who she was. She was a warrior.

"Siv," Mia muttered quietly.

Tears began to fall down my face, and I forced myself through everyone who had surrounded themselves around me. Mia followed my lead and rushed down the steps to the cellar. When we finally reached one another, we embraced so tightly that I was amazed either of us could breathe.

"I missed you so much," I sobbed into my sister's chest.

She pulled away from me and grabbed my cheeks with her palms, looking me over with tears brimming in her hazel eyes. "I've thought about you every single day, Sivvy."

I quickly noticed several small scratches and bruises that stretched from the tip of her collarbones all the way up to her face. My brows drew together from concern. "Mia, I've been so worried about you," I cried. "You're all cut up."

Mia smirked. "You should see the other guys," she teased as she grabbed my hand and led me back to the stairs and up into the pub. "Billy, pour my sister an ale, would you? She looks like she needs a drink."

I glanced behind the bar to see the familiar face of Nabilla. She must have dodged the crowd as we entered the cellar and made her way straight to the bar, which made me chuckle. In the short time I knew her, I'd gathered that she wasn't a social butterfly like Marco. Billy only spoke when there was something to be said, and any other conversation was more of a nuisance to her.

She slid a glass filled to the brim with a foamy golden drink, and my face scrunched in confusion as she wrapped her arms around my sister's waist and pulled her into an embrace from behind. The act was oddly sensual.

Noticing my puzzled expression, Mia smiled. "There's a lot we need to discuss," she said as she motioned me to sit, grabbing the seat next to me.

Billy's grip remained on her sides as she stood behind my sister. I stared at both of them expectantly. "Are you guys..."

"Together? Yes." Mia responded, causing my brows to shoot up in surprise. Both of them laughed, and she continued, "Nabilla and I have been together for... how long?" Mia asked.

"A little over two years," Billy answered proudly.

I shook my head. "Two years?" I asked. "Seriously, Mia?"

Her smile dropped, and she looked at me with guilt deeply embedded in her eyes. "Siv, there are so many things that I've wanted to tell you."

I huffed. "That's a bit of an understatement, Mia." Anger seethed out of me as I glared back at my sister, ignoring Billy completely.

"I know you're angry. I would be, too, if the roles were reversed," she reasoned. "But, please try to understand where I was coming from."

I laughed angrily. "Let me guess. You were just trying to protect me?"

Mia nodded. "Yes, actually."

I shook my head. "Unbelievable," I said, chugging the golden liquid from the glass and quickly cringing from the bitter taste.

"Siv, if I were to tell you that you had been chosen by fate to become the hero Saleda needed, not only would you not have believed me, but even if you did, you would have never been able to keep it together. Catrin and Cormac would have known right away that someone had revealed your true identity to you, and they would have locked you away and done who knows what with you," Mia said softly. "Keeping that information from you was the only way I could keep you safe." Mia pleaded.

"Keep me safe?" I asked. "What exactly did you keep me safe from?" Mia pulled back, and her brows pulled together. I knew my words hurt her, which made my chest ache. But I was hurt, too.

Billy stepped out from behind my sister. "That's not fair," she said with her jaw clenched. "Everything your sister has done has been for you. You have no idea the sacrifices she has made over the years for you."

I looked away from them, using the back of my hand to clear the tears that had begun to streak my pale face. "What about the sacrifices I've made? You say that I wouldn't have been able to handle the truth, but I took beatings for you my whole life, Mia. I'm stronger than you think I am."

My sister's face paled from the sting of my words. "You are strong, Siv. No one is disputing that, but we had to be careful. One wrong move, and the rebellion could have ended before it even began."

Billy sighed loudly. "We don't have time for this. The two of you need to put this behind you and focus on the bigger picture. Hundreds of people out there rely on you to win this war, and thousands more whose futures are in your hands."

Mia sat up. "She's right, Siv."

I nodded. "I know she is."

"Will you forgive me?" Mia asked, her brows knitted in a hopeful expression.

I peered at her for a moment before closing the gap between us and holding her close. I was still hurt by my sister's actions and what I felt was a lack of trust, but I didn't want to be angry with her. I had felt what it was like to be away from her, and now that I was here, I didn't want to let my feelings distance me again. "I'll never be able to not forgive you," I whispered. "But please, don't keep any-thing from me ever again."

She placed her chin on my head, tightening her arms around me. "There's still a lot you don't know, but I promise everything will be revealed within time," she whispered back.

I wanted to argue and demand that I be told everything, but I already felt like I was beginning to drown in all of the new information I had received. I thought that maybe they were right to slowly immerse me into this world that they had been living in. So, instead, I relaxed in her embrace and cherished the comfort she always seemed to provide me with.

Mia and I talked for hours over ale. Marco had left the pub with Florian at some point, and Billy made sure our glasses never stayed empty as she let us catch up. We laughed as we shared stories from years ago, as well as stories during our time away from one another, and cried when we spoke of the injustices that had been happening under Catrin's rule. She told me about how she and Billy had met right there in the pub, and I told her about my feelings for Jude, which she promptly followed up with by asking a series of inappropriate questions.

I allowed myself to forget why we were there in the first place. I knew the joy and ease I felt at that moment would not last. Tomorrow would eventually come, and when it did, we would no longer be just Mia and Siv. I would begin to learn what it was to be the Queen that Saledian's needed, and with that would come more responsibility than I had ever known.

CHAPTER 12

I'd never enjoyed more than a sip of alcohol here and there, and that morning, I was truly paying for indulging the night prior. The deep throbbing in my head was all I could focus on when loud voices woke me from my slumber. I tried my best to sit up, but my body did not respond to my demands. So I lay there, hands covering my eyes from the sunlight shining through the narrow windows of wherever I had ended up last night.

"Siv, you need to get up," Florian said softly. "Don't let the hangover win. We've got way too much to do today," he said, chuckling under his breath.

I groaned and turned over, pulling the sheets over my head. "Please go away."

I heard him laugh before he left the room, and I audibly sighed out of relief. I didn't think Florian was one to listen to anyone's demands, so I claimed victory and let myself drift back to sleep. However, it didn't last long. My few minutes of peace quickly ended when a bucket of ice water was dumped on me.

I drew in a deep breath out of shock, and my body swiftly sprang up out of the drenched bed. Florian stood in front of me, bent over, laughing. "What is wrong with you!" I yelled, reminding myself of the deep throb coming from my head.

Still laughing, he threw a towel in my direction. "You left me no choice!"

I noticed Florian had stopped laughing, and when I glanced back at him, he was staring with intense heat behind his warm green eyes. It was then that I realized I must have borrowed one of Mia's slips to sleep in, which was now almost completely see-through.

I hurriedly draped the towel over me, heat spreading across my cheeks. "Where are we? I need to bathe," I told him flatly.

Shaking off his feverish stare, Florian asked with an amused grin, "Do you really not remember?"

I shook my head as I glared back at him.

Florian looked to the doorway where I now noticed Marco was standing, and he promptly shrugged with a witty smile. "You're in the apartment above the pub. I carried you up here last night. I figured you had enough ale after you wouldn't stop talking about how Jude was the love of your life and how handsome you thought he was," Marco said, still grinning.

I covered my face with my hands. I was absolutely mortified, but when I finally looked up, I noticed Florian's features had been clouded by irritation.

Marco noticed the awkward tension and continued speaking, "Siv, if you think that's bad, you should have seen Florian the first time he got drunk," Marco elbowed Florian in the arm playfully. "He threw up on his own shoes and then proceeded to down another glass of ale directly afterward," he said, laughing in between words.

Florian abruptly elbowed Marco back quite a bit harder. "Thank you, Marco." Florian shook his head, smiling to himself, and pointed down the hall. "The washroom is the first door on the left. I brought up hot water for you to bathe in, but don't idle. We have much to do today."

Chuckling at the information Marco had just revealed, I left the crowded room and headed down the hall.

My headache had been slightly soothed by the hot bath Florian drew for me, but I still craved to be in bed and asleep. Despite my wishes, I slowly got dressed and walked down the steps of the apartment into the pub where I had heard voices. Marco, Florian, Billy, and Mia sat at a round table near the back and seemed to be too deep in a conversation to notice me walking toward them.

"What're you guys talking about?" I asked them, their eyes drifting from one another to me.

"You," Marco answered nonchalantly.

I sat down between Florian and Mia. "What about me?" I asked.

Mia took a deep breath before finally turning to me and offering a smile that failed to meet her hazel eyes. "We've come to the conclusion that in order to keep you safe from this point on, you need to understand the reality of the world you now live in."

A vast range of emotions were sparked inside of me. I was eager and excited to finally learn more about my situation. I was also scared and hesitant because I had been blissfully unaware of the danger surrounding me. It was one thing to be constantly told that, but it was another thing to be fully conscious of it.

"Where do we begin?" I finally asked.

Mia nodded, folding her hands on the table. "Let's start with the prophecy of your birth and destiny," she answered, giving Billy a pointed look.

Billy rose from the table and grabbed a large, worn book from a locked cabinet behind the bar. My heart began to race as she walked back to the table and began flipping through the pages before pointing to a specific text. "Here," she told me. "Read."

I placed my elbows on the wooden table and leaned in slightly to have a better view of the text.

When death falls upon the world, and blood soaks the ground that Kings once sat upon, all will be destroyed until dust fills the womb of every woman. But, the night the sky is colored brightly, hope will be born. What was thought to be lost will be found once more. Love will ignite healing upon the lands.

Kingdoms will clash, and blood will fall again, but the exiled will bring forth the fall of false leaders. The forgotten heir will be born without a name but be destined to rule. When the rightful King is joined with the foreign child, they will usher in a new age of peace and honor.

However, if the child's heart bleeds, they will release death and destruction upon the world.

My eyes stayed glued to the words on the worn page. I wasn't sure I understood them. I wasn't sure that this prophecy had answered any of my questions. If anything, I had more questions now than I had before.

My focus was finally broken when Mia grabbed my hand on the table. "I know this is a lot, Siv," she told me with sympathy in her eyes. "But, we're here for you. We can help you through it all. You're not alone."

I squeezed her hand slightly before letting go and sitting back in my chair. "Thank you. Thank all of you," I told them, looking at each face around the table. "But, I'm going to need more than some old text to explain what is expected from me. I don't understand what any of that means, and I don't understand what any of it has to do with me."

Mia nodded and glanced toward Billy who sat across from me. Billy's eyes stayed on my sister for a brief moment before she turned to me. "Catrin and her uncle Cormac tracked your birth and killed your parents in order to obtain you. They sought the power within you," she revealed without emotion. "We believe they kept Mia alive because they assumed the love between the two of you would ignite your abilities. When that failed, it was too late to kill her. They were afraid that her death would cause you to release death and destruction as the prophecy predicted."

A strange wave of grief came over me at the revelation that Catrin had my parents killed in order to take me. I never knew them, and I knew that they had died, but I had no idea that they had been murdered by the woman that I believed had taken me in. It made sense that she had lied to me about being friends with them, though. I knew she had lied to me about many things, but what I didn't expect was a slight feeling of relief. For years, I had wondered how my parents could have tolerated someone like the Queen, let alone be a friend to her. I often questioned what kind of people they truly were if they belonged in the Queen's tight-knit circle of corrupted confidants. I wasn't aware of the resentment I had been holding on to, but I found comfort in knowing they weren't associated with her.

Mia continued, "you were betrothed to Seth for two reasons. They saw how close you two had become, and they hoped that love would grow between you both, igniting your power. That was the first reason, and the second reason was to ensure he would be the rightful King of Saleda by joining him with you. You were Catrin's way of maintaining her power and control over this Kingdom."

"Did Seth know the reason for our betrothal?" I asked.

Mia shrugged. "I don't know." I nodded, accepting that I may never know the answer to that question.

Marco looked around the table expectantly before finally speaking up, "am I the only one who thinks we should speak about the other issue here?"

I turned to him, furrowing my brows. "What is the other issue?"

Marco began to speak, but Billy cut him off before he had a chance to get a word out. "Marco, not now. We have to take this one step at a time. Overwhelming her isn't going to do anything but slow down the rebellion," she scolded him.

Florian finally broke his silence. "No, I agree with Marco. We should discuss that part of the prophecy," he said, shifting his gaze to me. "I'm sure you noticed the part of the prophecy that states, *When the rightful King is joined with the foreign child, they will usher in a new age of peace and honor.* That means that you won't reach your full potential until you've been wed to the rightful King."

My chest tightened as his words set in. I hadn't thought about that part of the prophecy. It hadn't made sense to me until now, but it made me realize something. Ever since my wedding to Seth had been stopped, I had finally felt free. When we fled to Kantar, I was no longer Catrin's or Seth's. I was my own person for the first time in my life and now I was being told that I would have to give that freedom up in order to fulfill my destiny. My thoughts began to shift to who I would be forced to marry, and that's when it finally dawned on me. Florian was the late King's first son.

"I have to marry *you*?" I asked Florian, hoping that I was wrong.

He chuckled. "You don't have to. I won't force you into anything that you don't want. But that is the only way you'll be able to learn everything you're capable of," he answered.

Marco looked at Billy, who shook her head at him before his eyes landed on Florian. "Well, that may not be completely accurate," he finally said.

Florian's green eyes glared at Marco, and his nostrils flared before saying, "we all agreed this was the meaning of the prophecy, Marco. We have known this for years."

Completely unbothered by Florian's anger, Marco smirked. "Yes, but that was before-"

Billy stood from the table. "Regardless of our interpretations of the prophecy, Siv getting married is not our top priority. I think we can all agree on that. So let's move on and figure out our next move."

Mia nodded in agreement. "Billy's right. At this point, we don't need to be discussing any of this. My sister has enough on her plate as it is. We don't need to add to it."

I appreciated my sister trying to come to my aid, but I didn't like the feeling that I was still being held in the dark. It was infuriating to know that everyone at this table knew my fate besides me. "I'd like to know what Marco has to say," I announced. "I understand that my personal life doesn't take precedence, but if we're already talking about it, I would like to know."

Billy and Florian glared at Marco, but he continued anyway. "Before the Krig Territories fell, my Grandfather and Grandmother were the Chief and Chieftess. Jude's father was the firstborn, and he took the title among the Krigs in Kantar. After his death, that title had been passed down to Jude." Marco hesitated slightly when his eyes met Billy's. "Here in Saleda, our titles are meaningless. We never even thought to consider the possibility of Jude being the rightful King in the prophecy."

"Because he's not," Florian muttered under his breath.

Marco shrugged. "I'm not saying he is or isn't, but we have to discuss the possibility, Florian. I mean, it was his kiss that awakened her power in the first place." He began chuckling. "One thing is clear, though. Whoever wrote this prophecy was *not* a Krig. Their verbiage is definitely causing a lot of confusion," he joked.

Florian's jaw twitched. "The only person here who's confused is you. If fate would have chosen Jude, the prophecy would have said Chief, not King."

Billy had finally had it. "Florian, enough!" She shouted. "No one is denying your claim to Saleda's throne. We're just exploring the idea that it may not be Saleda's throne the prophecy was referring to. We could be talking about Lorus as a whole for all we know. Like it or not, when Jude claimed to be Siv's soulmate, it changed everything, and I think that tree was enough proof for us all to believe it."

Mia lifted an eyebrow at Florian. "My sister's hand is not a tool for you to use to get what you want, Florian. Is that all you see her as?" She asked him. "It would be a blessing for you to take her as a wife. It was never a promise or an obligation on her end, so why are you acting as if she belongs to you?"

"No, you're right." Florian's expression softened as his eyes shifted to me. "I'm sorry, Siv," he said softly. "My intention has never been to take you against your will. Sometimes, I get so focused on taking back the throne my father once sat on that I forget that this is every bit of your war, too. I hope you know that I don't see you as anything less than the Queen you were meant to be. Can you forgive me?"

The look of genuine remorse on his face made me feel for Florian, but I couldn't help but remember his words from only moments ago. I nodded, accepting his apology, but knew I would not forget.

CHAPTER 13

Eventually, everyone had left the table and I was left alone with the prophecy laid out in front of me. I read it over and over again, trying to make sense of it. I knew I had brought that Willow tree back to life, grew the wildflowers in the field from nothing, and even healed Jude's bruised face. But it didn't seem like enough to take Saleda back from Catrin. Although she was cruel and demanding, she had thousands who were loyal to her. I had faith in the rebellion's ability to fight, but I had no faith in my ability to help them. What was I going to do? Grow wildflowers on the battlefield? I wanted to do more. I wanted to reach my full potential, but I didn't want to marry in order to get there.

The thought of my only purpose being to stand beside a man really hurt. I had believed that every year leading up to my marriage with Seth and when I had finally escaped that situation, I thought there was more to my life. I had thought for a brief time that maybe my future wouldn't involve a forced marriage. However, if doing so would save the people of Saleda, I would, but it didn't make it sting any less. The only thing that did ease the hurt was the idea of marrying Jude. The possibility of calling him mine made my chest warm and my cheeks bright red. It was embarrassing how quickly I would forget about my desire to be a free woman and owned by no man when it came to him. The thought of marrying him felt different. It didn't feel like I would be handing my life over to him. It felt like I would be offering to share it with him and vice versa. I had to remind myself that I didn't know him very well despite feeling so intensely for him. Jude could very well be like any of the other men in the palace. Once he slid that ring on my finger, it could very well become shackles. I wouldn't let myself forget that possibility, no matter how right he felt.

However, the idea of marrying Florian needed no reminder of the horrible possibilities that could follow. He had reminded me so much of Seth these last few days. He was warm and friendly when he was happy, but the moment his mood turned sour, so did his words.

Suddenly, I remembered Jude's letter he had given me. He told me I'd know when to open it, and I figured now was the time, so I ran up to the bedroom and pulled it from my leather pouch. I ripped the red seal and began reading his written words.

Dear Siv,

I'm sure you're overwhelmed at this point. I can't imagine so many things being thrown at me all at once, but you're strong. By now, I'm sure you've heard of my ancestry, as well as my claim on you. While I have no idea what your reaction might be, I wanted a chance to be able to explain in my own words.

When I was young, I took a trip to the Lake of Longing. I'm not sure if you've heard of it, but there are myths surrounding this body of water. They say if you drink from it, the water will show you what you desire most. The thing is, the water won't show you anything that's out of your reach so you know you'll be able to obtain whatever it showed you. Well, the water showed me you. At the time, I just assumed I was longing for the comforts of a woman. I didn't think about it again until the day you walked down that path to my cottage.

My body knew you were my Erosa before I did. Minutes before I saw you, my hands began to sweat, my heart began to race, and I knew something was about to happen. Then I saw you, and even though it had been more than a decade, I recognized you instantly. My other half.

Before I knew you, we had all thought the prophecy was speaking of Florian as the rightful King. We had all accepted and agreed with your union if that is what you wanted. But I now know that my gods were telling me to step up as Chief. For years I saw my title as nothing but a symbol of what my people had lost, but I believe Rheis and Stes are pushing me to be more, to do more.

Despite this, I don't expect anything from you. I trust that my gods knew what they were doing when they intertwined our fates, but I would never force you into a union, even if that is what it took to fulfill the prophecy.

We will see each other again, but until then, know that I am thinking of you.

Love, Jude

I gently folded the letter and placed it in the pocket of my trousers. I felt the heat of tears that threatened to fall, but I refused to let them. I was tired of crying. I was tired of having decisions made for me, and I was tired of being the only one who didn't know what was going on. I had been told from the very beginning that I was to be the Queen everyone had been waiting for, and yet, they treated me like I was a child. Perhaps I had been acting like one.

I sat back at the table where the large book containing the prophecy was still laid out. I made sure to be gentle as I closed it. I wasn't sure how old it was, but by the looks of it, it had seen better days. The cover showed a title in large golden letters: *The History of Lorus.* Excitement guided my hands as I opened the large book once more and began reading.

Before I knew it, hours had gone by. I had only managed to finish a quarter of the book, but I had learned so many things I would have never heard of within the palace gates. There were four major ethnic groups that had originally resided in this world. The first ethnicity was the Krigs from the Krig Territories. Jude, Marco, and Billy's ancestors were a race of warriors. They were born with gifts such as speed, agility, strength, and leadership. They were brilliant when it came to war and strategy, much like Marco had described when he told me the story of their gods. The Krigs were the protectors of Lorus for thousands of years before the great war.

Another ethnic group was called Vaegarians from the Vaegarian Dynasty. These people were described as being incredibly intelligent, charming, cunning, and sometimes devious. They were great inventors and engineers, but oftentimes, the intentions behind their creations were flawed. The Vaegarians believed they were the true leaders of Lorus and they would frequently dispute about who should hold power over this world. Their land had eventually become so polluted by their machines and technologies that it was uninhabitable. So they turned their sights on the Nativus lands and ultimately took it for themselves after eliminating the people who had lived there for thousands of years.

The Nativus were a very mysterious and reserved race. Not much could be recorded about them because not much was known other than the fact that they were the original rulers of Lorus. They were said to be spiritually connected to the world and its nature, sometimes even to the point where they could manipulate its elements. The Nativus had no interest in power, and they rarely had issues with any of the other groups, which made them beloved and respected rulers. Their race was slaughtered by the hands of the Vaegarians, who viewed their elemental gifts as a threat, and they wished to have complete control over Lorus. That was the last thing written of their kind, which made my heart ache despite not ever knowing them.

Lastly, there were Saledians. We were described as creative, resilient, diverse, and at times erratic. I had never thought about Saledians as a whole. Probably because I had never met too many people outside of the palace. However, I thought that description was pretty accurate based on the limited knowledge I had about my country.

The History of Lorus had chapters on the great war and what had led up to it. When the Vaegarians had just begun killing off the Nativus, the Krigs were vocal about their outrage and did everything to protect their cherished rulers. They threatened the Vaegarians with death if they did not stop the genocide they had planned. They were no match when it came to the Krigs and their combat skills, as well as their close relationship with the Nativus. The Vaegarians had promised the Krigs that they would end their violence against the Nativus. But, when the Krigs had their backs turned, the Vaegarians attacked using weapons that were more advanced than anything anyone had ever seen. They used these weapons to kill almost half of the entire Krig population, and then they forced those who remained to leave their country and seek refuge in Saleda.

I wanted to keep reading. To learn everything there was about Lorus and my prophecy, but Mia interrupted me instead, "Siv," she said, looking at the open text in front of me. "I'm sorry to interrupt, but there's someone you need to meet." My sister motioned me to follow her outside the pub.

We walked to a home a few doors down from the pub, and I trailed closely behind my sister as she opened the door to the small house. Inside sat an elderly woman with long white hair on a wooden rocker. Her pale eyes creased as her wrinkled smile grew. "My child," she said, waving me closer to her. "I have been waiting to meet you for quite some time." I sat on the aged armchair beside her and allowed her to take my hands into her own, causing her eyes to widen. "The power that surges through you is strong," she mumbled before turning to my sister.

Mia nodded before glancing at me hesitantly. "We believe she may have unknowingly accelerated her abilities." I lifted an eyebrow as I peered back at my sister but remained silent.

The old woman smirked as she returned her focus back to me. "I see," she answered Mia. "My child, I'm sure you have many questions. Let's begin with my name," she said as she let go of my hands and sat back in her rocking chair. "I am called Iridia."

I mimicked the white-haired woman and sat back in the arm chair, trying my best to appear at ease despite my racing heart and sweaty palms. "It's nice to meet you, Iridia. My name is Siv."

She chuckled. "I know. You see, Siv, this is not the first time we have met."

A line appeared between my eyebrows as my eyes glanced back and forth between Mia and Iridia. "It's not?" Mia walked behind me, placing her hands on my shoulders in a bid to comfort me.

"We are family," she revealed. "Your mother was my granddaughter, and you and Mia are my great-granddaughters. I was there for your birth." Iridia gave me a few minutes to process what she had said before she continued, "I know this must be shocking to hear after going your entire life believing that Mia was your only relative, and I'm sorry for that. I wish we could have had this reunion much sooner, but fate has brought us here now instead."

I inhaled a shaky breath as I tried to keep my emotions in check. I desperately wanted to keep calm and collected in front of Iridia, but the mention of my mother already had me spiraling. For years, I had ignored any and every thought about my parents. I didn't want to know anything about them because I thought that if I did, I would begin to actually miss them. It had been Mia and I for so long that I had never mourned them, and I didn't want to start now.

Mia's grip on my shoulders tightened slightly. "Iridia will explain everything to you much better than I would be able to," she told me, stepping out from behind me. "I'm going to let you both have some time alone and I'll be back in a little to retrieve you."

I wanted to beg my sister to stay with me to help ease the shock I knew was to come, but I reminded myself that I must become comfortable without her by my side. So, I nodded my head and watched her walk out the door, leaving me alone with my great-grandmother.

Iridia smiled warmly and offered me a plate of strange-looking fruit. "It's called klurula. It's native to the Nativus land. I somehow managed to keep a few seeds, and I grew a couple of klurula trees in the back," she explained as she looked me over. "You look so much like your mother," she said with sadness in her pale eyes. "And she looked so much like my daughter."

I took a bite of the fruit and momentarily savored its sweet flavor before curiosity began to overcome the anxiety sitting heavily in my chest. I truly did want to know who I came from, but at the same time, I didn't want the pain that would come with that information. Finally, I lost the war in my head and asked, "what was she like? My mother?"

The old woman's deeply wrinkled face transformed with happiness. "She was everyone's friend, always putting others' needs before her own. Her smile was enough to make you forget about the filth surrounding us and her laugh. Oh, her laugh was better than any song I had ever heard. I miss her and my daughter more than anything. Your mother was a bright light in this dark world, " she said, looking straight ahead. "From what your sister has told me, so are you."

I looked down at my folded hands that sat on my lap. "I'm not so sure about that," I answered and peered up from my hands and leaned into the old woman. "Iridia, what am I?" I asked her.

The corners of her mouth lifted slightly. "We are the last of our kind, dear. We are Nativus."

My jaw dropped. I had only known about the Nativus race for a little more than an hour. Although I believed something within me knew the truth, hearing it out loud made it real. "How-"

Iridia stopped my question with a wave of her hand. "I'm not sure what you know and don't know about this world we live in, but I need you to let me speak. We don't have much time." She waited for me to nod before she continued, "as I'm sure you've noticed, I am an old woman, and my life is coming to an end, but before it does, I must complete my destiny." She smiled brightly at me. "And you, my sweet Queen, are my destiny."

My forehead creased, and my eyes widened as I stared at the elderly woman before me. I should have maintained my panic, but her smile and her tight grip on my hands were like a blanket of comfort. She was a stranger to me, and yet I felt at ease with her. I knew I could trust her.

"You see, I was a mere child when our kind were slaughtered, and I wondered for years why fate had spared me. Then, I began receiving visions. Visions about my granddaughter, you, and the death and rebirth of our world. A great shift is happening in Lorus, Siv. Power that has been in the wrong hands for centuries will be returned, and the darkness that has clouded our skies will begin to clear. Horizons will once again be seen, and justice will prevail."

I shut my eyes, trying my best to avoid the tears that were threatening to fall. I felt as though every time I was coming to terms with this prophecy and my duty to this world, another ball dropped. I was exhausted and defeated. This was bigger than me. This was more than I could handle.

"Iridia, I truly believe there's been a mistake. I can't do this. I don't even know what I'm expected to do! I have yet to receive an answer from anyone. I don't know what is expected of me besides marrying some king. Is that all there is? Am I to be some man's wife in order to save Saleda?" I looked away from her as my tears finally fell down my face. I hated the thought of my only purpose being to stand beside a man.

She slowly rose from her rocking chair and stood in front of me. "No mistake has been made, child. You're exactly who and what you need to be," she said calmly before dropping her smile. "Your union is not so you can stand behind a man; it is so your man stands behind *you*. His love and support will show you what it is to be taken care of, and you will have the chance to replicate that love and care for the people of Lorus."

The color drained from my face as I listened. This was even bigger than I had thought, and I couldn't stop the fear that occupied my body. I didn't think I was capable of taking over Saleda, but now I'm supposed to take back power over the entire world?... That would be close to impossible.

Iridia's cheerful demeanor gradually faded as she looked at me. "I must warn you, though. Power is never free. The more power you seek, the more you must sacrifice to obtain it," she warned.

I shook my head. "But I don't want power. I didn't ask for any of this. I just want to give these people peace."

Iridia's somber expression deepened. "You may not have asked for it, but fate has given it to you anyway. Now it is up to you what to do with it."

My nose wrinkled as I watched the old woman. "What does that mean?" I asked her.

She laughed before shaking her head. "You've much to learn, child." Iridia sat back down in her rocking chair, and her eyes began to close. "But now, I must rest, and you must leave. I will see you on the other side," she said with quiet snores quickly following.

CHAPTER 14

I had so many more questions to ask Iridia, but it didn't feel right to wake an old woman up from her slumber. I sat beside her for a while, reflecting on everything she had revealed. She was definitely strange, but her presence put me at ease. Even as she slept, it was like she provided me with a sense of safety I hadn't felt before.

I finally stood from the worn armchair and let myself out of her small home. I knew I should wait for Mia to retrieve me, but I had a strong urge to explore the city on my own. I had grown used to always having someone to hold my hand through mundane tasks, such as walking through town. I wanted to meet people and I wanted to see where I had lived my entire life. If my destiny was to free these people, I figured I should know them.

I had only walked a few steps when a loud bang erupted, and a flash of light blinded me before I was forcefully thrown into the brick building across from me. The silence was replaced by a loud ringing in my ears. I tried to breathe through the dust and smoke that now filled the air. In my state of panic and confusion, I propped myself up on my elbow, looking for whoever had pushed me. Scraps of paper that were on fire rained down on me as I struggled to come to terms with my surroundings. It wasn't until I saw the rubble that had once been the pub and Iridia's home that I realized no one had pushed me; we had been bombed.

My mind was hazy, and although I had yet to feel any pain, my body was stiff and slow to rise. I looked around at the ruins surrounding me, trying my hardest to think straight. Panic replaced my confusion as I remembered Iridia had fallen asleep inside her home minutes before I had left. Then I thought of my sister. Where was Mia? Had she been inside the pub? I forced my legs to carry me to the remains of what had once been the rebellion's safe house. I ignored the grief that had built up in my chest as I stumbled past Iridia's home and climbed through the wreckage of the pub. I knew she was dead, but I wasn't sure of my sister's fate.

My hands began to bleed as I dug through bricks, glass, and burnt, splintered wood. I still felt no pain, but the crimson liquid that covered my fingers screamed at me to stop. I wouldn't though, not until I was sure that my sister was safe.

Tears streaked my ash-covered face when I spotted brown hair among the rubble. My weak legs could only carry me so far before I stumbled and fell feet away from the body that I was desperately trying to reach. I forced myself up with every last bit of strength my body had, and when I fell before the buried figure, I began to dig frantically. I had barely made a dent when a pair of arms pulled me away from the remains. I didn't care who was behind me, dragging me away. I didn't even think to look as I tried to jerk and thrash myself out of their grip. I couldn't hear anything but the steady ringing in my ears, but I knew I was screaming.

Finally, a larger and firmer set of arms harshly pulled me away and threw me over their shoulder. The only thought that occupied my mind was if that body had been my sister. I didn't care who was carrying me. I didn't care where they were taking me. All I knew was that my sister could be dead, and I was being taken further and further from her. Billy, Marco, and even Florian could be lying there, lifeless with her. The entire walk from the wreckage had been a blur. The only memories remaining from that time were being fully immersed in dread and horror. Before I could comprehend anything that had just happened, I was gently set down on a chair in a room that I didn't recognize.

It was only when Marco's face came into view that I realized he was *alive*. He started to speak, but I lunged for him, wrapping my arms around his waist and resting my head against his chest. Surprised, he slightly staggered before he regained his footing and eased into my hold, wrapping his arms around my shoulders.

"You're not dead," I said, unable to hear anything but the constant ringing.

I could feel the vibration from Marco's voice, and although I looked forward to hearing him speak again, I was happy just to know he hadn't been in the safehouse.

Pulling away from him, I asked, "Wa-was Mia inside?"

He began talking, but I pointed to my ears and shook my head. After a second or two, he seemed to comprehend that I couldn't hear him and gestured to me that Mia was okay, as well as Billy and Florian. The reprieve of anxiety and anguish left my body feeling light. My head fell backward, and tears of joy left more stripes down my ashy face before the pain and exhaustion had finally set in. The adrenaline that had made it possible to dig through stone and glass had long left me.

Marco seemed to understand because before I could utter another word, he gently picked me up and carried me into a bedroom at the end of a long hallway. When he set me down on the firm bed in the corner of the room, I tried to overcome the fatigue that had come over me. Every movement I made sent a throbbing pain down my spine and limbs, and finally, it was too much, and I had no control over the deep sleep that claimed me.

I stretched my arms out above my head as I finally began to wake up, and I slowly forced my groggy eyes to open. A weight in my palm forced my eyes down to my hands that had been carefully wrapped in my sleep. I realized my sister was asleep next to me, holding me tightly. I thanked whatever gods had been looking out for her before I slowly slipped from her grip. I climbed out of bed, ignoring the dull aches that echoed throughout my body.

"What're you doing?" Mia asked before I had even made it two steps from the bed.

I turned around quickly at the sound of her voice and wrapped my arms around her tightly. "I thought you had died in the explosion, Mia," I told her. "I thought I saw you in the rubble, and I tried to dig you out." I lifted my wrapped hands that had begun to bleed through the bandages.

My sister pulled away from my embrace, gazing over my injured hands. Then, her eyes shifted to the numerous other bruises and cuts on my body. "Siv, I was the one who grabbed you before Marco took you here," she muttered, clearly traumatized. "As soon as I heard the blast, I ran to you. I thought I had lost you until I found you sobbing over the wreckage of the pub, soaked in your own blood." Mia looked away from me, quickly wiping away a stray tear. "I have done and seen a lot of terrible things for this rebellion, but nothing has ever made me as scared as I was when I thought you had been inside Iridia's home still."

In all the chaos and confusion that had surrounded me after the bomb had gone off, I somehow had forgotten about Iridia. "She's gone, isn't she?" I asked.

Mia closed her eyes, nodding her head. "Yes," she answered before pulling me back into her body and gripping my sides tightly as if she were afraid we'd be torn apart. "Iridia wasn't afraid of death. In fact, she looked forward to seeing her family again. Our family."

Her words only offered me a moment of comfort. It was strange to mourn the loss of someone you hadn't even known the day prior to their passing, but the pain I felt at her loss was deep. She was the only family member besides Mia, and I wasn't sure if I was grieving her death or, more selfishly, how I had only gotten to have one conversation with her before she was taken from me.

I took in a shaky breath before asking, "how many did we lose?"

Her smile faded, and her expression hardened. "Six bodies were recovered from the pub, and the cellar is still buried, but if anyone were down there, there's no way they could have survived," she answered grimly.

The color drained from my face as I realized their deaths were because of me. That explosion was meant for me, but they lost their lives instead. I wasn't sure how to cope with that.

Mia loosened her grip on me, pulling away just enough to look me in the eyes. "Siv, you've been out for two days. One of the cuts on your back was pretty bad and it had gotten infected. The rebellion's healer had an elixir that healed the infection, but it forced you into a deep sleep," she revealed. "As much as you deserve time to process the events that have occurred, I need you to bathe and get dressed. We have a lot that needs to be discussed.

I knew I had been asleep for a while based on the bandages covering my hands, but I didn't think two days had passed. I pushed down the panic that had been a recurring guest in my chest, and I decided to focus on the small, mundane things that needed to be done before anything else. "I don't have any clothes. My bag was in the apartment above the pub," I told her.

"This house belonged to a member of the rebellion. She gave us permission to use this place before she lost her life in the last battle," Mia said with a sad smile as if she were remembering an old friend. "She was roughly the same size as you. I'll grab something for you while you bathe."

It felt strange to be in the home of someone who was no longer alive. It felt even stranger to accept the clothes that they had once worn, but I didn't have too many options, so I was forced to agree.

After I had a much-needed bath, I dried myself and looked at the clothing Mia had left in the washroom for me. I was surprised to see that she had left me a sundress. It wasn't like I had anything against dresses; I actually enjoyed them before Seth began picking them out for me. But I hadn't worn one since the night of the coup, and I had gotten used to wearing trousers. I pulled it over my head and nervously messed with the hem of the light purple fabric as I made my way down the stairs, where I heard hushed whispers.

The whispers stopped, and everyone's eyes fell upon me as I descended the stairs. I smiled when I saw Billy and Florian among Marco and Mia, but it quickly fell when I noticed their sullen faces. "What's going on?" I asked, feeling uncomfortable.

"We found the traitor," Billy said as she began to pace back and forth between the kitchen and living room. "Things are a lot worse than we thought."

I turned to Mia. "Who is it? What does this mean?"

Billy spoke, relieving my sister of having to answer me. "It was Luis. You met him-"

I interrupted him. "I remember him. He was the one who had red hair, right?"

She nodded. "Yeah, that's him," he said, exhaling loudly. "He's not who we thought he was," she said quietly.

I looked at Florian, trying to read his expression, but came up blank. He hid his feelings well, especially in stressful situations. "There's not much we can do about it at the moment. We need to focus on our next move."

Marco turned to Florian. "If Luis really was the rat, he knows almost everything." He cursed under his breath as he ran his hands through his hair.

"He is," Billy chimed in. "I had my suspicions about him for quite some time now, and although they were always dismissed," Billy looked pointedly at Florian. "I decided to follow him when I spotted him close by the rubble moments after the explosion. I was confused at first because the apartment he entered was one of our friends; his name was Arthur. He was a good man who had a strange interest in fire and explosives. At first, I was angry because I thought he may have been working with Luis, but his lifeless body told me otherwise."

I wondered if Arthur was the same man Mia had told me about as she joked about blowing the palace up. I didn't know the man, but judging from the somber mood in the room, he was a close friend to them. I couldn't help but feel guilty that yet another life had been lost.

Marco continued, "We'll have to warn each of the safe houses. We'll have to scrap every plan of attack we had before now. We're done for."

Florian looked up to the stone ceiling and shook his head. "I admit I overlooked him. He charmed me, along with many others. I should have been smarter than this. If Siv had been inside the pub during the attack," Florian cut himself off and massaged his temples. "This should have never happened. That we can all agree on, but we're not done for. Not yet. We can still win this war," he said to no one in particular.

"I'm sure we're all grateful it wasn't Siv who was inside the pub at the time, but lives *were* lost," Marco said, grabbing a long sword from the wall. "Now, we need to decide what we're going to do about it."

"That's not all," Billy groaned. "I dragged Luis to the stockade at the edge of town and placed him in the cell. He spent all of yesterday with no blankets, food or water. This morning, after a few hard hits and the promise of a hot meal and water, he was pretty talkative," she confessed without an ounce of remorse. "He told me that he is Catrin's brother."

I thought back to the night I had met him. His red hair and blue eyes were identical to Catrin's and I hated that I didn't recognize that until now. I should have known. I could have saved the lives that were lost in the pub if I had recognized their similarities sooner.

"Luis claimed that they're from the Vaegarian Dynasty. They grew up there before they moved to Saleda." Billy covered her face with her hands. "They're of Vaegarian descent."

All of the blood drained from Florian's face as he looked up. "If that's true then..." His voice faded and he didn't finish his sentence.

Billy nodded and glanced over to me. "Our fight is no longer with Catrin; it is with her country of origin."

CHAPTER 15

I could tell that Billy's news of Luis and Catrin's ethnic origin was a game changer, but I wasn't quite sure why. Despite the possibility of adding more soldiers to Catrin's army, I wasn't sure what her being of Vaegarian descent would change. "What exactly does that mean?" I asked.

Mia looked at me with a pained expression. "Siv, if Catrin is acting on orders from the Vaegarian Dynasty, this war is about to look very different. They've been quiet and kept to themselves since the Great War, but even back then, they had technology and tools that we can't compete with."

Although I had read about their technology and inventions in *The History of Lorus*, I hadn't comprehended just how dangerous they were. Mia's knitted brows and hazel eyes that had become consumed with fear confirmed just how bad this was for us.

Marco stood from the table and placed his hand on my shoulder. "But that was before we had you," he said with a lop-sided smile. "Their attempt on your life a couple of days ago should show you just how much of a threat they see you as. Once you manage to strengthen your power and use it with intention, their weapons won't mean anything, and they know that."

His attempt to comfort me had only made me more anxious. "How am I supposed to strengthen my power or learn to use it purposefully?" I asked him as I continued to nervously mess with the hem of my dress.

Florian stood from the table and disappeared into the kitchen before reappearing with a knife. "I think I know a way." He took a deep breath before running the sharp end of the knife across the skin on his forearm.

I gasped as I watched his blood drip onto the wood floor. Rushing to cover his wound with my hands, I yelled, "what are you thinking!" Florian shrugged as he looked down at my now bloody hands covering his wound.

"Mia, go grab some clean cloth!" I shouted.

I was sure my heart was about to beat right out of my chest from the fear nestled tightly inside. There was so much blood, and I began to fear that Florian's life would be yet another life lost. I was afraid to loosen my grip when I asked, "Florian, do you feel light-headed at all? Maybe we should sit down."

He shrugged. "I feel fine, actually."

Mia came rushing back with a bundle of clean cloths and a small parcel that I assumed held medical supplies. "You need to remove your hands, Siv. He needs stitches." She said as he rolled out the parcel.

We had both gained a lot of practice when it came to cleaning and sewing wounds. Catrin's punishments gradually became more violent, and we would be left to our own devices when it came to avoiding infection or bleeding out. So, I was confident in Mia's skills as I gently let go of Florian's arm. I couldn't help but cringe when Mia began to inspect the wound, wiping the blood out of the way. "Florian, your-"

Florian cut her off with loud laughter. "She healed me, didn't she?" He asked, pulling his arm from Mia and running his fingers where the wound should have been.

I yanked his arm from him and inspected it. The blood had begun to dry in the hair that covered his arm, but there was no longer a gash left from the knife. I stared at the missing wound for a moment before I turned my attention back to Florian. "If you ever do anything that dumb again, I will be the one cutting you with a knife!" I shouted at him.

Florian shrugged again while chuckling. "It worked, though, didn't it?"

Mia sighed loudly as her body began to relax. "I agree with Siv on this one. That was extremely stupid."

As the panic began to subside within me, the weight of what I had just done settled. I had summoned my power without even thinking of it. A smile grew on my face as my confidence grew slightly. Maybe I could be a weapon for the rebellion. Perhaps I had been putting too much thought into it. Perhaps it came down to instinct rather than skill.

"If you can do this now, imagine what you could do after you've agreed to a union," Florian said nonchalantly.

Mia groaned loudly. "Give it a rest, Florian. It's not going to happen."

He winked at me, and I rolled my eyes at his arrogance. "That could have ended very badly," I told him flatly. "At the very least, you'd have to get stitches, but what would have happened if you lost too much blood? You need to start thinking things through a little more."

Marco exhaled loudly. "He's never been very good at that," he said in a dry tone.

Ignoring the banter between Florian and Marco, I turned to Billy and Mia. "What are we going to do in response to the explosion at the pub?" I asked, and the two men quickly quieted down, eager to hear their response.

Billy answered quickly, "for now, nothing." I began to disagree but she held her hand up, stopping me. "If the Vaegarians are truly involved in this war, we cannot risk being rash. Every move we make has to be carefully calculated from here on out. We cannot act out on our emotions."

"She's right," Mia agreed. "If we make ourselves vulnerable to them at the wrong time, our entire army could be wiped out."

I crossed my arms. "Then let's make a plan."

"Plans take time," Billy responded.

I laughed out of frustration. "Then what do you propose, Billy? I refuse to hide while Catrin is doing who knows what! If the Vaegarians are as dangerous as you make them out to be, then shouldn't we strike when they least expect it? They'd never see us coming right now. They think we're scared and hiding. They think we're doing exactly what you want us to do," I seethed.

Florian smirked. "She's got a point, Billy," he told her. "The entire point of this explosion, besides killing Siv, was to create fear. There's also a chance they still don't know Luis was captured, which means they don't know about their inclusion with Catrin."

"I actually agree with them," Marco chimed in, earning a glare from my sister.

Mia lifted her chin before she spoke. "If we get this wrong, we're done for. You all realize this, right?"

I did realize that, and it could be that I was letting my emotions get the better of me, but I couldn't let Iridia's death be for nothing. I couldn't let the lives lost in the pub and cellar be for nothing. I felt as though I was to blame for their demise, and not doing anything would only make that guilt grow. I wanted to prove myself. I wanted to help.

"But if we get this right, we may win this war," I interjected, earning another smile from Florian.

Billy shook her head and threw her arms up in defeat. "I've said my piece. The rest is out of my hands," she sighed. "Marco, come up with a plan and timeframe. I'm afraid my expertise will be hindered by my disapproval," she ordered before leaving the room.

Marco sarcastically saluted her before turning to my sister, who shook her head and followed after Billy, making me chuckle slightly.

Florian stared at me, not caring if I noticed, and I finally asked, "what?"

His green eyes finally shifted to the table in front of him as a grin appeared on his unusually stubbly face. "Nothing," he answered. "I'm just enjoying you taking charge finally. You spoke your piece a moment ago and demanded that we listen. A week ago, you would have never done that."

Although the compliment came from Florian, who I had my own issues with, it made me feel proud. He was right. A week ago, I would have silently agreed to wait it out. After years of abuse by Catrin's hands, I had become convinced no one wanted or cared to hear what I had to say. I now know that's not true. I now know that I must raise my voice if I'm to be heard, and I enjoy being heard.

A slight blush appeared on my cheeks. I still wasn't used to being praised and his words had made me flustered. "Thank you."

Florian's green eyes darkened as his gaze once again burned into me. "You're very welcome, my Queen."

The next two days were consumed with preparations for our upcoming ambush on the palace. Mia, Florian, and I helped map out the palace grounds so that our army was familiar with their surroundings once we had flooded the gates. Marco and Billy trained their soldiers and rehearsed their battle strategy.

Although we were busy and everyone was on edge about the impending ambush, we worked as a team. It was neat seeing so many people work toward one common goal, and I thoroughly enjoyed the camaraderie our preparations had created. These people were becoming my family, which made me want to fight for them even more. They deserved a life of peace and happiness, but they had been living lives filled with hunger and pain instead. I wanted to change that.

I was startled by a large hand gently resting on my shoulder, but as soon as I saw Marco's familiar eyes and mischievous grin, I relaxed on the small chair at the dining table.

"What're you daydreaming about?" He asked, taking a seat next to me.

I shrugged. "Several things," I told him. "I was thinking about how close I've gotten to everyone in this rebellion and how tomorrow's ambush on the palace may end with some of their lives being lost. I'm nervous, Marco. I know this was my idea but the closer tomorrow gets, the more afraid I become. What if Mia and Billy were right? What if we should have waited?"

Marco leaned in, leaving barely any space between us. "You can't think like that, Siv. I've fought many battles, and I've lost many friends, but I have never regretted standing up for what I believe in." He looked around us, making sure we were alone. "I love your sister like she was my own, but her love for you clouds her vision sometimes. Her need to protect you is more important to her than the rebellion's cause. And Billy, although a great warrior, has always chosen peace over bloodshed. While that is not always a bad thing, it's not possible in this war. No compromise or negotiation will ever be good enough to redeem Catrin or even the Vaegarian Dynasty."

I considered what he had said. I could see the truth in his words, but my sister's opinion was important to me, regardless of why she thought the way she did. I began to wonder what Jude would have thought if he were here. If he would have agreed with me, Marco, and Florian or if he would have taken the side of caution with Mia and Billy.

"Marco, do you think Jude would approve of our plan?" I asked him.

He thought for a minute or two before answering, "if it were any other situation, I think he would have preferred more time before an attack. Jude is a planner and a perfectionist. He likes to make sure a plan is ironproof before acting on it. But, because this fight is with Catrin and possibly the Vaegarian Dynasty, I believe Jude would have already infiltrated the palace on his own and ripped Catrin's throat out before anyone had noticed he was there."

I cringed at the morbid picture Marco had painted in my head, but I supposed he was right. I felt better knowing Jude would have supported my decision, but now, instead of anxiety, I ached for Jude's calming presence.

"Do you think I'll ever see him again?"

Marco chuckled. "If you truly are his Erosa, and I have no doubt that you are, he will move mountains to see you again."

That was all the comfort I needed. As long as I could look forward to seeing him again, I could carry on.

CHAPTER 16

As the sun began to set, the buzz inside of the town began to quiet. Although our numbers had significantly risen from volunteers all over Saleda, you could hear a pin drop. Everyone was aware that within hours, everything would be different. Some of us may not be here any longer and others would be injured, but we all hoped for the same thing. We wanted Catrin out of the palace. We wanted Saleda to be free.

My feet felt heavy as I joined Mia, Marco, Billy, Florian and a few others at the dinner table. They were all huddled over a map of the palace that we had drawn up, finalizing our plans for the ambush. I looked at their faces, which were lit up by the candles surrounding the large map. It was as if we had all aged ten years overnight. We each had bags underneath our eyes, and the lines between our brows had deepened from stress. Regardless of the brave faces each of them adorned, I knew they were worried, afraid even. I knew I was.

As they finished talking, Mia turned to me and grabbed my hands. "You will stay with Marco at all times, okay? He will make sure nothing will happen to you," she said with the look of concern clouding her features.

I nodded, even though I wasn't thrilled about being assigned a babysitter. Originally, I was to stay outside of the palace gates until after they had infiltrated it and seized it from Catrin, those who were loyal to her, and her guards. Mia and Florian had both argued that I was their only asset and that to put me in harm's way would be ignorant. Much to my dismay, I had to remind them that I wasn't an 'asset' but a living, breathing person who was just as much a part of this rebellion as they were and several arguments later, this had been our compromise.

Mia tightened her grip on my hands for a moment, offering me a smile that failed to meet her eyes. "This is going to work," she said under her breath and I nodded again even though I knew she was talking to herself more than me.

"It's time," Billy said as she walked past us, opening the door and walking out to the large crowd that had gathered outside of the house we were staying at.

Florian grinned as he walked behind Billy and despite not having the best relationship with him, I admired how he could conjure up so much confidence at a time like this. Mia squeezed my hands one last time before following Marco and gesturing for me to come along.

"Well, the time is here. We have all known tonight would come, and for some, it is sooner than expected, while for others, it is far past due," Florian addresses the crowd. "As I look out at the faces standing before me, I see bravery, I see conviction, and I see hunger for justice. We have been starved, robbed, beaten, flogged, stabbed, and hung while those inside the palace gates enjoy their lavish dinners and grand balls. Tonight, that changes. Tonight, we take back what is ours!" Florian roars.

The vibrations from the crowd's cheers traveled through my body, and the nerves that had been begging me to stay behind like the original plan allowed. I was still nervous, but now, a fire had been lit inside me.

"But to be brave does not mean that fear is not present. To be brave is to feel that fear and still have the courage to carry on. So I ask you all, will we carry on tonight?" Florian asks the hundreds of people surrounding us.

"*Yes!*" They screamed in unison.

Florian smiled. "I'm glad to hear it," he said before turning back to me. "I think they deserve to hear from their Queen before they run into battle for you."

My face immediately felt hot, and I knew my skin had turned a deep shade of red as I looked back at him. "I can't, I don't-"

Florian stepped closer, placing his hands on my shoulder. "They're putting their lives on the line because they believe in you. It's time you believe in yourself."

With shaky hands and sweaty palms, I stepped beside Florian and looked out to the faces staring back at me. Their eyes held a deep sadness that only someone who has experienced tremendous pain could hold, but it held something else, too. Their eyes also blazed with fortitude, and I couldn't help but feel proud. Everyone here had lost something, but here we were, fighting for what we believed in. Fighting for what was right.

"Hello," I began, but my voice cracked. Now embarrassed, I bit my lip and looked back to my sister, who encouraged me to continue. "I have met most of you, but for those I have yet to introduce myself to, my name is Siv."

Silence followed my words and I once again looked back to Mia. "Keep going," she whispered with a small smile.

"When our safehouse was attacked, and our friends' lives were lost, we had a choice to make. We could either play it safe and wait it out, or we could fight. We chose to fight," I told them, clutching the loose fabric of the tunic I wore underneath the leather bodice Mia made me wear. "I won't lie to you, the choice we made is a dangerous one, but it is the choice that needed to be made if change was ever to come. Tonight, we will march and ride our way into battle. For many of us, this will be our first, and for many, it may be their last. But every single one of us will be joined by the spirits of our ancestors who had been starved, tortured, hung, and burned, just as we have for simply living. Tonight, in this fight, we will bring down our enemy and bring freedom to our families and our friends, and we will give our ancestors peace at last."

To my surprise, the crowd hollered in agreement, which consoled my nerves and helped me continue. "It is easy to feel as though the odds are stacked against us. It is no secret that Catrin has us outnumbered; she has more resources, and she has better weapons. But she also has a fatal flaw that she exposed to us the night of the coup. Catrin never expected us to fight back. She has underestimated us from the very beginning, and tonight, we will use that in our favor."

As the crowd roared, I turned to my side to see Florian smiling proudly at me. "When you begin to believe in yourself, they begin to believe that this war can be won," he said, gesturing at the lively crowd. "Now let's make Catrin wish she never stepped foot in Saleda."

The thunder of hundreds marching toward the palace reverberated through the streets of Mendacia. With the amount of soldiers we now had, we knew the element of surprise would be quickly withdrawn as we marched into battle, but it was better than nothing.

"When we get to the gates, I want you to keep your cloak over your head. I want to keep your identity hidden for as long as possible," Florian told me.

I knew this battle meant more to Florian than most. He had imagined this day for two decades. Today he would finally get the chance to take back his home that had belonged to his family for centuries before Catrin, or rather the Vaegarian Dynasty, had stolen it. Yet, here he was, worried about me and my safety. The wall that I had built up around me when it came to him lowered slightly. I still disliked the way he dealt with his anger at times, but I was beginning to think that he might be a good person despite all his faults.

After a short ride from the village, we could see the large gates to the palace grounds. Everyone lowered their bodies as well as their voices while Marco and Billy evaluated the situation. I had expected to see hundreds of guards out in front, but there couldn't have been more than twenty. I looked at Billy and Marco, who looked just as confused as I was.

"This can't be right," Billy muttered.

Florian pressed his hand on Marco's shoulder. "How many were on patrol last week?"

He shook his head. "At least three times this many," he answered.

"What if we truly caught them off guard? What if they didn't have enough time to man the gates?" I asked.

Marco cursed under his breath and combed his hands through his short hair. "Even if we did catch them off guard, they would have manned the gates. At no point in time has it ever been this vacant."

"What does that mean?" I pressed.

Florian's brows snapped together, and his posture stiffened. "It means nothing. We must continue."

Billy gently placed her hand on Florian's shoulder. "We need to reevaluate the situation. Fewer guards could mean-"

He cut her off. "It means *nothing*, and we must continue," he repeated. "Regardless of why their numbers have decreased, we must carry on. We have waited long enough, and too many lives have been lost in the meantime. If we fall back now, that shows weakness. We cannot afford to show weakness at this point in the war."

"He's right. There's too many of us for them to have not heard us coming. If we turn back now, we will look weak, and they will see that as an invitation to attack once more," Marco chimed in. "As much as I dislike our position at the moment, I don't think we have any other choice than to keep marching."

I looked around and saw that many nodded their heads in agreement, but I felt Mia stiffen behind me. "What do you think?" I asked her.

Mia took in a deep breath, and her expression was filled with concern. "If I'm being honest, I don't like it," she said. "But I also think Marco and Florian are right. We can't turn back now." Mia signaled to keep moving, and a second or two later, the ground was shaking once again from the movement of people marching into the unknown.

Guards began shouting commands as we neared the gates, and moments later, burning arrows began falling upon us. Florian quickly pulled his shield up to cover both of us as we continued to march on.

"It doesn't look like anyone's been hit yet," Florian whispered, soothing my nerves.

Shouts and cries replaced the whistling sounds of the arrows, and before I realized it, I was now sitting alone as Florian jumped out from under the shield and immediately shoved his sword into one of the guards rushing towards us. I quickly looked away when Florian's blade exited the man's body, and thick red fluid was sprayed across Florian's face. I was well aware that today would be filled with death, but I was not used to the cries of the men who had just realized they were dying or the coppery smell of blood surrounding their lifeless bodies.

Florian reached for my hand, and when I failed to take it, he grabbed me by the waist, gently shaking me. "Are you okay?"

I looked around as members of the rebellion finished off the last couple of guards and shook my head. "I don't know," I told him, unable to blink.

"She's in shock," Mia chimed in. "She's never been involved in a battle. We should have prepared her more."

"When did we have time for that?" Florian replied with a cutting tone.

I shook my head and tried my best to gather myself. "I'm fine. I'll be okay," I told them with fake confidence, hoping they wouldn't see right through me.

Marco turned to Florian. "You know the plan. We'll meet at the entrance when all is said and done," he told him, motioning for Florian to let go of my waist that I hadn't even realized he still had a hold of.

Florian nodded, letting go of me and turning back toward the soldiers behind us. We continued to march towards the tall, elaborate doors leading to the Great Hall without Florian. Once inside, we all looked at one another. We were once again met with only a handful of guards. Mia wasted no time and charged them with her long sword and took down two guards by the time Billy joined her. Marco stood in front of me, guarding me from any blows as he studied each doorway, looking for more guards.

"This makes no sense," he said to himself.

Billy pulled a guard by his chained armor and dropped him in front of Marco. "Tell him what you just told me," she spat.

The wounded guard looked up at Marco with tears brimming in his eyes. "Queen Catrin knew you'd come after the explosion. It's a trap."

Marco looked him over briefly as if he was trying to unravel Catrin's plan. "So she placed you all here for what? A brief distraction?"

The man slumped and looked to the ground, now covered in blood. "I don't know. I just followed orders," he answered.

Marco shook his head in disgust. "You knew you'd die today."

The injured man nodded, looking defeated.

I swallowed down the bile that had been making its way from my stomach. It wasn't that Catrin's cruelty was new to me. I had grown up with her brutal tendencies, and I had always known what she was capable of. But seeing others suffer at the hands of her cut-throat ways was always difficult to watch. This man had suited up in his armor and took guard, knowing that today would be his last. Yet, I'm sure Catrin hasn't wasted a moment of thought on any of the lives being thrown away at her expense. They are only a brief consequence of getting what she wants.

Billy looked to Marco, and the two shared a moment before she nodded and he turned toward the somber guard. "It looks like today's your lucky day, then," Marco told him. "Leave the capital, take whoever you can, and don't look back. If we meet again, I won't be so generous."

Marco turned from the guard, who was now running away quickly, and he motioned me to follow him and Billy through the corridors to the left wing.

Though we were more cautious now, we still had a mission to seize the palace. We were convinced that it could still be done, regardless of whether Catrin was expecting us or not. Mia and I were well rehearsed in palace drills from our time living there. So, we knew that the palace's safe room was in the center. While everyone else who had accompanied us inside followed orders to clear and seize the remaining left and right wings of the palace, Mia wanted to arrest and imprison the nobles who lived there herself. Many of them had not been cordial to either of us, but especially her while we were growing up. They were aware that we were not of noble blood, and they disliked sharing their space with two lowborns. Although we would have much rather grown up anywhere but there, the noble children and oftentimes adults would let us know we were not one of them. Ironically, Seth was the only child who ever invited us to play.

No words were spoken as Mia led the way. Everyone remained alert, knowing that we could run into a surprise attack at any moment, but my head was anywhere but there. I kept squeezing my eyes shut as the faces of the guards who had just killed flashed through my mind. I knew that Billy, Marco, Florian, and especially Mia took no joy in taking the lives of those guards and would have much rather let them *all* go. We all knew that it was no fault of their own that they were in that position, which made it that much harder for me to come to terms with it. But it was hard to know who was a loyalist and who was just doing what they had to survive.

My breathing was becoming more and more erratic as the image of their blood seeping onto the white marble floors flooded my thoughts, and their cries filled my ears. Marco suddenly stopped, causing me to run straight into his back, fumbling backward and tripping over my own ankle. Cursing, I lifted my ankle to my chest and hissed in pain. When he turned around, his harsh expression immediately softened when he saw the distress I was in.

"What is it?" Mia asked, turning around to see what the noise was about.

If I wasn't desperately trying to ignore the sharp pain in my ankle, I would have been embarrassed. "I twisted my ankle," I gasped as I tried to put weight on it before scrunching my face up in pain. "I can't walk on it."

Marco forced me down to a sitting position on the ground and looked up at Mia. "I can stay with her. That was the plan all along, anyway. Go ahead, and we will meet you at the entrance," he urged her. "She'll be safe with me. I promise."

I could see the hesitation written all over her face as she struggled to make a decision on whether or not she should stay with me, so I told her to go. I told her I'd be fine with Marco, even though, deep down, I had hoped she would stay.

"I'll see you soon. Okay?" Mia looked back at Marco with a stern expression that made it hard to believe there was a romantic relationship between the two. "Don't let anything happen to my sister," she told him before taking off after Billy.

CHAPTER 17

Marco picked me up and carried me back down the corridor that we had come from. He decided it would be best for us to wait at the entrance until everyone had completed their missions. Despite being angry and embarrassed at first that I hadn't actually helped at all and instead became a hindrance, I knew that he was right. We were both quiet as he lugged me along against his chest. I figured his unusual silence was either because he was annoyed that I had prevented him from helping seize the palace or, at the very least, being there for my sister, but my silence was due to a completely different reason. Something felt off to me, but not in a bad way. It was as if the instability that had been brewing inside of me was balancing out, and I couldn't figure out why. Knowing myself, I should have still felt the stinging buzz of shame as I was being carried away from the fight. Instead, I felt the warm comfort that only one other person had ever endowed me with.

"Jude," I finally said, breaking the stillness between us.

He stopped briefly, looking down at me and assessing if I was in any pain. "What? Am I hurting you?"

I shook my head. "No, no, I'm fine," I told him. "But I-I don't know why, but I think Jude is close."

Marco's dark eyes widened, making their red tint bolder. "He was right," he said under his breath before picking up his pace. "He was right about you being his Erosa," he finally said to me.

"Why are you running? Is that bad?"

Marco kept his gaze straight ahead as he ran effortlessly with me against his chest. "If Jude is here, that means he brought his army. If a Krig army is here, the last place we need to be is in the middle of that battle." He finally looked down at me. "When a Krig is in combat, we're volatile. Jude would tear me to pieces if you were to obtain even a scratch. Me, and whoever may have hurt you. I'm trying to avoid a potentially messy situation," he explained.

"So he's here then?"

Marco laughed. "Is that all you got out of what I just told you?" Shaking his head, he said, "if you feel Jude's presence, he's here."

A wide smile formed on my face and I felt as if my body had become lighter somehow, but it didn't last long. A guard who was almost as large and tall as Marco stepped out from a doorway, striking Marco's upper chest with his shield. Although Marco's arms spared me from the brunt of the blow, it took him off his feet. He swiftly rose and positioned himself over my body, guarding me from whoever had taken us by surprise. However, my head hit the white marble floor before the rest of my body, and I didn't realize what was happening until my vision finally cleared.

I heard Catrin's voice before I saw her tall and gaunt body slowly walking toward us. "Well, would you look at my little Siv. You're all grown up now, aren't you?"

Marco's body tensed and he shifted slightly in an attempt to block my body from both her and the guard at the same time. "A Krig army is on their way to the palace as we speak," Marco warned her. "If I were you, I wouldn't waste my time on us, and I'd catch the next ship out of Saleda."

Catrin's harsh laugh sent shivers down my spine. I had heard that laugh numerous times in my life, and it almost always preceded immense pain. "You Krigs have always thought you were more of a threat than you actually are," she seethed. "I'm not afraid of you or your oversized savage friends."

Marco's breathing became shallow and his fists were balled at his sides. "I believe that," he told her. "But perhaps your lack of fear will be your demise."

Catrin's pale blue eyes shifted to the other side of us. "Kill them both," she ordered.

I tried to shout, but no sound would come. I was frozen in horror as Marco wasted no time, pursuing the guard in a brawl. Although he obviously had more skill and technique, the guard had a shield and a sword. After a few cuts to his arms, Marco began to slow, which allowed the guard to kick out his knee, forcing him to the ground once again. The guard pulled his sword back just as Marco looked back at me and whispered, "I'm sorry."

I heard the hiss of the sword, and my heart sank. His badly timed humor had quickly become something I had looked forward to in every conversation he was in, but he was also sweet and caring. Marco was like the brother I had always wished for growing up. He had somehow become such a significant part of my life, and even though I didn't even know who he was a month ago, I wasn't sure how I'd be able to live without him, but I quickly remembered I wouldn't have to. Catrin ordered my death as well.

Warm tears flooded my eyes as I burrowed my head in between my legs and waited for my own execution. To my surprise, the sharp edge of the guard's sword never came, but instead, two large arms snatched me from the ground. I lifted my head and gasped when I realized it was Marco who had picked me up from the ground. I cocked my head to see behind Marco's massive form, and to my surprise, Seth was holding a bloodied sword while the guard laid lifeless in front of him with a fatal wound to the back. My brows scrunched in confusion, but Seth's attention was not on me. He looked to his mother, who stood behind Marco and me.

Catrin's cold laugh once again echoed off the stone walls, making me cringe. "What is this?" She asked, glaring at her only son. "Have you come to play hero for your sweet bride?"

Seth straightened up and wiped the blood off his sword with a handkerchief. "No, mother," he answered. "I've come to put an end to you."

Marco stepped back from Catrin and slowly moved both of us so that we were now behind Seth. All we could do was stand there and helplessly watch as they both blocked our only escape route.

Catrin's smile dropped, and she clenched her teeth. "Seth, there will be only one victor in this war, and we both know it will not be them. Choose your next move wisely."

"Maybe not, but it will not be you either," he answered, bringing his sword back up to his face and inspecting it closely. "You made your decision when you sought out Siv's death."

"You wouldn't," Catrin whispered. "You would betray your own mother? For what? For her? You didn't even want her when I served her to you on a silver platter!" She yelled, pointing her finger at me.

Seth's calm demeanor faded, and wrath took over each of his features. "I would betray you a hundred times over if it meant saving her life. I never wanted Siv on a silver platter! I loved her, but I had to keep my distance just to keep her safe from you and-" Seth paused, shaking his head. "It doesn't matter," he whispered.

"You are weak. You've always been weak! You want to kill me? Then go ahead and do it because I don't think you have the courage or the willpower to go through with it," Catrin threatened with rage.

Before Marco and I even had a chance to react, Seth's sword sliced through his mother's neck. The sound of silver hitting the floor echoed through the now silent corridor as her crown hit the floor seconds after her head. All three of us stood there silently, staring at Catrin's bloody and headless body. There were no words to be said.

Finally, Seth cleaned his sword with shaky hands before quickly sheathing it and turning to Marco and me. "Follow me. No guards will attack us if they see me with you. They'll think you surrendered or my mother ordered me to take you," he said, walking away from his mother's corpse without even a second glance.

"Do you trust him?" Marco asked, holding me close to him as if he still felt the need to shield me.

I thought for a moment and watched as Seth stopped and turned to us, waiting for us to follow him. In spite of him being a pompous pig for the last several years, I still saw him as my childhood friend. I still saw him as the only child in the palace who never judged me and Mia for being a commoner or having no wealth, titles, or prominent name. I had tried to hate him for years, but I never could.

"I do," I told Marco. "I don't know if I should, but I do."

My answer didn't seem to help Marco. He stood still as he sized Seth up. "If you try anything, I will gut you before you even have the chance to draw your sword. Understand?" Seth's green eyes widened before he nodded.

I knew exactly where we were going as Seth led us through the twists and turns of the palace corridors. "Seth, Why are you leading us back to the entrance of the palace? Mia and many others are going to want your head the moment they see you."

"It's the safest place for you," he answered without turning back to look at me. "Catrin's guards won't touch us as long as I'm with you. They may be confused, but they wouldn't harm me in fear of my mother."

Marco halted. "How do we know you're not leading us straight into a trap?"

Seth stopped and finally turned to face us. "What reason would I have to trap *you*?" He asked Marco. "And if I wished to trap Siv, I would have let that guard kill you back there. But here we are, alive, thanks to me." Marco rolled his eyes but continued to follow Seth.

The marble floors no longer held their pristine shine but were littered with the blood of both rebellion fighters and Catrin's soldiers. I wasn't sure what I was expecting, but I felt ashamed when I remembered how excited I was for this battle to happen. My head had been so clouded by the desire to seize the palace and take whatever power Catrin had held over me since my birth that I had overlooked the toll that it would take on me, as well as everyone else. I knew lives were going to be lost. I tried my best to prepare myself for it, but nothing could have prepared me for the mass amount of casualties lying all around us. My heart sank every time I recognized a body, and by the time we had arrived at the entry of the palace, despair had taken hold of me.

I sat in the corner of the large open room. It was one of the only portions of the entrance that didn't have red stains on the floors or walls and there were no bodies close enough for me to possibly identify them. I brought my knees up to my chest and rested my cheek on one.

"Can we talk?" Seth asked, crouching down beside me.

I shifted my eyes to meet him, but instead, I spotted a bitter-looking Marco not standing far behind him, glaring daggers. "It's your life you're risking," I answered half-heartedly.

Seth turned around to meet Marco's glare and shrugged his shoulders. "I honestly didn't think I'd live through today anyway. I'm not sure I really wanted to," he answered sullenly. "But I can't die without explaining myself to you. Will you allow me that?"

I picked my head up from my knees and allowed myself to take in his appearance. Seth's once-manicured blonde hair was now longer and unkept. The wrinkled clothes he wore were unusually baggy on him, and I realized it was because he had lost weight since the last time I saw him. The beds of his fingernails were red and scabbed over due to him chewing on them. He only ever did that when he was under extreme amounts of stress. His green eyes were accompanied by large bags underneath them, but you could barely notice them because of the bruises adorning his face. All this time I had never thought to wonder what he had been going through or if he was suffering any consequences of the rebellion's actions. My harsh expression softened slightly, and I nodded, gesturing for him to continue.

"First, I want to apologize for the last five years. I'm very much aware of how I acted towards you and those around me, but I need you to know that there was a reason for it. There was a reason for why I pulled away from you after our betrothal, and it had nothing to do with me not wanting to marry you," he told me, his features heavy with remorse. "I had found out about the prophecy, about you, and about her plans for you. My mother never knew that I had found out her reasons for urging me to create a romantic relationship with you, to make you fall in love with me, to see me as your partner in life. She believed that this would ignite your power, and from there, she planned to use you." Seth ran his hands through his messy blonde hair, staring at the floor as he continued, "but I couldn't do that to you, Siv. I've loved you since I was a child and despite wanting to love you for the rest of my life, I couldn't do it if it meant you'd be used for the rest of yours. I had only been a tool for my mother to use as she pleases from the moment I was born, and I didn't want the same fate for you. So, instead of creating a loving relationship with you, I tried my best to get you to despise me instead. It was the only way I could think to protect you regardless of how much it hurt."

I stared back at him, speechless. All these years, I had assumed his shift in demeanor toward me was because he resented our forced betrothal or, at the very least, he had begun to hate me for being a commoner like the others in the palace.

My heart sank when I realized he had only done and said all of those hurtful things because he was trying to protect me. He distanced himself in order to save me from his mother. Perhaps this is why I could never hate him, why I could only ever see him as my friend even after all of the horrible things he'd done and said. I could no longer hold myself back, and I wrapped my arms around him, embracing him.

Seth quickly relaxed into me. "I've missed you so much," he whispered into my ear.

I smiled against his chest. "I've missed you too," I told him truthfully before pulling away from him. "Seth, did you know? Did you know who your mother was?" I asked.

He took a deep breath before itching the back of his head. "She told me when she told me of the prophecy," Seth turned from me. "It's not something I'm proud of."

CHAPTER 18

My conversation with Seth abruptly ended when I was ripped from Seth's arms and pushed behind a burly man's body. If I wasn't already in shock from the sheer amount of death that surrounded me, I'm sure I would have known it was Jude the moment his hands grazed my skin, but I didn't. So, instead, I instinctively retreated several steps back and wrapped my arms around my torso, preparing myself for whatever blows may come my way.

"Jude!" Marco shouted, running up from behind me. "Siv's been through enough today. You'll only traumatize her more if you pick a fight with that rat."

Recognition dawned on my face, and I dropped my arms from my chest. Jude was still facing away from me, glaring down at a terrified-looking Seth. "Jude?" I asked quietly. "You're back?"

He turned slowly to face me, revealing his dark brown eyes with a hint of scarlett blazing within them. I couldn't wait a second longer, and I threw my arms around him. My hands tightly gripped the thin white fabric of his shirt as if I feared him being taken away from me once again. After a while, he finally tugged me away from him and scanned my body, looking for any signs of injuries.

"What happened to your leg?" He asked, noticing me favoring my other leg.

"She sprained her ankle not too long ago," Marco answered for me. "She hasn't learned how to heal herself quite yet."

I looked back at Marco with raised eyebrows. "You think I'll be able to heal *myself*?"

Marco chuckled. "Why wouldn't you?"

Jude interrupted us and pointed to Seth, who was now backed against the wall, avoiding our eyes. "Why is he not in the cells with the rest of the prisoners?"

Marco placed his hand on his cousin's shoulder but kept his eyes on Seth. "He saved our lives," he admitted. "He killed Catrin and led us to safety."

Jude scowled as he looked down on the blonde man in front of him. His hands were balled into fists, and the redness in his eyes swirled furiously. "I've heard of you. It was you who sat back and allowed Siv to be abused for years and never did anything to help her," he spat. "Do you think this one act of courage should stop me from slitting your throat at this instant?"

I stepped in front of Jude, blocking him from Seth, and placed my hands on his chest. "Jude, there's a lot more to it. Seth did more to help me than I ever realized," I explained, looking behind me at the man I was once promised to. "You will not lay a hand on him. Promise me, Jude."

Jude scowled at Seth one last time before shifting his focus back to me. His hard expression quickly softened, and he nodded. "If that is what you want, then I will not harm him," he told me. "But I will make no promises as to what I will do if he ever does anything to put you in danger."

I accepted his words and offered him a genuine smile. Regardless of the grim situation, I was overjoyed to have him near me once again. The gruesome images of the deceased bodies surrounding me faded as I took in his appearance before me. His thick black hair was tied back as usual, but loose strands fell on his tanned face. It made him look a little more tussled than I was used to, but I liked it. I hadn't noticed the dark red splatters on the fabric of his tunic and trousers, but I chose to ignore them as I appreciated his form. I began to feel guilty for the happiness I felt at that moment while there was so much to be somber about.

"Marco, do not let the *Prince* out of your sight," Jude ordered, hissing Seth's title sarcastically. "He may not be a prisoner, but I still do not trust him." Then, without another word, Jude picked me up effortlessly and carried me outside of the palace.

"Where are we going?" I asked him even though I honestly couldn't care less.

"Away from the stench of death," he answered. "We both need to bathe, and then I'd like to speak with you alone."

We allowed silence to fill the space between us as he carried me back to the village and into an unfamiliar home on the other side of town. It was much larger than the home we had been staying at in town. It had two stories as well as a cellar, and the decor was refined yet comfortable. He seemed to know his way around inside as he quickly opened a door on the main level and placed me down on a sunbed near a window.

Almost as if he could read my mind, he said, "This was Luis's house. I stayed here with Billy and Marco a while back, and now that he is residing in a cell, I figured we could find some privacy within these walls," he revealed before leaving to fetch warm water for a bath.

When he returned, he began to lift me, but I shook my head. "You should bathe first," I insisted. "I did nothing but distract and get hurt." My cheeks reddened from embarrassment. "You actually fought. You deserve clean water to bathe in."

"You have the heart of a warrior, regardless if you fought or not. It takes courage to step foot into battle," he said, his eyes never leaving mine. "Besides, there's another bath upstairs."

I allowed him to carry me into the main washroom, and when he lowered me to the ground, his eyes lingered on my lips. The awkwardness and uncertainty of what would come next quickly disappeared as Jude gently grabbed my neck and pressed his lips harshly against my own. Backing me up against the tiled wall, his hands traced the curves of my body.

Jude's lips rapidly moved like he was famished, and my body was the only nourishment he'd accept. He shifted his attention to the space between my neck and collarbone, and my chest moved up and down rapidly as I did my best to fill my lungs with the air that had been denied only seconds before. Both of his hands grabbed the back of my thighs, and he lifted me up, forcing my legs to wrap around him. His mouth migrated to my shoulder, scattering kisses all the way down my arm before he finally tore his lips from my skin.

His eyes were still filled with desire, but now a hint of apprehension appeared as well. "I'm sorry," he said with a strained tone. "I should have more restraint." Jude placed me down and stepped away from me.

The distance he had created between us left me feeling cold and vulnerable. "Why?" I asked, feeling slightly rejected. "Why do you feel the need to restrain yourself from me?"

Jude bit his lip, and his gaze fell to the floor. "Although it is easy to forget when I am around you, I have to remind myself that our relationship comes with many responsibilities," he answered. "It's also easy to forget that you're unaware of the depths of your abilities. The closer you and I become, the more powerful you will grow, and it would be thoughtless and unfair of me to push that power on you before you're ready."

My eyes narrowed on him and the fire of passion that lit my body only moments ago was now fueled by annoyance. "I *am* ready," I told him bluntly.

Jude finally looked up from the ground and placed a hand on my cheek. "Siv, this isn't about you and I. Our relationship could shape the next phase of not only Saleda but all of Lorus. I'm not sure why or even how, but we must remain focused on the needs of the people. Not our own desires."

His gentle touch left my skin, and he made his way out of the washroom, leaving me flustered and confused. I had never been touched like that before. In fact, the only person I had ever even kissed before Jude was Seth. His touch was never driven by the passion that I felt at that moment with Jude. Any intimacy shared with Seth had always felt forced, and now I knew why. He had been holding himself back and making himself seem crude and uncaring our entire betrothal in hopes of protecting me from Catrin's plots to exploit me.

At one point, I had been so hopeful for a future with Seth, but his sullied touch and cold demeanor killed any thoughts of happiness with him. I was beginning to feel as if Jude was pulling away in order to protect me as well, and that thought worried me. I craved everything about the man, but especially the heat of desire that he sparked within me. I wouldn't allow him to rob me of that for the sake of my safety. I was ready for more power. I could handle anything if it meant that he wouldn't regulate our interactions to only those of a friend.

I undressed and slid my weary body into the warm bath water. I did my best to ease myself into a state of relaxation, but my mind wouldn't allow for it. As I scrubbed my skin clean of any evidence of the battle I had just left, my thoughts prepared me for a different kind of battle. One that included advocating for myself, which wasn't something that I had been well-rehearsed in. Exiting the now murky water, I clothed myself in the black satin robe that hung beside the door.

When I made my way into the living room, a clean-shaven and freshly bathed Jude was already sitting beside the fireplace that had recently been lit. He grinned when he noticed me walking toward him but quickly dropped it when he noticed my stern expression. "What's wrong?" He asked, genuinely worried.

I waited to answer until I was inches away from him. Ignoring his gesture to sit beside him, I remained standing. "I need you to listen while I'm speaking and wait until I am finished before you say anything," I ordered.

I couldn't help but notice a hint of a smile as his dark eyebrows shot up in surprise, but he nodded his head in agreement.

"I am not a child, and I refuse to be treated as one any longer. I have been told what to say, how to act, and who to be ever since I was born. Up until recently, I was blind to just how wrong that is. I was content with having every decision made for me because of the certainty that came with being dependent on everyone but myself. I have made so many sacrifices in the name of my own safety that I have allowed myself to be molded into someone that I don't even recognize." I paused and went to tuck my hair behind my ears until I remembered it had been taken from me as well. "Jude, I may be your *Erosa*, but that doesn't mean that you get to decide what is best for me or for us. Regardless of the situation, I will make my own choices from here on out and the first choice I am making is to be with you. I understand this choice may accelerate things in this war or that it may put me at more risk with the Vaegarian Dynasty, but those are all chances that I am willing to take if it means that you won't avoid looking at me or speaking with me, or touching me."

I forced myself to maintain eye contact with him as he peered down at me. His expression was hard to read and I began to worry that I had said the wrong thing or that he may reject me. My mind began to race as I realized his loyalty to the rebellion and to this war might be stronger than his loyalty to me. I started to believe that I had been foolish to believe this man, whom I hadn't even known for more than a month, would disrupt the rebels' battle strategy in order to be with me.

My gaze dropped, and I stepped back from his large form that sat in front of me. "I-I'm sorry. I was wrong to-"

Jude didn't let me finish before he stood and closed the gap between us. "Siv, are you sure?" He asked, studying my face. "We have no idea what this could do to you. I mean, look what our moment in the washroom did," he said, pointing to my ankle that I had forgotten all about.

I rotated my foot, testing out the sprain that seemed to no longer exist. "I healed it?" I asked no one in particular.

Jude nodded. "The remaining bruises and scars from your previous injuries are no longer visible, either. You were unable to heal yourself before, but one moment between the two of us and here we are." Jude removed his shirt, revealing nothing but his broad and toned torso. "You managed to heal every cut and nick I obtained from training and today's battle as well."

I became noticeably more flustered from the view of his naked chest in front of me, and I began chuckling. "You just wanted an excuse to remove your clothing," I teased, hoping to ease the tension that had grown between us.

Jude smirked, taking notice of my nervousness. "Perhaps," he said before his stern expression returned. "But we have no idea the extent of what you may be able to do. Not only that, but you have no control over it. We can't be this reckless. We're putting everyone's lives in danger just by being close to one another."

I knew he was right, and I knew the smart thing to do in that instant was to take things slow with Jude, but I was unable to think that clearly. The intensity of my desire clouded every thought that entered my mind and I forced myself into believing that I was strong enough and prepared enough for whatever power our relationship may inflict upon me.

"I'll learn to control it," I answered him. "I'm stronger than I look."

Jude seemed to be entertaining a battle of his own as his heated gaze shifted to my lips, his brows furrowed, and his fists were balled at his sides. "I have no doubt, but until then, we can't be anything more to one another than friends."

His words hit me like an arrow to the chest. "Friends? Jude, it could be years before I'm able to control my abilities. Or what if I'm never able to? Do you want to just be friends until then? You'd be okay with just being friends for the rest of our lives?"

Jude nodded, but the pained expression on his face betrayed him.

I felt my eyes begin to tear up, so I turned my back on him. Since the moment I met Jude, I felt connected to him. I had thought it would be impossible to feel lonely if he were near, but here I was. Jude was standing less than a foot away from me, but I had never felt so alone. Not even in my days at the palace. At least inside those pristine walls, I knew where I stood among my enemies, but this was new territory for me. I loved Jude, that much I knew to be true. But at the same time, I felt rejected and abandoned by him.

I couldn't even be upset with him because deep down, I knew he was right. I knew he was making a noble sacrifice for the rebellion, for Saleda, and for Lorus. If I were as virtuous as him, I would have been able to accept a friendship with him wholeheartedly. But I wasn't. I wanted to be selfish. I wanted to be with him regardless of the consequences for those surrounding me.

"Okay," I finally answered him as my heart broke silently. "Friends then. Nothing more." My teeth clenched as I swallowed the lie I had just told him. I knew I'd never be able to be just friends with Jude. My feelings for him were too deep and it would be impossible to pull them back up to the surface level and meaningless conversations that came with the kind of friendship we'd have to have.

Jude squeezed my shoulder from behind me before walking away. I was glad he didn't say anything. Nothing would be able to fill the gap we had just agreed to wedge between ourselves. As seconds, minutes, and eventually, hours had passed since he had left me alone in a traitor's home, my heart hardened, and I promised myself I'd no longer be so naive. I couldn't allow myself to continue to believe in love, soulmates, or happy endings. These beliefs would only cause me heartbreak, and I didn't have time for that. Not now, and if we were to win this war, maybe never.

CHAPTER 19

"Siv! Wake up!"

My groggy eyes reluctantly opened as my arms stretched over my head. My chest seized when I didn't recognize my surroundings before I looked down at the leather sofa I must have fallen asleep on and recognized Luis's expensive furniture. The conversation with Jude from the evening before replayed in my head, but I had no time to feel the lingering emotions before Marco marched over to me.

"Siv! Get up and get dressed," he urged with uncharacteristic seriousness. "You need to see something."

I quickly lifted myself from the sofa and jogged to what I supposed was Luis's bedroom. His closet was full of men's clothing that looked as if it had never been worn. My fingers ran across the unblemished fabric of the mundane tunics and trousers. I began to wonder if he had been a spy long before the rebellion even began based on his unworn clothes and how his home had barely looked lived in.

I decided to bring up my concerns later as I threw on the fresh cotton tunic and trousers before ripping up some fabric to use as a scarf for my head. Although my hair had begun growing back, it was still extremely short, and while I didn't mind it, I loathed the way some would look at me with pity. I was trying my best to seem like a strong and brave leader. That was hard to do when the people I was to lead only saw me as a victim of the Queen. Wearing a scarf at least allowed me to feel somewhat normal and avoid sympathy.

As I finished tying the scarf around my head, nothing could have prepared me for what waited on the other side of that door. My breath halted in my chest as my eyes landed on hundreds of people lining the streets outside of the house.

"What's going on?" I asked Marco who leaned against the cobblestone house, waiting on me.

Marco's quietness only made me more anxious as he stood beside me, looking at the crowds in amazement. "Words out," he quietly replied while avoiding my eyes. "The surrounding cities heard the child from the prophecy has finally come to liberate Saleda. They're here for you, Siv. They came to fight for you."

My eyes widened at Jude's revelation. "They want to fight?"

He nodded. "Most just want to be on the right side of history this time when they heard the war had officially begun. But yes, they're here to fight." Marco answered as he gestured for me to follow him down the worn streets. "I have to warn you, though, not everyone believes you're the true Queen. There are some who do not believe in the prophecy and while they wish to liberate Sleda, they don't think you should be who rules in the aftermath."

We rounded the corner of the town square the crowds began to follow us, and several people began to stare at me. Some of them started slowly backing away from me, suspicion and wariness in their eyes. I subconsciously hid myself behind Marco's towering figure before he pulled me out in front of him.

"You are their Queen," he reminded me. "No more hiding. You need to address them." Marco pointed toward the center of the town square.

I nodded, but my chest tightened at the look of fear on some of their faces. These people were afraid of me, just as they had been afraid of Catrin. I had barely even scratched the surface of my abilities, and I had absolutely no control over when or what I could do. They had every right to be afraid of me, but my heart still broke at the thought of being compared to Catrin. I reminded myself that it was up to me to win them over once again.

I ran my fingers over my arms for comfort and I reluctantly left Marcos' side. Shivers ran down my back as I climbed the stairs to the tall wooden platform that had supported Seth and me on our wedding, as well as the floggings and hangings of the townspeople. That was enough to remind me of the change I must bring.

I stood tall as I looked out at the growing crowd in front of me. "I'm sure you have all noticed a slight change around our city," I joked, earning a few stifled laughs. "I want to assure you that I mean no harm to anyone. The rumors are true. I am the child from the prophecy, and I have been blessed with abilities that I plan to use to help each and every one of you. Although I may not know how to control it yet, it was given to me to protect you, to save you from the injustices that we've lived with for far too long. So that is what I will do." I looked down to find Marco smiling up at me, encouraging me to continue. "Yesterday was evidence of just how strong we can be when we work together. We walked into a trap and still came out as victors. But the war is not won yet and we must continue to persevere. There will be many more challenges ahead of us, and we will become tired, but we must carry on anyway." I took a deep breath before continuing, "I believe in each and every one of you, and the only thing I ask is for you to believe in me as well. I did not ask for this title and I did not ask for this power, but I will do everything I can to earn your trust and your loyalty. I am *not* like Catrin. I will not punish you if you do not wish to follow me. You will not be hung for treason if you speak out against me. I have never wished to bring harm to any of my people. If you wish to leave, you may do so. If you wish to end your fight for our cause, no one will stop you. But, if you wish to stay and fight with me, I will owe you my life."

The crowd remained silent as they digested my words. It stung when a few walked out from the crowd, obviously choosing to leave and dismiss me as their leader. But that sting faded when a woman weaved her way out of the crowd and stepped forward. "I choose you as my Queen," she proclaimed, taking a knee and bowing. "I choose to stay and fight for *you*."

I gestured my thanks to her, and to my surprise, many followed her lead. Despite the few that had left, the majority of the crowd was now kneeling before me, pledging their allegiance. I couldn't help but laugh with joy when I spotted Billy, Florian, Mia, and even Jude among them. Suddenly, numerous imposing figures filled the space behind the kneeling crowd. They're large and muscular bodies contrasted with the civilians who had filled the space before them. I realized they must be Jude's Krig army that he gathered and marched into yesterday's battle with. Each of the massive soldiers placed their fists over their hearts before kneeling as well.

Jude pushed his way from the crowd and joined me on the platform. "First, we free Saleda, then we free all of Lorus, including Krigsmen. Their loyalty belongs to you as long as mine does," Jude whispered in my ear before he placed his own fist over his heart and knelt beside me. "Alla hoallar helande Vallisa!" He shouted.

"*Alla hoallar helande Vallisa!*" The Krig warriors repeated.

Looking down at him, I whispered, "what does that mean?"

He beamed up at me. "It's a Krig phrase that is difficult to translate, but it is a sign of respect and admiration."

Jude, as well as all the other soldiers, stayed kneeling until he finally stood and motioned for his army to disperse, the rebellion members quickly following behind them. I stood there for a moment longer while everyone else resumed their daily activities. Despite the dull ache I felt in my chest when I saw Jude, I couldn't help but feel honored when I replayed the scene that had just occurred. For the first time, I truly felt like a Queen, and it felt natural. I was unfamiliar with the feeling of certainty, especially when it pertained to me, but I knew I was meant to be here for this exact reason.

"Siv, we need you," Mia said, regaining my attention. "We need to discuss what happens next."

CHAPTER 20

We arrived at an abandoned building near the edge of town that had been turned into the new safe house. My sister, Jude, Billy, Marco, and Florian took a seat at the large round table in the front room while others stood against the wall. Silence filled the air until I realized they were all looking at me.

"What?" I asked.

Jude chuckled beside me, and Marco chimed in, "so what all do you think you can do? Can you just heal or can you alter body parts too? Because I think Jude could use some alter-" Jude slapped Marco on the back of his head, making him unable to finish.

Billy glared at Marco, clearly unimpressed with his humor. "What Marco means is that we still do not know the extent of your power or what you can do with it," she explained. "Until we do, we think it's best that you stay at the palace and train."

The happiness that I had felt only moments before had suddenly vanished, and I was left with an empty feeling of dread. "You're not serious." I turned to Mia, desperate for someone to have my back. "You're really going to lock me inside of the palace just like Catrin did?"

Mia shook her head. "No one is locking you up," she began, but I cut her off.

"Can I leave whenever I wish?" I asked.

She hesitated. "No, but this isn't to keep you prisoner. This is to keep both you and everyone else safe. If there were a better way, we wouldn't even consider this, but we are in the middle of the war. You are the only weapon that gives us a fighting chance, and you have no idea how to control your power. We don't know the dangers that come along with it."

My shoulders slumped as I struggled to find another way to keep everyone else safe from myself. "Jude, what if we went to your cottage?" I was unable to find any comfort from his glance, I could only see guilt.

"Siv, I can't. It's too risky to travel there alone, and we need you here," he replied.

"This is not a punishment but it is a consequence of your power being ignited too much too quickly," Billy added. "Thankfully, you've been in a good mood during every episode, but what do you think you'll do when you're angry? This is for the greater good."

"I'm pretty upset right now, Nabilla. Do you see me throwing fireballs around or impaling anyone with my mind?" I asked as Billy leaned back in her seat, but Marco couldn't contain his laughter, which earned him another slap on the back of his head from Mia.

My heart sank as I was reminded of how I felt when I was kept at the palace previously. The feelings of panic, nervousness, and sorrow were much stronger now, though. I had felt a taste of freedom, friendship, and love, but I was being forced back into a space of loneliness and captivity. However, I accepted my fate and told myself I was being selfish and this was only for the good of the rebellion, but my heart couldn't believe that. I had never hurt anyone before. What reason did they have to believe that I would hurt someone now?

CHAPTER 21

Moving me back into the palace was an easy task since the only belongings I had were the clothing that I wore, and even then, they were taken from someone else. I tried my best not to act like a child and accept my situation with as much grace as I could, but there was something about the cold architecture of the palace that made me want to run away as fast as I could. Despite how senseless running away would be, it sounded better than reliving the horror that was my childhood in this place.

I had chosen a room in the same wing of the palace as my old bed chambers since that was the only wing I knew my way around, but I refused to step foot in that old familiar room. It was bad enough to have to live here once again, but I didn't need to sleep in the same bed that I had cried myself to sleep in almost every night.

I looked out the tall window to the courtyard and chuckled when I remembered making fun of Seth with Mia while he practiced his battle skills with his trainer. It felt like a lifetime ago, but it had only been months.

"It's good to hear you laugh again," Jude said, standing in the doorway. "I know this isn't how you imagined being Queen, but after all this is over you can build yourself a proper castle and make it your own. It will be free of any memories from your past, and it will have plenty of room to make new memories."

"Will you be in any of them?" I mumbled, still looking out the window.

Jude joined me on the narrow bench overlooking the courtyard. "I'd like to be," he answered. "I still see a future with you, Siv. But until we know that you can control your abilities and nobody's life will be in danger, we have to-"

"Do what's right, be smart, make sacrifices. Should I continue?"

Jude exhaled loudly as his shoulders slumped. "I'm sorry. I wish it didn't have to be this way. I truly do."

His apology only saddened me further. "You could have chosen me, Jude. You could have picked me over all of this," I cried. "Why didn't you? If I really am your soulmate, your Erosa, or whatever you'd like to call it, then why wouldn't you pick me?"

"You know why, Siv." His eyes were brimmed with tears as he looked at me. "I'm not just a man, and you're not just a woman. I'm a Chief, and you're a Queen. We both have responsibilities that take priority over our own wants and needs."

I wiped my face free from tears. I knew this, and I knew that I had no right to be angry with him. But I was still hurt, and I was maddened that it seemed so much harder for me to walk away from him. It made me feel rejected and shunned despite having gained our soldiers' trust and loyalty hours before.

"I know," I finally replied. "I understand why, but that doesn't ease the misery I'm in while I'm inside these gates. I just-" I took a deep breath in an attempt to calm my nerves. "I just need some time alone."

Jude nodded, but he did nothing to hide the gloom in his expression from being dismissed by me. "I'm sorry," he uttered before leaving me with nothing but my own despair.

It had only been a few minutes when I heard my door open again. Expecting Jude, I turned around, ready to apologize for sending him away and instead asking him to stay with me. But it was not Jude who entered my room; it was Seth.

"What're you doing in here?" I asked him, genuinely curious about his presence.

Seth looked out into the corridor one last time before quietly shutting the door behind him, carefully carrying a steaming mug. "Your sister confined me to the palace grounds," he explained, chuckling. "I don't think any of them know what to do with me. They hate me, but they also know I'm the reason they were able to seize this place. They can't put me in a cell, but they don't want to see me in town either."

"Looks like we're both being held captive," I half-heartedly joked.

Seth's green eyes narrowed. "They won't let you leave?"

I shook my head. "For my safety and the safety of everyone else, apparently."

He nodded. "Can I sit?" He asked, gesturing to the spot that Jude had been only moments before. "We didn't get much of a chance to speak yesterday after… everything. I figured that I might as well offer you some closure while I'm stuck in this marble prison." I allowed him to sit beside me but kept my eyes on the courtyard below. "I brought you some tea." He said, pushing the mug toward me.

I gratefully took the mug from him, smiling as the hot liquid warmed my body. "Honey chamomile," I whispered, savoring the familiar and comforting flavors.

"I remembered that it was your favorite," he said, smiling.

My brows snapped together. "How did you know? I never told you, and I know for a fact that you never made me tea before," I hissed, remembering his mistreatment.

Seth shifted on the bench and looked down. "I know a lot more about you than you think," he said quietly. "I never wanted to be unkind to you, Siv. You were always my best friend, even after I was no longer yours."

My expression softened slightly. "I know," I whispered to him. "I'm sorry."

"You have nothing to be sorry for. My explanation does nothing to ease the pain I caused you all these years," he told me. "You have every right to hate me. That was my goal, after all."

"I don't hate you, Seth. It's just going to take some time to process everything before I can look at you without being reminded of the worst years of my life," I admitted. "But I think someday I'll be able to."

He did his best to offer me a smile, but I knew it wasn't genuine. I now knew it had hurt him to be the vile person his mother had unknowingly forced him to be. Maybe Seth was truly a kind and good man. He just had trouble navigating the life he was dealt, and if anyone could understand that, it was me.

"So I hear you've won over the hearts and minds of the Kingdom," Seth said, looking out the window. "I wish I could have seen you change this place, Siv. You really were born to be Queen."

My brows creased as I turned from the window to look at him. "Why wouldn't you be able to?"

"I'm so sorry," he said as a tear trailed from his green eyes. "I never wanted any of this."

A deep pit began to form in my stomach as I took in his distressed demeanor. I stood from the bench in an attempt to distance myself from him, but suddenly, my body felt incredibly heavy, and my legs gave out from under me. Seth caught my fall and carried my limp body to the bed. "What did you do?" I struggled to ask him, realizing that something must have been put into my tea.

He looked down at me, his features clouded with remorse. "Siv, there is so much more to this war than you realize," he told me with a shaky voice. "I know it's hard to understand right now but know that I am only doing this to save your life and the lives of everyone else in this war."

My mind began to fade as I looked up at him in disbelief. "Seth, don't do this," I pleaded, trying my best to stay awake.

"If I don't, you will die. Everyone will die," he replied shortly before I lost consciousness and fell into a deep sleep.

CHAPTER 22

I awoke in a large canopied bed with dark blue silk sheets. I stretched out my limbs, savoring the way the fabric felt on my bare skin. My head throbbed as I sat up, and the pain emanating from my skull reminded me that Seth had taken me from the palace. I frantically scanned the elaborate room when the light fixtures caught my eye. There was no flame that emitted the lights, just a bright form of energy that floated in between the glass that held each one. I had never seen anything like it and I instantly knew that I was no longer in Mendacia or even Saleda. I threw my legs around the side of the bed and stood, ignoring the dull ache that traveled throughout my body. I immediately noticed that I had been changed into a matching dark blue silk nightgown, and I quickly examined the rest of my body. When I had come to the conclusion that no other part of me had been harmed, I ran to the thick curtains that covered the floor-length windows and pulled them aside.

I wasn't prepared for what waited on the other side of that glass. I had to have been at least fifty stories up, and although the people looked like ants below me, I could see machines running through the neatly paved streets. It was as if they had taken boats from the water and placed wheels on them, but they ran effortlessly. I watched the scene beneath me in amazement as a familiar voice jolted me from behind.

"It's remarkable, isn't it?" Seth asked.

I turned to see that he had obviously bathed, shaved, and trimmed his hair since I had last seen him in my bed chambers. He was dressed elegantly, too. Noble Mendacia's clothing was never anything less than intricate, but this clothing was different. He didn't wear a neatly pressed tunic like he had before. Instead, he wore a white buttoned-up shirt accompanied with a deep green velvet jacket that fit him like a glove. His trousers didn't match the jacket like they would have if we were in Saleda, but the deep black complemented it perfectly, as did the polished back shoes he wore.

Seth noticed me taking in his appearance and nervously messed with the crystal cufflink on his sleeve. "Welcome to the Vaegarian Dynasty, Siv." He made his way beside me and opened the curtains all the way, putting the city on display.

I took a step away from him. "Why am I here? Why would you bring me here of all places, Seth?"

His blank expression turned somber. "I had no choice," he replied. "It was this or the death of thousands." When I didn't respond, Seth turned to the window, looking down below at the busy roads. "Sit down, Siv. I'll explain everything."

"I'm fine standing, thank you," I said, wrapping my arms around myself.

"Suit yourself," Seth said as he made himself comfortable on the lavish velvet chair in the center of the large room. "I'm of Vaegarian descent. You found that out, but what you and the others failed to uncover was that I'm of royal Vaegarian blood."

When I failed to respond to his revelation, he continued, "I wasn't even aware of my lineage until my mother betrothed us. Up until then, I was blissfully unaware of the storm that was brewing to the west of us." He cleared his throat before continuing, "Apparently, I am the great-great-grandson of the Emperor of Vaegaria. My mother, her brother, and uncle were all sent to Saleda in a long-term plan to take complete control over Lorus. I, unknowingly, was the last piece in the puzzle before their plot for power was completed. As King, I was supposed to link the Kingdom of Saleda with the Vaegarian Dynasty. At least until you were born," he revealed.

"Why? What do I have to do with your plan to take over the Kingdom?" I asked with wide eyes.

Still sitting, Seth turned to me. "First of all, it's not *my* plan. I'm as much of a chess piece in this game as you are," he argued. "The Vaegarian people have never believed in any gods, only science. However, the powers that the Nativus possessed were always a mystery that they could not figure out. They captured hundreds of thousands of Nativus and experimented on them after they had taken over this land. They could never figure out where the power came from or how to harness it and remove it from their bodies. Almost every Nativus they tested on died. They eventually were forced to give up their studies when their last subject perished." He stood and made his way across the room to me. "Despite their belief in science, they still studied the great prophecy in the event that it came to fruition and the greatest and most powerful Nativus to have ever existed was brought to Lorus. The night you were born, my mother and her uncle were tasked with finding you and keeping you close until your power had fully matured. They believed that you would be their greatest tool in enquiring about the power that they seek. Since then, my title as King has meant little to them. It's you they want."

The hairs on my arms stood straight up, and I slowly backed away from Seth. I was in far more danger than I had thought. These people were going to dissect my body until they found what they wanted, and there was no escape. Even if I somehow managed to sneak out of this tower, where could I go?

"Seth, they're going to kill me," I trembled. "You delivered me to my death."

Seth gently grabbed my arm and pulled me so close to him that I could feel his breath on my face. "No one will lay a hand on you," he promised. "They have no desire to test or experiment on you. That is in the past. They promised me."

"They promised you?" I asked. "You can't trust these people! They'll tell you whatever you want to hear in order to get you to do their bidding!" I shouted.

His hand hurriedly covered my mouth. "You cannot speak like that here," he whispered. "Treason is one offense they will not allow. If you thought my mother was cruel, you haven't seen anything." Seth looked at the door and waited a few moments before he turned his gaze back to me and removed his hand from my mouth. "As long as you do what they ask, you'll be safe."

"And what will they ask of me?"

Seth nervously chewed on his lip before answering, "you are to marry me."

Anger flooded my veins, and before I realized what I was doing, I pushed Seth as hard as I could and started to slap him, but I didn't get too far before a flood of women came through the door, and he used the distraction to pull my body into his, making it look as if we had been embracing when they entered.

Seth slowly let me go and the women hurriedly began taking measurements of my body. They all wore the same gray uniform except for the tall woman who entered my chambers last. Her long black hair curled perfectly along her back, and she wore a loose purple gown that complimented her pale skin. "My name is Opal, and I have been assigned to..." She looked me over, her eyes settling on my closely cropped blonde hair before giving an obvious fake smile. "I've been assigned to you as your stylist."

I tried my best to ignore all of the other women fidgeting with me as I stared back at Opal. "Stylist?" I asked.

Opal chuckled before she instructed the women to take me to the bathing room. I hardly put up a fight as they dragged me along. I watched as they pressed a button on the large bathtub, and my eyes widened when it began filling with warm, soapy water. "I've heard your ways back in Saleda are a lot less... civilized," she said as she felt the water with her hand. "Get in, the temperature is perfect."

I tried to ask how any of this was possible, but before the words left my mouth, Opal harshly forced me into the tub. "I don't have the time to be answering all of your ignorant questions. You've slept an entire day away. The Emperor and Empress are waiting to meet you tonight, and if there is one thing you need to know, it is to not disappoint them in any way," she said as one woman began hurriedly scrubbing at my skin while another tweezed at the hair in between my eyebrows.

I cringed as they scrubbed my skin raw. "That hurts," I hissed, but they continued on until I yanked my arm from them. "I told you that hurts!"

Opal chuckled at my outburst and gestured for the woman to stop. "We'll have to do something about your hair," she said, still smiling at my struggle. "I'm afraid the Emperor isn't fond of it," she paused, scanning my head again. "This style of haircut," she finally finished.

I was then taken from the bath and placed into a dark blue satin robe. Opal gave out orders to the women surrounding me. Some were instructed to paint my nails, and others began to paint my face, but what really bothered me was the women who fitted my head with an itchy but realistic-looking wig. The color matched my hair exactly, but the length fell to my waist.

When she finally handed me a mirror, my mouth dropped. I didn't look like myself at all. My short blonde hair was now long and shiny, and my blue eyes were buried underneath thick black lashes, and black paint covered my eyelids. My cheeks were an unnatural shade of pink, and my lips were bright red. I shook my head as I realized that my reflection reminded me of what Catrin had looked like.

"Take it off," I begged Opal as I tugged at the hair that was now tightly secured to my head. "Please, remove all of this!"

She placed her hand on my shoulder as she looked at me through the mirror. Her expression faltered for a moment, and I thought I saw a hint of compassion before her stone-cold look reappeared. "Don't bother messing with the hair. It won't come off without the right tools. Vaegarian technology applies to our cosmetology as well," she said with a wink. "Now for the finishing touches." Opal took out a crystal box that held a heavy-looking diamond tiara. She placed it on my head as tears began to fall down my face.

"Do not ruin all of the hard work my girls have done by crying. There is no room for tears in this country. You will learn that soon enough," she said as she lifted me up and steered me toward a dark blue gown that was hung up. "They will get you dressed, and Seth will be here to escort you to the Grand Hall shortly."

Opal turned to leave, but I grabbed her wrist. "Please help me. I need to leave this place," I begged her.

She grabbed my hand from her wrist and looked around at the women surrounding the room. "Leave us!" She ordered. Once we were the only two left, she sat me down. "You cannot trust anyone. The Emperor has eyes everywhere, and if he believes you are trying to escape, your chambers will be replaced with a cell, and this jewelry will be replaced with cuffs."

I shook my head. "Opal, please. My sister and my friends have no idea where I am. I have people depending on me. I cannot let them down. Please," I pleaded with her.

Opal looked around again before she placed her hands on top of mine. "For your own sake, as well as mine, you will learn to tolerate it here. You will do as you're told, and you will not disrespect the Emperor or the Empress. They may need you alive for the time being, but they don't need to make you comfortable in the meantime. Things could be so much worse," she whispered.

I let my head drop into my hands. "I failed everyone," I sobbed.

I felt Opal's hands on my back, rubbing soothing circles into the Satin fabric that separated her touch from my skin. "I wish I could do more for you. I really do," she whispered. "But for now, let's get you into this gown." She carried the long-sleeved gown from the hanger and helped me step into it before tying the extravagant laces in the back until I could hardly breathe.

I stared at myself in the mirror and cringed at my reflection once again. I looked eerily similar to the woman who stood for everything that I had worked so hard to destroy, and I hated it. I wanted to tear out the hair that was not mine, I wanted to wash my skin of all the paint, and I wanted my simple and comfortable wardrobe back. This was not me, and it never would be.

The knock at the door pulled my eyes from the mirror, and they landed on Seth, who now donned a jacket that matched my blue gown perfectly. "You look ravishing," he said as he dismissed Opal with a nod. "You are easily the most beautiful woman in the entire country. Don't tell the Empress I said that," he teased as he held out his arm for me. "Before you even think of trying anything tonight, the entire tower is laced with ettacao."

I hesitated before I reluctantly took his arm. "Am I supposed to know what that is?"

"It's an herb that was chemically engineered to render any Nativus abilities. They created it during the height of the Great War and have been pumping the tower full of it ever since," he answered nonchalantly.

His calm demeanor did nothing but make me even more uneasy. I was confused as to how he could become so comfortable surrounded by these people.

We stopped in front of what I thought to be an empty coat room, and Seth attempted to pull me inside with him, but I refused.

"Siv, stop being so stubborn and just trust me," he told me.

I laughed. "Trust *you*?"

He rolled his eyes before harshly grabbing my arm and pulling me into the small room with him. Once we were inside, the door closed, and Seth pressed a button on the wall. There was a brief pause before the room began to move downward, and I clasped onto his arm.

Seth chuckled quietly. "You seem pretty eager to hold onto me now."

I let go of his arm and placed my hands on the two walls beside me as I hunched in the corner of the small room. "How are we moving?" I asked.

"It's a lift. It transports you from each story of the tower. It's much more efficient than taking the stairs down fifty-two stories," Seth answered as he took enjoyment of my panic. "Come take my arm before the door opens. I don't want the Dynasty's first glance of you to be in the corner of the lift clawing at the walls," he said, gesturing to his arm.

I grudgingly grabbed onto him as I breathed in deeply, trying to calm my nerves. "Who all am I meeting? What am I supposed to say?" I asked him.

"We're meeting the Emperor and the Empress of the Vaegarian Dynasty first and foremost. Everyone after that doesn't matter; our titles are either equal or above them so I could care less what you say. But let me do all the talking when it comes to the Emperor and Empress," Seth answered.

I nodded. I'd gladly let him do all the talking for tonight. It wasn't lost on me that this entire country was made up of my enemies. I may have to remain civil with them for the time being in order to stay alive and keep whatever freedoms I may have at the moment, but I would never become docile here. I would never stop fighting for Saleda.

The door opened, and loud music, people chatting, and glasses clinking filled my ears. I looked around the room, and everyone was extremely tall and had pale skin that matched Opal's. This must be what full-blooded Vaegarians looked like. I shivered at the thought of being in a room filled with people whose ancestors killed off my entire race.

Seth whipped me around to face him. "Siv, I know this is hard, but you have to wipe the look of disgust off your face. Our survival depends on tonight going well. If we mess this up, not only will I suffer, but you will be passed on to whoever else they find to rule Saleda," he told me quietly.

I looked around at all of the men who had taken notice of our arrival. They all looked me up and down as if I were to be their next meal. Some of them even licked their lips as they eyed me.

"All of a sudden, I'm looking pretty good to you, aren't I?" Seth asked. His grip around my waist became tighter as if he was taking ownership of me, and he leaned down to my ear. "Do not leave my side tonight."

I did my best to wipe my face of emotion and follow Seth to the end of the hall. Two large thrones made completely of crystal sat upon a deep purple rug. I clenched my jaw as I observed the man and woman who sat upon them. The man had thick white hair and a beard that matched. He wore a large crystal crown that made his hazel eyes appear even brighter. I couldn't help but think they resembled Mia's, but when they made contact with me, they made me shiver from their coldness. The woman's hair was bright red, and she wore it in a tight bun underneath a matching crystal crown. Her eyes were a light blue, much like Catrin's. Something was off about their appearances, though, and I couldn't put my finger on exactly what it was. They looked as if they had been created in a lab rather than born. Their pale skin had no signs of life. No veins could be seen, no wrinkles, no scars, no freckles or moles. It was strange.

"Ah, this must be the Queen I've been so *hungry* to meet," The Emperor said as he rose from his throne and offered a hand to his wife.

I could see the resemblance to Catrin as they looked me up and down. It took everything I had to not bolt off, running in the opposite direction from both of them. Seth nudged me, and I bit my lip as I made my way into a deep curtsy, just as I used to do for his mother. When I rose, the Emperor stood in front of me with his wife beside him.

As uncomfortable as I was, I had years of experience when it came to flattering royalty. I remembered how Catrin used to revel in the flattery of her court, so I smiled with a fake shyness I knew he'd love, and I looked into his eyes. "It is an honor to be in the same room as you, Emperor." I then focused on the Empress and bowed. "The rumors of your beauty do not do you justice, Empress." I lied between my teeth, trying my best to fool them into believing I'd be submissive to them.

They both smiled from ear to ear and ushered me and Seth to an adjacent room. There was no door, but the music that played loudly was muted enough to where you could hear one another speak. I sat beside Seth at a silver table that stood on top of a deep purple rug, and the Emperor and Empress sat across from us.

"Please, call me Andrew when we are among friends," the Emperor told me before gesturing to his wife. "And this is my lovely wife, Marie."

I nodded. "You can call me Siv," I offered quietly.

"Seth spared us the details, but I did hear that it was a long and challenging journey to get you here, Siv," Andrew said as he gestured toward a servant who then filled the chalices on the table with wine.

I swallowed, trying to come up with a response, but Seth answered for me. "That it was, but she is worth it," he said before he kissed my cheek gently.

Marie seemed to accept his reply as she smiled warmly at his affection toward me. "It is so nice to see a young Royal couple such as yourselves in love. I cannot tell you how many dinners we've had to endure with nobles who absolutely loathe one another. It's insufferable!" She roared.

Andrew placed his hand over his wives. "Yes, tell us how you two became so compatible after all of the uproar in Saleda's cities. Siv, you were taken by the rebels the same night of your wedding, no?"

I stiffened. How was I to act in love with Seth while my friends were dealing with who knows what back in Mendacia? How was I to pretend they took me against my will? I had no idea how I'd lie about any of it when my emotions were so obviously invested in the rebellion.

"She was," Seth answered. "They held me at knifepoint and ambushed our guards. Before we even knew what had happened, Siv was gone. The best day of my life had turned sour in less than a minute. I don't like to think about that day very often."

I remembered how Seth had scurried off like a scared child as Florian retrieved me, but I bit my tongue as I listened to his lies.

The Empress shook her head. "That had to have been terrifying," she said and glanced at me with sympathy. "Forgive me for asking, but what was it like being their captive? I'm not sure I would have survived being in their hands for so long."

I looked at Seth, hoping he'd answer for me, but he and I both knew I'd have to speak for myself. "I was frightened at first, but then I accepted the reality of my situation. I knew I needed to keep my mind clear if I were to ever escape. So, that's what I did. I'm very thankful for Seth's rescue." The inaccuracy of my words tasted bitter, and I wanted to vomit as I spoke them, but I kept my expression blank as I stared back at the Empress.

She smiled. "How lovely. Your sweet beau is now your eternal hero. We must celebrate your safe return to your King!"

Andrew nodded in agreement with his wife. "Indeed. I shall make a toast," he said as Marie began clapping.

We followed him out to the Great Hall, and the crowd went silent as several servants began chiming a small bell. Hundreds of eyes were now on The Emperor and Empress as Seth and I stood awkwardly beside them.

"I'm sure you are all aware of the long-awaited arrival of our new Saledian Queen and her King," he announced, and the crowd cheered before quieting down once again. "It was a long and grueling journey for the both of them. Our sweet Queen was held prisoner by those wild beasts that call themselves rebels! The same feral group of people who murdered my great-granddaughter."

My eyes widened. I had assumed when Seth told me his great-great-grandfather was the Emperor he was referring to the past. How could they possibly still be alive and why do they not look a day over fifty? They also had no idea that it was Seth who killed his mother, not us, but I supposed that was probably a good thing. I cringed as my mind raced but Seth elbowed me in the side. "Keep it together," he whispered, and I straightened up.

The Emperor continued. "Her heroic King rescued her from their clutches and brought her home to us!" The crowd cheered once again. "But now, the real challenge begins for them, and they will need all of our support as they attempt to conceive our sacred heir! It is their son who will lead this country into a victory no one has ever known before. It is their son who will have great power coursing through their veins, and it is their son who will unite every Kingdom under our own."

My head turned toward Seth as Andrew spoke. He had left a very important part out of their plan when he explained we were to be married. He had told me that they wanted my power to win this war, not an heir. This was all wrong.

I began to panic when Seth grabbed my arm behind my back. "One wrong move tonight, and we are both doomed. I'll be discarded, and you'll be chained to the floor and used until you breed their heir. Be smart, Siv. An outburst would not do anyone any good. *Breathe*," Seth ordered harshly. "I'll explain everything later, but for right now, do your best to make them believe we love one another."

I turned to him. "Why do they want an heir?"

Seth rolled his eyes. "They believe a Vaegarian born with Nativus power is the true key to ultimate power over Lorus," he whispered. "I'll answer more questions after we get through tonight. But please, for both our sakes, be on your best behavior." I turned back toward the crowd and watched as they cheered at the Emperor's words.

"I know it is a bit *unusual* to celebrate a half-breed King and a Nativus Queen," The Emperor joked, igniting a roar of laughter throughout the crowds and making Seth stiffen. "But we now know that our previous efforts with the Nativus race were in vain. The true answer to securing Lorus is much similar. We only need to let nature do the work for us, and we will become and remain the most powerful Dynasty the world has ever known. So, it goes without saying, they will be a welcomed and celebrated addition to our line, and I expect them to be treated as such," Andrew warned the crowd before lifting his cup. "Cheers to new beginnings, and we will see all of you at their wedding!" He said, staring at Seth and me.

We lifted our chalices and nodded toward him before sipping the wine. "Can we please leave?" I whispered to Seth.

"I want to get out of here just as badly as you do, but we can't seem suspicious. We have to make our rounds," he replied.

"When is this wedding?"

"Soon," he answered bluntly.

Empress Marie took me by the arm before I could ask any more questions. "Come, dear. I'm going to introduce you to my court," she said, whisking me out of Seth's grip.

I turned back to him with wide eyes, and he mouthed, "*Behave,*" before he turned back to the Emperor and pretended to laugh at whatever joke he had just told.

CHAPTER 23

Empress Marie led me to a group of tall and pale women who all donned elaborate purple gowns. Each of them plastered a wide smile on their faces as she greeted them and introduced me. The women curtsied toward me and introduced themselves, but instead of memorizing their names, I scanned the Great Hall, doing my best to memorize the layout. I wasn't sure how long I'd have to play the role of their Sweet Saledian Queen, but I promised myself that I would find a way back to Mendacia and to the rebellion. If I died because of my efforts, so be it. I could not stay here in this hostile country when it had been built on the blood and bones of what I now knew to be my ancestors, the Nativus. I would not allow myself to contribute to the suffering and the torment of my people back in Saleda. They needed me, and I would find my way back to them somehow.

"Siv, did you hear Lady Audrey's question?" Empress Marie asked, gently patting my arm to gain my attention.

I turned my focus back on the group of women standing in front of me and smiled apologetically. "You must forgive me. I've only just woken up a few hours ago. I must still be a little exhausted from my journey. Would you mind repeating the question?" I asked, looking at no one specific since I wasn't sure which of them was Lady Audrey.

A strawberry blonde giggled. "I just asked how you were looking forward to married life with King Seth. He's very handsome. The Emperor and Empress' good looks most certainly didn't skip him even though he is very much Saledian," she teased, and all the women giggled along with her.

I plastered a fake smile on my face and answered, "I'm very much looking forward to marrying him. He has been my best friend for as long as I can remember, and the thought of spending the rest of my life with him feels like a dream." I half lied.

Marie smiled, but it failed to reach her eyes as she looked down at me. "Has he shared his family history with you at all? We Vaegarians take our lineage very seriously, and it is important for you to know it as well." Without offering me any time to reply, she continued, "Seth is my great-great-grandson. While Seth's

Saledian father was a calculated move, Catrin's own Saledian heritage was out of our hands. It's a shame that our sacred heir will barely be Vaegarian, but he'll be enough to carry this Dynasty to glory," she answered confidently.

My eyebrows raised in surprise and I thought now was as good a time as any to ponder about their age. "I apologize if this is a rude question, but you look so young. How is it possible for you to have a great-great-grandchild?"

All of the women began laughing, and Empress Marie gave them a dirty look, which quieted them down in an instant. Then she turned back to me. "You really know nothing of our kind, do you?" She asked. "Vaegarians do not age like Saledians. If you're born into the right family, you can live for hundreds of years. We have the tools and technology to reverse the aging process, but it does cost you," she answered ominously.

My mouth fell as I took in her words. *Hundreds* of years. Andrew and Marie could have easily been alive during the genocide of the Nativus. They could have been there for the war against the Krig Territories. My chest seized as I realized just who I could be speaking to. Marie could have had a hand in ending my ancestor's lives. I wanted to get as far away from this woman as I could, but I reminded myself of the various warnings I had received about her, so I smiled instead.

"How interesting," I replied. "Are any of your other children or grandchildren here tonight?" I asked. The silence that followed my question made me instantly aware of my misstep, and I tried to backtrack. "I'm sorry. That was a very personal question. Please forgive my foolishness."

Empress Marie studied me for a moment before painting that tight-lipped smile on her pale face once again. "No, darling. It's okay, and I know that Seth hasn't told you much about his family. How would you like a lesson in our lineage?" She asked as she excused us and led me down a long hallway where portraits lined the walls.

The Empress pointed to the first portrait that portrayed a much younger version of her and her husband. He was holding a staff and standing behind Marie, who sat in front of him. Neither of them had a smile on their faces, but instead, a cold, stoic expression that gave me chills just looking at them. "This was my love and I after our wedding and coronation. We are the first crowned Emperor and Empress in this land," she explained, smiling slightly. "We take great pride in what we have given our people."

My jaw clenched as she revealed that she and her husband were indeed the ones who stole Nativus' land, killed my entire race, banished Krigs from their own country, and have been killing and tormenting them ever since. My heart ached as I thought of Jude witnessing his entire family murdered in front of him. Not to mention the countless other Krigs with similar stories, like Billy and Marco. This woman and these people were not only alive during these atrocities, but they ordered them. Fire ran through my veins as I stared at the portrait on the wall.

"We look so young there. Don't we?" She asked, ignorant of my rage-filled thoughts.

I smiled and nodded. "You do," I answered curtly.

Empress Marie led me to the next portrait on the wall, which showed a young man with a smaller but extravagant crown that sat on dark brown hair. His blue eyes matched Marie's, but his expression was much warmer. "This was our son, King Edmond," she said, pointing to the brunette man. "He was such a lovely boy, but he was much too weak to rule." She stood there staring at her son before she slightly shook her head and looked down at me. "He is the one who introduced the weak Saledian blood into our line. He fell in love with a servant woman, and she bore twins before we could terminate her altogether. My grandchildren were then born half-Saledian, of course. A shame to us all, but they were Vaegarians nevertheless."

The Empress pointed to the next portrait that showed two figures standing side by side. I instantly recognized Cormac with his lifeless and cold expression, but not the woman standing next to him. She looked almost identical to Marie, with bright red hair and blue eyes.

"I'm sure you recognize my grandson, Cormac. This was his twin sister Sybell who was Catrin's mother," Marie said, holding her gaze on the young woman who looked eerily similar to herself. "Sybell was my everything despite her being half Saledian. I never held that against her. The Vaegarian in her was strong enough to overshadow most of the weak Saledian traits and she quickly became the daughter I never had. That was until she became pregnant with Catrin." The

Empress' expression turned cold as she looked away from her granddaughter's image. "You see, for whatever reason, nature has been working against our kind for centuries. It has become harder and harder for Vaegarians to conceive naturally, but my lovely Sybell fell pregnant almost immediately after her marriage. We were all so overjoyed that we didn't even think about the possibility of her losing her life during labor. Her half-Saledian body was not strong enough to bear a Vaegarian child. I will never forgive my son for her death," she said grimly.

We slowly came upon the portrait of Catrin as a young girl. Her infamous red hair was worn down, and it flowed along her back. I was used to seeing it worn in a tight bun, much like Marie's, but the long flowing locks made her look innocent, and it made me wonder if there was a time when she had actually been a decent person. Surely, a child isn't capable of being evil, but this family made me believe otherwise.

Empress Marie huffed when she looked up at her great-granddaughter. "It was difficult having Catrin here after her mother had so tragically passed," she said, looking away from the portrait and back down at me. "It made it all the easier to send her away to Saleda with Cormac. Perhaps fate had done that on purpose to pave the way for your arrival," she said, smiling down at me.

She then led me to a blank space on the wall. "We will have a portrait commissioned for you and Seth here after your nuptials. Perhaps we should wait until you are with the child. I'd love the portrait to capture a glimpse of our sacred heir," Marie said eagerly, looking down at my abdomen. "I know you and Seth have yet to marry, but you have been together for quite some time. Have you consummated your relationship yet?" She asked and upon seeing my shocked face, she laughed loudly. "We have no religion or gods to strike you down for enjoying one another, my sweet Siv. You will learn that Vaegarians are much more progressive than your Saledian counterparts."

My shock slightly faded once I had digested her words, and I couldn't help but internally roll my eyes at just how *progressive* killing off an entire race and tormenting another was. Despite the anger still pumping through my veins, I did my best to pull off a shy blush and shook my head at her question.

Her expression dulled as she once again looked down at my stomach before looking back at me. "I must admit that surprises me with how fond you are of one another, but perhaps that is normal in Saleda with all of their foolish customs," she said, guiding me back to the Great Hall. "I'm hoping since Seth is mostly Saledian, conceiving will be easy. But fear not, if your womb continues to be empty after three moons, we have the technology to aid in such things here."

I stopped in my tracks, and my mind began to race. What did she mean by that? How could they possibly force a child upon me? I had never heard of such a thing and if she was telling the truth, that meant I only had three months to figure a way out of this country. If I failed, I would inevitably end up pregnant with Seth's child. That thought alone made me want to hurl the contents from my stomach. I had never thought much about being a mother, but it seemed terribly wrong to imagine my child being related to these people. Yet I'd be required to marry Seth and bear him a child if I wanted to live. It felt disgusting regardless of how my situation was being forced upon me.

I quickly realized that the idea of bearing Seth's child was not only foul because of his Vaegarian family, who wished to claim the child as their own, but because it felt wrong to think of sharing a future with anyone but Jude. Despite how our last conversation had ended, I still loved him. My heart ached when I remembered that not only did he have no idea where I was, but even if he did, he could not save me. The Crystal Tower was secured with technology that made no sense to me or anyone who had not grown up in this country. It would be up to me to save myself and I had no idea where to even begin.

The Empress paused and turned to see that I wasn't directly behind her anymore. She must have mistaken my expression of horror for a look of shock because she walked back to me and placed a hand on my shoulder. "Vaegarians are known to be far more academically inclined than our... peers in Saleda. I know it must sound too good to be true, but you will find out that this country will have substantially more to offer than Mendacia. I'm excited for you to become accustomed to everything we have here." Marie gently pulled a lock of my blonde hair and rubbed it between her fingers. "Once you become well-adjusted in your new home, you'll forget about everything and everyone you've known before."

My fists balled up at my sides, and I forced deep breaths through my lungs. I knew the Empress was baiting me. I knew that if I said one wrong thing, it would become significantly harder to escape this dreadful country. So, I unballed my hands and forced a sweet smile instead.

"I'm sure you're right," I replied.

Marie paused for a moment and studied my face before leading me back to the Great Hall. "As much as I'd love to show you around the Crystal Tower and introduce you to all our subjects, I also know that you have had a very long journey, and you are probably wishing for some time alone with my great-great-grandson. I only ask that you remember what I said about us being progressive here. No judgment will fall upon you for giving into your desires before your big day," she told me with a wink as she nodded toward Seth, who was chatting with other men along with the Emperor. "I'll allow for you and your beau to take an early leave for the night and if you need absolutely anything at all, servants will be stationed by your door at all times."

I internally groaned. Of course, she would have people outside my door at all times. It would be impossible to go anywhere without them knowing. I'd have to find another way out of that room without being detected.

She left my side to go stand beside her husband, so I quickly found my place beside Seth and tugged on his cuff so that he would bend down to my level. "The Empress gave us permission to leave early," I whispered in his ear. Seth looked down at me and nodded before he politely excused us and graciously thanked the Emperor and Empress for their hospitality.

Once we were inside the small lift, Seth turned to me. "What did you and the Empress speak about?" He asked nervously.

I shrugged. "You mean your great-great-grandmother? You failed to mention many things when you spoke of their grand plan to indoctrinate me into this messed-up family."

Seth looked down at his polished shoes. "Yes, technically, she is my great-great-grandmother, but this is the first time I've been in this country, and this is the first time I am meeting them. Neither of them was especially fond of my mother, and they only tolerated me because I held the crown of Saleda after my mother's death and that you would happily fall beside me as my Queen. If I were to embarrass them in any way or if you were to express any hesitation to their plans for you, they would not hesitate to have me killed and replaced with someone else who'd be happy to force you into compliance," he answered solemnly. "Now, please, tell me what you two spoke about."

I almost started to feel bad for him until I remembered how he had manipulated my feelings toward him before in order to get me alone, drug me, and whisk me away to this godsforsaken place. I straightened my back and stared straight forward. "She just told me about your lineage. That was pretty much it. That and her sacred heir that you and I are expected to conceive for them any day now," I replied coldly.

Seth shuffled uncomfortably beside me and awkward silence filled the air between us before he exhaled loudly. "I know you're not happy about our predicament, and believe it or not, I'm not thrilled about our private lives being a free topic of discussion for the entire country. But this is the fate we've been given. This is what our destinies look like, and sulking about it won't change anything."

I swiftly turned to him and pushed him as hard as I could. "*This* is not my destiny!" I screamed. "I am the Queen of Saleda! My *destiny* is to deliver them peace and unity! I refuse to turn my back on my people, and I definitely refuse to conceive *anything* with you or anyone else from this revolting country and its abominable people! Not to mention, I am in love with someone else!"

Seth slammed my body up against the wall of the lift and covered my mouth with his hand. "Shh!" he whispered harshly, and he pressed a button that made the lift come to a halt. "You cannot say things like that in the Crystal Tower. You will get me killed, and you'll find yourself being used repeatedly down in the dungeons until you give them what they want." Seth's grip on me loosened, and he let me slide out of his reach. "Siv, I may be the bad guy in your eyes, but I am not the bad guy in this country. I'm trying my best for you. You realize that if I hadn't taken you here myself, much worse things would have happened to you and many others. This was my only way to save your life!"

I let out a malicious laugh. "Save my life? I would rather be dead than live a life for these people. I understand that you believe you did the right thing, but I do not see it that way," I told him, glaring into his glossy eyes. "If you were trying your best for me, neither of us would be in the position we are in now. You would have found another way. At the very least, you would have confided in me, and we could have figured something out together, but you didn't, and now we're here."

Seth looked away and quickly wiped a stray tear that had fallen. "Siv, if I wouldn't have forced you to come with me when I did, everyone you love would be dead right now. The Emperor gave me a month to arrive at the Vaegary Dynasty with you or he'd send an army of his own not only to retrieve you but everyone in the rebellion. Do you know what that would have looked like for Saleda? Thousands would have been slaughtered within days. The war would have been over, and there would be no Saledians left. The only reason this war is still happening is because they find it entertaining. Otherwise, they would have ended it the moment the uprisings began." Seth turned back to me, his tears freely falling down his somber face now. "So yes, I was trying my best for you. I tried everything to not have to force you here. I thought that if somehow I had your love, you'd be more understanding toward all of this. Maybe you would even want this with me. But I had to think of another way to get you here when I realized you'd never love me. Not with that Krig around anyway."

My brows snapped together as I tried to process everything he had just revealed. Perhaps Seth wasn't my enemy here, but he definitely was not my friend either. "You could have told me, Seth," I whispered. "We could have figured something out."

He shook his head. "Siv, you're not getting it. There is no winning against them. They have technology so far advanced from anything we have in Saleda. They have the numbers, the tools, and the power to kill every single member of the rebellion with the snap of their fingers. The only way to avoid that is to submit to their will. That is how you keep your friends alive. If they believe the rebellion is nothing but a minor inconvenience, they won't bother sending their soldiers to Saleda. But if they think for a second that they're an actual threat, everyone will die."

He pressed another button that made the lift continue its course up to our floor, and I followed him silently to my room. I had been so naive about everything. Of course, the Vaegarians had the ability to stop the rebellion. The technology that I had seen just in a few hours was more advanced than anything we had back in my country. All of a sudden, any plan I had to leave here and continue the fight back home seemed not only impossible but pointless. It would be like leading a herd of sheep straight into a lion's den. Every bit of hope I had about succeeding in this war was gone in an instant.

Seth held the door open for me, and to my surprise, he followed behind me. "What're you doing?" I asked him.

"These are our chambers, Siv. They expect us to conceive. Do you really think they'd give us separate rooms?" He asked. When I didn't respond, Seth hung his jacket up on the coat rack by the door and then looked at me with sympathetic eyes. "I won't lay a finger on you, but if any of the servants come in here and witness us acting like we hate each other, we'll be a lot worse off than this."

I wanted to argue with him. I wanted to hit and slap him until he gave up and left the room, but I knew he was right. The thought of the Emperor and Empress taking my fertility into their own hands was enough to make me sick.

When I was finally alone in the bathing room, I fell to my knees and began to sob. I missed my sister, I missed my friends, but most of all, I missed Jude. He always knew what to say to make me feel better, and his touch was enough to make me forget everything. I needed him, but I knew that I may never see him again, and that made me sob even harder.

I never thought about how difficult it may have been for him to distance himself from me; I had only thought of my own pain. I hated myself for fighting with him, for making an already difficult situation harder for both of us. I hated myself for not fighting harder for the rebellion, for not seeing the bigger picture like he had. I hated the person I saw in the reflection of the floor-length mirror in this ostentatious bathroom. I was becoming exactly what I set out to destroy, and I couldn't see a way to stop any of it.

I must have cried myself to sleep on the cold tiled floors because the next thing I knew, Seth was carrying me into the bed.

CHAPTER 24

Acouple of weeks had passed, and my hopes of leaving this country and these morbid people had started to lessen. Every day was more of the same. The Empress and Emperor would parade me around the tower and in front of their people, who would stare and prod me with questions of my fertility as well as Seth and I's intimate relationship, which, unbeknownst to them, did not exist. We'd spend hours looking at different decor, food, and dress options for our impending wedding which always served as a warning of the closing window I had to escape this place. The Emperor and Empress withheld the date of our nuptials from both Seth and I. They said it was to surprise us, but I had a suspicion that perhaps they were catching on, and this was their way to make sure we did not flee before then.

My mornings began with a knock on the door with two small men walking in with crystal breakfast platters. I would have no complaints about this part of my day because of the mouthwatering assortments of food given to me if it weren't for the two small white tablets that also came along with it.

"The Empress told me to have you take these," one of the men had told me when I had asked. Avoiding my eyes, he pushed his palm closer to me. "They're supplements to assist with conceiving."

I had instinctively pulled away from him, but Seth offered his own palm to the male servant. "I'll make sure she takes them. Thank you."

The servant briefly paused before shaking his head. "That won't do. The Empress asked me to make sure the Queen took them before I left your chambers."

Seth looked at me apologetically, and I reluctantly took the tablets from the man and placed them in my mouth before giving him a tight-lipped smile. I turned away from him, expecting him to leave, but to my surprise, he remained by my side. "I'm going to need you to open your mouth and lift your tongue," he commanded.

"You can't be serious?" Seth asked the man.

I inhaled, trying to think of a way to discard the tablets without swallowing but I quickly realized there'd be no way out of it. So I quickly swallowed and washed them down with the tall glass of juice before showing the servant my empty mouth.

"Thank you, Queen Siv. I apologize for my thoroughness, but I'm sure you know how important it is for you to have a safe and healthy pregnancy. The Emperor and Empress will do everything they can to make sure that happens," the small man said before excusing himself from our chambers.

I shook my head before turning my attention to Seth. "Those tablets won't get me pregnant will they?" I asked him.

Seth chuckled before he shook his head. "No, Siv. They're not magic. You'd still have to...you know."

Although I had grown used to their aggressive manner in regard to the tablets each morning, I still dreaded it. They were a consistent reminder of what I was doing here in this country as well as a reminder that I may never return to my own country and my people could very well be doomed to a continuous cycle of suffering. These thoughts consumed my mind every second of every day, and my mental state started to deteriorate after the first week. I was in a permanent state of distress, all while having to try and keep an image of calm and collectedness. I was miserable.

I sighed as I examined the food that had been brought in, and my chest tightened when I noticed a klurula mixed in with the rest of the fruit. Iridia had introduced me to it, and it reminded me of her death back in Caliot, which reminded me of the unanswered questions that I never had the chance to ask.

I turned in bed and faced Seth, who was sitting beside the large window overlooking the busy city below. "Seth, did you have a part in the explosion in town?"

Seth's chewing came to a halt as he looked at me, and he swallowed quickly. "Why are you asking me this?" His brows furrowed as he examined me and he sat up from his chair, making his way toward the bed. "No, Siv. I had no idea that my mother's brother was a spy, and I definitely had no idea about their plot to kill you. I had only found out after the fact. My mother had become so jealous of her family's interest in you and lack of interest in herself that she was willing to go against their wishes and have you killed. Had I known earlier, I would have found a way to warn you or to stop it altogether," he explained. "Do you believe me?"

I studied his face. He looked genuinely sorry, but I couldn't be sure if he was putting on another act. So I shrugged and began picking at the fruit on the platter. "It's not like it would matter if I believed you or not. It doesn't really change anything."

Seth set his platter aside and moved closer to me on the bed. "It matters to me," he said. "I have had to play the part of a monster several times in my life in order to survive, but I am not that person. I don't kill or torture people for fun like they do here. I'm just trying my best to keep you safe, Siv."

I didn't want to believe him. I didn't want to fall into another one of his traps again, but what other choice did I have? I had no friends here, and no matter how much I disliked him, he was the only piece of home that I had left. In fact, he had gone out of his way to try and make me comfortable in this horrible place but I couldn't forget that he was the reason I was here. But if there was even a sliver of a chance that Seth could be on my side, I was going to take it.

"I believe you," I told him. "I don't want to, but I do."

Seth smiled and squeezed my hand before he sat beside me and continued eating his breakfast. "Today, the Emperor and Empress have invited us to lunch in the city. There's a chance they might separate us once again, and if that happens, just remember to act like we are deeply in love and doing everything we can to give them their heir," he said in between bites. "Marie is extremely manipulative and good at getting the truth out of people, so be on guard around her, and if you ever find yourself alone with Andrew, speak as little as possible and do whatever he says. I have heard stories of that man's cruelty, and the last thing I want is for you to be his next victim."

I sighed loudly. Seth wasn't telling me anything I hadn't already figured out on my own. As far as I was concerned, everyone in this place was cruel and heartless, and I'd do my best to avoid them all. However, as much as I hated this country, their food was delicious.

After we had eaten everything the servants had brought us, Opal arrived and ordered me into the tub. I laughed as she kicked Seth out of the room and began fussing over me. As harsh as she was, she was quickly becoming a friend to me. I didn't let myself forget that she was a Vaegarian, but I also didn't let that keep me from enjoying her company. I didn't have much hope for an escape anymore, but I knew having a friend on the inside couldn't hurt.

Opal and her girls had finished up my hair, makeup, and clothing after about an hour. I didn't look as extreme as I had before, but I still cringed slightly at my reflection. I doubted I'd ever get used to seeing myself look like this.

"Seth should be back any minute now to escort you," Opal told me as her girls all left my chambers. "Open this before he gets here," she said, handing me a folded piece of paper that had been sealed with dark red wax and an emblem of a willow tree in the middle of it.

My mind immediately went to the necklace that I had left on my nightstand before Seth had drugged and dragged me to this godsforsaken place. It was obvious that whoever had written this letter was somehow associated with the rebellion. "What is this?" I asked her.

Opal looked back to the door, making sure no one was around before she turned back to me. "Not all Vaegarians support the Emperor and Empress. There are some of us who have loyalties elsewhere," she explained. "I don't have to tell you how important it is that this information stays between the two of us. Burn this letter after you've read it."

I watched her leave with wide eyes before I hurriedly tore open the willow-sealed letter and read the contents.

My dearest Queen,

I'm sure you understand how dire the circumstances of your survival and well-being are not only for the country of Saleda but for the entire world as a whole. But, if innocence still clouds your view of reality, let me explain it to you.

You hold a power so mighty that not even the technology and resources of the Vaegarian Dynasty will be able to combat it. The Emperor and Empress wish to keep you sheltered, just as you were in the Mendacian palace. They wish to keep you ignorant of just how strong you can be. If they succeed with their methods of obtaining a sacred heir, all will be lost.

While you are in town with the Emperor and Empress, you will receive a signal. You will be given an excuse to leave the city and be brought back to your quarters. I have arranged for someone who has been adamant to see you to be waiting for you, but you must be haste with your visit.

You have friends here, my Queen. You have friends all over Lorus. But you also have many enemies. Tell no one of this letter. Trust no one.

I stared at the letter in shock. The hope that I had forcefully banished from my heart had returned. Someone knew of a way to stop the Emperor and Empress. Someone knew how to get me back to Jude, my sister, my friends, and my people. I couldn't stop the smile that had formed on my face and I laughed from joy as I realized there was a chance for me to actually achieve what I had set out to do in the first place. Perhaps I really would give the people of Saleda peace and unity. Perhaps I could give the entire *world* that.

The sound of the door opening ripped me from my bliss, and I quickly threw the letter into the flames of the fireplace at the end of my chambers.

"What was that?" Seth asked, eying the heightened blaze of the fire.

I paused for a moment before smiling at him and wiping my hands. "Opal gave me some undergarments that looked more like thin scraps of lace than anything. She said they were more for you than me, so I figured I'd watch them burn instead," I lied.

Seth chuckled and shook his head. "Of course," he said, walking up to me and offering me his arm. "Are you ready?"

I nodded and took his arm. He led me to the lift, where we went all the way down to the first floor. This was the first time I was seeing the very bottom of the Crystal Tower and I was excited to be so close to the ground, so close to the outside. The theme of the tower stretched to every floor it seemed, because the walls and floors all shined with the same clear and glistening materials. Several purple rugs were laid out, and silver furniture filled the expansive layout. Expensive-looking paintings covered the walls, and several tall Vaegarians were drinking from chalices and chatting amongst one another. I noticed that all the women wore sleeveless gowns, unlike the long-sleeved gown I was wearing, but I was thankful for the extra material because the tower was unusually frigid.

Seth noticed me shivering, so he began rubbing my sleeved arms. The friction helped warm my skin slightly but I looked around to see that no one else seemed to be bothered by the chilly atmosphere.

"Why is no one else cold?" I whispered to him.

He looked around at everyone before looking back down at me. "Vaegarian's don't become cold like Saledian's. They thrive in cold settings, and they lose strength when they become warm. I'm not sure how or why, but I've heard that they slowly begin to deteriorate if their body reaches a certain temperature. I'm sure it has something to do with the measures they take to maintain their youth," he explained. "I don't know if that's common knowledge or not, so please don't repeat that." I nodded just as everyone's attention turned toward the Emperor and Empress, who entered through the grand doorway.

"Good afternoon!" Emperor Andrew greeted the room. "For those of you who have not yet met our special guests, now is your chance. The young King and Queen of Saleda will be joining us in the city for our meal. Now, it is their first time in this country, but they are welcomed guests here, and this will be their home. At least until our sacred heir is born to us," he said, looking at both Seth and I. "Now, let's show them our proud city, shall we?"

About a dozen of those who had been sipping on their chalices and chatting amongst themselves joined the Emperor and Empress as they ushered us into several different unattached carriages.

"Where are the horses?" I asked Seth quietly as I looked around.

Empress Marie laughed loudly in her seat, seemingly eavesdropping. "These carriages do not need horses in order to take us from one destination to another," she explained boorishly. "You are no longer in Saleda. You must get used to our civilized way of life here. Perhaps we will allow you and Seth to bring some of our technology back to Saleda with you after you have bore us our heir." She turned back in her seat in front of us without saying another word, and I couldn't help but bite my tongue, holding back every nasty response I wished to give her.

Emperor Andrew finally joined the Empress and sat next to her as we began to move. I couldn't help but watch as my view of the Crystal Tower began to fade behind us as the carriages sped down the perfectly paved roads into the city. I was unfamiliar with just how smooth and not to mention how fast the ride was to our destination. Despite hating this country and most of the people who lived here, I couldn't ignore how magnificent their machines were. In a horse-led carriage, the journey into this city would have taken at least half an hour but we had arrived in less than ten minutes with barely any bumps or impacts along the way.

CHAPTER 25

The view of the city from my and Seth's chambers didn't do it justice. My mouth hung open as I observed the streets littered with automatic carriages, and the homes, apartments, stores, and factories were all made of metals and glass rather than wood or masonry like in Saleda. Life here seemed a lot more fast-paced and organized but it was lacking the warmth and comforts that I had witnessed outside of the palace in Mendacia. The people surrounding us did not speak to one another. In fact, they merely looked at each other as they went about their day. It was strange, and it made me feel uneasy as I followed Seth into a large building made of silver metal with barely any windows. I quickly realized that the building must have been some sort of dining hall because of the savory smells that filled the space, but the tables were all empty as we made our way inside.

The Emperor stood beside me, smiling down at me as I took in my surroundings. "When we dine in the city, we make sure to clear the location we will be at. It is a great honor to eat with us. Not many get the chance," he told me, obviously aware of my confusion due to the lack of people. "And yet, I am the one feeling honored to dine with you, my little Queen," he added with a wink, sending an ominous chill down my spine.

An elaborate feast was brought out only moments after we had taken our seats, and despite itching to leave and head back to my quarters to discover who was waiting for me, my mouth watered at the sight. A steaming turkey sat on a decorated platter with stuffing, vegetables, fruits, puddings, and pastries surrounding it. I didn't think I'd ever get used to the food served here, but my body had started to become accustomed as Opal had to let out the seams of most of my gowns.

I had finished my plate before everyone else at the table, and I began to zone out as their meaningless and superficial conversations dragged on. I probably could have benefitted from listening to them. Perhaps I could have learned a thing or two that could have helped in a potential escape plan, but I couldn't stop thinking about home. I couldn't stop thinking about all of the people suffering while I was drowning in foods and drinks they'd never know. I felt dirty as I looked down at my empty plate and glass before me. Just as I started to chastise myself for indulging in their hedonistic lifestyle, a servant spilled ale on my gown after attempting to fill my empty glass. The cold liquid had stunned me and I didn't even realize the piece of paper she had slipped into the palm of my hand as she patted down the damp fabric of my dress until the Emperor had barked orders for her to leave.

I tried my best to ignore the rage on Emperor Andrew's face as I stood from the table. "Is there a washroom close by that I can try and clean myself up in?" I asked no one in particular.

"Of course," the Emperor answered. "It is the first door on the right down the hall," he said, pointing toward the other side of the room. I nodded and excused myself, all while safely keeping the note concealed inside the long sleeve of my now-drenched gown.

As soon as I shut the door behind me, I scrambled to unfold the note.

Go is all that was written.

My excitement began to build, and I took a deep breath, focusing on my un-recognizable reflection in the large mirror that hung on the tiled wall. I smoothed down the long locks of blonde that had been sewn into my much shorter hair and fixed the black smudges that had been created by the crease in my eyelids. I couldn't help but laugh at what Mia would have to say if she were to see me at this moment. Tearing the simple handwritten note into shreds, I tossed it into the bin at the corner of the washroom and headed back to the table.

"I hope you all can forgive me," I began, looking at everyone around the table. "I did my best to dry the fabric of my gown in the washroom, but I am quite un-comfortable, and the last thing I want is to catch a cold. Would it be possible for someone to escort me back to the tower?" I asked with a honeyed voice.

I was relieved when the Emperor promptly agreed and called for a young servant girl to accompany me, but that relief was short-lived when the Empress stood from her seat and made her way over to me.

"I keep forgetting how fragile your kind is," she said as her eyes settled on my stomach. "The last thing we'd want is for an illness to interfere with conceiving a child. I'll have my servant fetch our physician after she delivers you to your quarters. We cannot be too careful." I internally cursed but faked a bright smile.

Seth rose from the table with questions in his expression. "Perhaps I should take leave as well," he started to say, but the Emperor shook his head and motioned for him to sit back down.

"You will stay and enjoy this meal with us. Our sweet Queen has an excuse, but my lovely friends here would still like to get to know the two of you and your plans to rule Saleda in the following years," Emperor Andrew ordered.

Seth reluctantly sat back down, but his eyes never left mine. I could tell he was worried about me being in the tower alone, but little did he know that I had someone waiting in our chambers for me. I gave him a reassuring smile before following the young servant out of the building.

Once we were inside the carriage, I exhaled loudly. I was happy to be excused, but I was anxious to see who awaited me in my room. We wouldn't have much time if the Empress was going to send someone to come check on me, but I hoped I would still have enough time to figure out who had written that letter.

I decided I should try and make small talk with the servant. I didn't want to seem too eager to get to my chambers, and it wouldn't hurt to make friends with the staff around the tower. They probably knew the ins and outs of this place, and that could be used to my advantage, but I was alarmed when I took in her appearance. She couldn't have been more than fifteen years old, and she was obviously Saledian due to her short and frail stature. Her skin looked like it had been an olive tone, but it looked almost transparent. Blue veins could be seen on every bit of skin that wasn't concealed by her white uniform. She looked extremely sick, and I wondered how they could make her work in that condition.

"What's your name?" I asked her with a comforting smile.

Her gaze remained on the front of the carriage as she answered, "Lise, Your Majesty."

"It's nice to meet you, Lise. You can call me Siv," I responded. "Are you from Saleda as well? I've noticed most of the servants do not look or act Vaegarian."

She finally looked at me and nodded her head with a look of fear written all over her face. "Yes, my Queen," she answered before returning her gaze forward.

"How did you end up here, of all places?"

Avoiding my gaze, she looked down to her feet. "We are not to speak of our pasts," she whispered.

"Why?" I asked her.

The young girl looked to the driver, who sat in the front row of the carriage, before looking back at me and furrowing her brows as if she were trying to figure something out. "Do you truly not know?" She asked me, and I shook my head. She looked to the driver once again before leaning closer to me. "We were taken," she whispered. "All of us were taken from Saleda. Some became servants while others..." She looked out of the window, a tear running down her face before she quickly wiped it away and shook her head as if she was shaking the fear off her body. "Others were not so lucky," she whispered.

My eyes widened from her revelation, and my pulse began to race. All of those missing Saledians that we had just assumed fled from Mendacia or had been killed by Catrin had actually been stolen from their homes and shipped off to become slaves or who knows what else. The part of me that had started to become complacent with my situation raged, and a new fire was sparked from within. Not only did I need to escape from this country, but I needed to figure out a way to help these people.

"I'm going to help you," I finally said to Lise. "I'm not sure how yet, but I will find a way to free you. Free all of you," I promised her.

The young girl looked as if she wouldn't allow herself to gain any hope from my words, and my heart sank for her. She must have endured so much at such a young age, and there was nothing that I could say to offer her any comfort. I knew what it felt like to lose hope, and I knew the only way to help her or any of them was to get myself out of the predicament I was in at the moment.

I reminded myself to focus on the task at hand. I couldn't help Lise or anyone, for that matter, if I couldn't figure a way out of here. The rest of the ride back to the tower was silent as my mind raced on how I would not only escape but free those who I now knew were enslaved to the Vaegarians. I took a deep breath before I opened my door and stepped outside and followed Lise to the lift that brought us to the floor of my room.

"I'll send the physician up shortly," she said, avoiding my eyes before she walked back to the lift.

I slowly walked into my quarters before a familiar scent hit me, and all of a sudden, every worry that had occupied my mind left my body, and I felt at ease. I immediately knew who was waiting for me and my steps sped up until I was facing the broad, handsome man who stood in my living room.

"Jude?"

He turned from the fireplace and the large scar running down his forehead to his chin stretched as a wide smile transformed his face. "Siv," he answered, hastily closing the gap between us and pulling me into his arms. I sank into his embrace, allowing myself to soak up the comfort that only he could give me. "I think you forgot this," he said, holding my necklace out to me.

I couldn't help the wide smile that formed as I quickly grabbed my necklace and put it on before turning my attention back to him. "How are you here?" I asked him, my voice muffled by the fabric of his thin tunic.

"It's a long story, but for the sake of time, I'll give you the short version," he answered, pulling away from me and sitting down on the sofa before pulling me back into his lap. "A couple of days after you were taken, we received a letter from the disgraced Prince of Vaegary, Edward. He'd been in hiding for centuries, but your arrival has brought him out and he offered his help in our war. He was the one who wrote the letter you received, and he's the one who got me in here. He told us that you were being held here in the tower, among other things." Jude's face wrinkled in disgust. "I know what they want from you and that rat. I know they expect you to bear a child with him."

I placed my hands on his stubbly cheeks and forced his red-hued eyes to focus on me. "Seth hasn't laid a hand on me, Jude. He hasn't forced himself on me or made me do anything. I promise," I told him in an attempt to reassure him.

"It doesn't matter," he answered. "If we don't get you out of here soon, Edward said they'll use their own means to get what they want from you. We don't have time to waste." Jude pulled me closer to him and rested his head in the crook of my neck. "We're all here, Siv. My army, your sister, Billy, Marco, Florian, we're all here, and we're ending this tonight."

I pulled back from his grip. "Tonight?"

"If we wait, they'll find out we're here, and every opportunity we have of an ambush will be lost, and they'll force a child upon you the first chance they get. We need to act now," he answered.

Lise's sickly face entered my mind. "Jude, the servants here, they're the missing Saledians. They were shipped here by Catrin and they've been forced into servitude and who knows what else. It's not just me that needs to escape this tower," I explained to him.

He seemed to think about what I had just revealed to him before he nodded. "We'll get them out of here. I'm not sure yet, but I'll find a way." Jude stood from the sofa, gently placing me down in front of him. "They're planning your wedding to Seth this evening," Jude growled, looking pained before clearing his face of emotion. "The entire country has been invited, so the tower will be filled to the brim with Vaegarians. You're going to use that to your advantage, okay? There will be a small opening in between the toast and the serving of the feast before the ceremony. Everyone will close their eyes for a very brief moment to honor their sacred heir. That is your chance to leave the Grand Hall and go down to the hallway where the portraits are. Do you know what I'm talking about?"

I nodded, avoiding any and every thought about the impending wedding ceremony that Jude had just revealed to me. "The Empress took me there last night."

Jude smiled slightly. "Good, that's good. There will be an envelope hidden behind Edward's portrait, and inside will be a key. Take it with you, and then go all the way down that hallway and to the left. You'll find the servants' stairwell, which will lead all the way down to the back end of the first floor. It's very important that you do not stop until you're all the way at the bottom of that stairwell. Your stylist, Opal, will be waiting for you with a servant's uniform so you'll blend in better but still try your best not to be seen. Most of the servants here are loyal to me, but some will do anything to gain the Emperor and Empress' good graces, which would include dragging you back to the feast and presenting you as a traitor."

I listened as best as I could, but doubt began to creep its way into my mind. "Are you sure we can trust Edward? He's a Vaegarian. Aren't they known for being deceitful?"

Jude looked to the door and placed his hands on my shoulders. "People don't always coincide with their stereotypes. Besides, he fell in love with a Saledian once. She was his everything, and she opened his eyes to the atrocities his parents had committed. Shortly after she gave birth to his children, they had her killed. He'll bring them down one way or another," he said, returning his gaze back to me. "I know what it's like to love someone with everything you have and then have them taken away from you. I know what that can do to someone, and although I may not trust him when it comes to anything else, I trust that the demise of his family is his top priority right now. We share a goal at the time being and he is all we have when it comes to the ins and outs of this place. We have no choice but to trust him at this point in time," he told me before continuing, "when you get to the first floor of the tower, you'll need the key to open the door leading to the underground dungeon."

I felt the blood drain from my face. I had been warned about these dungeons since the moment I arrived here, and now I'd be voluntarily going down into them. I swallowed loudly and continued to listen despite the alarms going off in my head.

"You will see things down there. Terrible and awful things, but I need you to keep your head straight and stay focused, okay?" He waited for me to nod before he continued. "There is a wall all the way at the end that holds several levers. You need to pull three of them, and this part is very important. The first lever is yellow, and it is the power source for the entire tower. There is a backup generator, but the power source will be stunted, which means the lights, lifts, defenses, and so on will all be slower and less efficient. The second lever is red; it will unlock the servants' quarters, so all who serve me will be allowed access to the floors that are off limits, and they have their own orders to execute. Lastly, the third lever you need to pull is purple. It will lift the gates to the tower, which will allow my army entrance to the private grounds of the tower. Once those levers have been pulled, you will only have minutes before my parents realize what is happening and send guards to the dungeons. There is only one way in and out, so you will need to be quick. Do not stop for anything, Siv. Do you hear me? Stop for nothing." He stared at me intensely.

"I'll stop for nothing," I repeated, and he nodded.

"When you're out, you'll run to the very back of the first floor. Once you've stepped outside, I'll be there waiting for you. From there, it is up to us how this ends. They have the manpower and the technology to erase entire races from this world, but we have both the element of surprise as well as your power within."

"What about Seth?" I asked him.

Jude raised an eyebrow, and his face began to redden from either annoyance, anger, or both. "What about him?"

I tilted my head. "Where does he fit into this plan of yours?"

"He doesn't fit into this plan at all. Do you not remember that he is the one who brought you here in the first place?" He asked, seemingly irritated. "We can't trust him. Not with something as important as this. He should die with the rest of them for all I'm concerned."

I shook my head. "No, he only did that because he thought it was the only way to keep me and the rebellion safe," I explained. I hated that I was coming to his aid, but I knew that if Seth didn't come with me tonight, they'd have him killed the moment they realized I was missing, and as much as I disliked the choices he had made, I knew he didn't deserve to die. I believed he had always done what he thought was best, no matter how wrong he had been. "I won't leave him to die at the hands of the Emperor and Empress. I know it's hard for you to understand, but he is my friend. Please," I pleaded with him.

Jude began to pace. "This complicates everything," he said under his breath before stopping and looking down at me. "Fine. I'll make it work. But just know, if he betrays you tonight, not only will many die but the future of our countries will be lost." I nodded, and Jude crouched down in front of me once again. "And if he does anything to hurt you, I will tear him apart, limb by limb."

"He won't," I told him.

Jude ignored my answer, and to my surprise, he pulled me in, roughly kissing me before pulling away, leaving me wanting much more. "I love you, Siv. I'm sorry it took me so long to find you," he told me, his gruff voice turning soft as he studied my face. "If anything happens tonight, I need you to know that I was wrong. I realized just how wrong when you went missing. You're my everything, and I choose you. I choose you over everything."

Before I had time to answer him, the handle to my door began to move. I turned around to see a tall man with a bald head and glasses entering my chambers. When I turned back, Jude was gone, and the floor-length window to my side had been opened. The breeze gently swayed with the curtains before the tall man huffed and quickly closed the window.

The bald man huffed. "I have heard it is a common practice for your kind to allow outside air into your homes. Some even believe it is good for their health, but that is simply not the case," the man stated before he turned to look at me. "I am the Emperor and Empress' personal physician. It is a great honor to have them call for me on your behalf. I hope you are grateful for all of the privileges they have given you."

I stood and gave him a small curtsy. "I am very thankful for everything they have done and continue to do for me," I lied. "It is an honor to have your attention..." I waited for him to tell me his name.

He looked me over before sticking his chin up in the air. "My name is Sir Vincent," he answered before grabbing my wrist and harshly leading me to my bed. "Undress and lay flat for the examination," he ordered.

I reluctantly untied the back of my gown and quickly hurried underneath the covers with just my slip-on. He set down a large case on the bedside table and began fiddling with several instruments. "You may feel a pinch," he said as he slid a needle into the crease of my arm. He ignored my hiss of pain and continued to draw blood from me. When he was satisfied with the amount he had received in a small glass tube, he held it up, observing the crimson liquid.

"What do you need my blood for?" I asked him.

The man placed the tube inside the case and retrieved another instrument. "Your blood will confirm or cancel out a pregnancy," he finally answered. "And if you end up having trouble conceiving, your blood will aid in our endeavors."

I tried not to cringe from his revelation and forcefully reminded myself that if I succeeded tonight, he wouldn't get the chance to do anything with my blood. Vincent then pulled my slip up and began to spread a clear jelly-like substance onto my abdomen and pushed it down with some sort of tool. "There doesn't seem to be a heartbeat of any kind; Nativus and Saledian pregnancies are said to develop at a much faster rate than a Vaegarian pregnancy. I'm not well rehearsed in your kind biological makeup, but I do know it is very similar to that of a Saledian. But worry not, I have been studying in order to educate myself on the differences of your race."

My brows drew together. "What do you mean by studying?"

He looked down at me with a blank expression. "If you want me to be prepared to aid you through a healthy pregnancy and birth, I must learn through trial and error," he explained with no emotion. "I have begun testing fertility experiments on several servants, and some are carrying healthy pregnancies as we speak. They'll be very useful for my education of human births. The Empress does not want you or your child to be harmed during the birth. It would be detrimental to the future of this country."

I was disgusted and my chest tightened when I realized Luce had to be one of the servants he was experimenting on. Anger began to cloud my mind when I thought about how young she had to have been. I took a deep breath before I looked back at the despicable man standing before me. "You don't hurt them, do you?" I asked, even though I was sure that I already knew the answer.

He roughly wiped the substance off my abdomen and shrugged. "Not all of them," he answered as he packed his case and left, shutting the door on his way out.

CHAPTER 26

I wasn't sure how long I had laid frozen in my bed. Vincent's words mortified me, and I couldn't stop thinking about all of the women he had experimented on because of the Empress' obsession with a sacred heir. Luce's frail face kept entering my mind, and I couldn't help but feel like I had a hand in all of it. If it weren't for me, they'd be safe.

"There you are," Seth said, entering the room and shutting the door behind him. "How're you feeling?" He asked, sitting beside me on the bed.

I stared at him for a moment before I worked up the nerve to speak. "Seth, can we have an honest conversation?"

His smile faded, and his eyes filled with concern. "What's wrong? Is this about tonight?" He asked, guilt taking over his features. "I swear I only found out that they were planning for our wedding today at lunch. I was going to tell-"

I cut him off with a wave of my hand before continuing, "Promise me that you won't betray me, Seth," I demanded. "Promise that there will be no more lying and no more ulterior motives."

Seth stood from the bed and looked down at me. "What's going on?" He asked.

I shook my head. "Promise me!" I shouted.

He looked toward the door before sitting down once again. "Okay, okay. I promise," he whispered.

I looked into his green eyes and once again found myself wondering if I could truly trust Seth after everything that had happened between us. But I also knew I couldn't leave him here to die. "Jude is here," I admitted. "Tonight, there's going to be an attack on the Crystal Tower."

Seth's eyes widened, and he began shaking his head. "No, Siv. That's not something you can just do on a whim. You're going to get people killed. How do you expect to do anything without them noticing? You are their prized possession. They have eyes on you at all times. Not to mention the type of weapons they have here; they are so much more advanced than anything you've seen in battle." He ranted.

I grabbed his hands with mine. "Listen, I have help from the inside. It's going to work. We will have the element of surprise, and they won't see it coming. You don't have to come with me. You don't even have to help me if you don't want to, but I couldn't leave you here without giving you the option."

Seth studied my face before he closed his eyes. "Why?" He asked. "Why would you put everything at risk to include me when I have done nothing but lie to you?"

His question had caught me off guard. I wasn't sure how to answer at first. Seth had always been a part of my life. He wasn't always a good part, but he was there nevertheless. We went from childhood friends to betrothed, to enemies, to friends again, then back to enemies, and now whatever this was. He would always be a piece of me, and I couldn't leave him behind.

"You have made some very bad decisions, Seth, and you have hurt me too many times to count. But I realize that you have only ever made those decisions because you were backed against a wall. You did the best you could with what you were given, and I can't overlook that," I squeezed his hands. "It's going to take time to regain my trust, but as for my friendship, you have it."

Guilt once again clouded his features as he took in what I had just told him. "I never lied about my feelings for you, Siv. I have loved you ever since we were kids, but I have failed you over and over again. I am so sorry for everything, and I truly mean that. I've always meant that," he admitted, looking down at our hands. "Tell me the plan," he said, looking back at me. "I want to be on the right side this time."

I repeated exactly what Jude had told me to do, and Seth listened carefully to everything. I would never admit to it, but his working with me provided me with both comfort and confidence. The fear that I had felt when I thought about going down to the dungeons on my own was slightly lifted as well. I was thankful that he agreed to help me, no matter how risky it was. I refused to think about how many things could go wrong. Instead, I let the excitement of being reunited with Jude fuel my motivation to go through with it.

I smiled at Opal as she put the finishing touches on my face and topped my head with the same diamond tiara I had worn the night before, but this time, it was adorned with a long and transparent veil. "You girls can go ahead and leave us now," she told the servants, who were still fidgeting with the extravagant white wedding gown I was wearing. Once everyone had been ushered out of my chambers, she turned to me. "You know what to do?" She asked.

I nodded my head. "I do," I told her as I pulled her in for a hug. "Thank you."

She stilled for a moment before she returned the hug. "Don't thank me," she whispered. "I've taken part in the atrocious acts of this country for too long now. It's long overdue to put an end to it all," she said before she pulled away and held me at arm's length. "Don't underestimate yourself tonight. Remember who you are, Siv."

Her choice of words was too concise to be a coincidence. Iridia had said the exact same thing to me before she had died. She had told me that my ancestors were rooting for me and that she was too. I closed my eyes and smiled, silently thanking Iridia before looking back to Opal. "I know who I am," I told her.

Opal's eyes were brimmed with tears, and her lips slightly quivered before she turned away from me. "Good, now let's make sure *they* know who you are," she said with conviction as she led me to the front of the room where Seth had been waiting for me.

He wore a white jacket that matched my gown perfectly, and his hair had been slicked back, which added an emphasis to his handsome face. In another life, I would have swooned at his appearance. Instead, I took in each of his features and memorized them, hoping that I'd see them once again after this was all over. I knew the risks of tonight, and I knew the odds of us both leaving this place were slim.

I pushed those thoughts from my mind and took his arm. "You look very handsome," I told him with a genuine smile.

He returned my smile, but it didn't reach his eyes. Seth's face was filled with sadness as he looked me over. "I only wish we could truly enjoy ourselves for once," he told me. "You make a stunning bride, Siv."

I chuckled and rolled my eyes. "I look like one of those glass dolls they never let us play with back at the palace," I answered him. "But thank you."

Seth snickered at my comment. "I can't argue with that." I started walking toward the door, but he pulled me back to him. "Siv, if tonight doesn't go well-"

I put my hand up to stop him. "Tonight is going to go perfectly. We're going to be okay and when this is all over with, we'll finally get to start fresh," I told him. "It'll be a new world and you can be whatever and whoever you want to be. We won't have anyone standing over us, telling us what to do or punishing us if we refuse. You will get to be your own person, Seth."

Seth stared at me for a long time before he finally nodded. "You're right," he said, once again offering his arm and leading me out the door and to the lift.

The lift opened, revealing the Grand Hall filled with Vaegarians. Their laughter echoed through my ears, and the sweet aroma of pastries and desserts filled the air. It would have been easy to forget that tonight would end in a battle if it weren't for my shaking hands and sweaty palms. A servant with a platter of chalices walked in front of us, and I grabbed one before she walked in the opposite direction.

Seth looked at me hesitantly. "I'm going to need some liquid courage if we're going to go through with this," I told him, trying to justify my actions.

I took a large swig of the liquid inside of the chalice and instantly regretted my decision. It was not wine that had been inside, but blood. I ran to the nearest bin, which happened to be in the farthest corner of the hall and vomited while Seth did his best to hold my hair out of my face. I was disgusted and couldn't stop hurling, even after the contents of my stomach had been completely emptied.

I lifted my head when I heard an uproar of laughter. The Empress and her court of Ladies all stood behind me and seemed to find great amusement in my body's reaction to their repulsive diet.

"Someone should have warned you, my dear. I will find someone to get you a special glass that only contains libations suited for your kind. What do you like, wine, ale, malt liquor?" Empress Marie asked with a look of pure enjoyment.

I wiped my mouth with the back of my hand. "Why was that chalice filled with blood?" I asked, trying my best to hide my shock and disgust.

Her expression transformed into annoyance when she took in my tone, and she straightened her back as she looked down at me with harsh eyes. "How do you think we maintain our youth, my child? The blood of the young and innocent fuel our eternal lives," she said with a cold smile. "However, every now and then, we dine on the blood of our own. It's a special delicacy, and this batch is extremely fresh, making the taste absolutely divine. It does nothing for our beauty, but it is a real treat nevertheless." She began to walk away, but she turned back to face me. "Actually, I believe that you knew the Vaegarian we're drinking from. What was that stylist's name?" She asked one of her Ladies.

The strawberry blonde giggled slightly before she answered, "Opal, Empress. Her name was Opal."

My face went pale, and I backed into Seth's chest, who placed his arms supportively around my waist. "Breathe, Siv," he whispered in my ear.

The Empress slightly smirked as she watched Seth try his best to comfort me. "One of her girls accused her of making contact with a known traitor," she said, examining my expression. "My husband and I do not take insubordination lightly, Siv. Opal knew the risks of her actions, and now you do too." She turned back to her Ladies and continued walking into the crowds of people.

I waited until I could no longer see her before I turned and buried my face into Seth's chest. I quietly sobbed for my friend as he held me. "Does this mean she knows, Seth? I asked him. "Did she just tell us she knows about our plan?"

Seth pulled me from his chest and bent down to look me in the eyes. "No. She doesn't know anything. If she did, you would have been locked up, and I would have been drained and inside several of those chalices by now," he told me sternly. "She said herself, they don't take insubordination lightly. Do you really think we'd be freely wandering around if they knew anything?"

I nodded, choosing to believe he was right. Seth had to be right. There wasn't another plan if this one didn't work, and I knew that the best way to make sure Opal's death was not in vain was to succeed. I owed her that. I owed it to everyone back in Saleda. There was no going back now, and Seth and I knew that. So, I wiped my eyes, trying my best not to ruin the last works of Opal, and I marched straight into the crowd with him following close behind. My eyes roamed the crowd until I found the Emperor, and I began pushing through bodies to get to him.

Seth pulled me back by my shoulder and turned me around. "What're you doing?"

I pointed in the direction of the Emperor. "I'm going to go speak to him."

His eyebrows creased, and he looked down at me as if I was insane. "Why? How could that possibly help us at the moment? Let's just hang back in the shadows until it's time for the toast."

"The Empress may not know our plan, but she's obviously on the fence about our loyalty. Hiding in the shadows is the worst way to prove we're not traitors. Now, I'm going to go speak to the Emperor, and you're going to come with me. We're going to act like nothing is going on and like we're just some soon-to-be-wed couple who are hopelessly in love with one another," I whispered to him with a stern look on my face.

Although I didn't want to admit it, Opal's death made me worry about the safety of Jude and everyone else with him outside of this tower. I didn't want to speak with the Emperor or his wife, but I knew it would make us seem inconspicuous, and I would do anything to keep our position hidden until the time was right. So I continued to march into the crowd of tall and pale bodies until Seth, and I joined the group that surrounded the Emperor.

His eyes landed on me immediately, and he brushed off the man he had been speaking to and turned toward us. "Ah, I was wondering when I would see you two!" He shouted.

I curtsied, and Seth bowed, which seemed to please him. "How is my exquisite little Queen? I've been worried about you since you left the city," he said as he made his way beside me, pushing Seth out of the way. I began to feel nauseous when the Emperor began rubbing my arm in a very sensual manner.

Seth cleared his throat in an obvious attempt to redirect Emperor Andrew's attention. "We're both very grateful that you sent your own personal physician to check up on Siv. Your hospitality means the world to us."

The Emperor briefly acknowledged Seth's comment with a nod before he diverted his gaze back to me. "I've been meaning to ask your sweet bride if she would allow me the pleasure of having a moment alone with her. I've been very eager to get to know her," he told Seth while he looked me up and down.

Seth looked between me and his great-great-grandfather before he forced a grin. "I'm sure there will be plenty more opportunities for that. Why don't we enjoy the feast and save the talk for a more quiet and calm occasion," he offered hopefully.

Emperor Andrew's gaze left my body and swiftly landed on Seth. His lips drew back in a snarl for a brief moment before his face lost all emotion. "Surely you're not denying your Emperor, Seth," he said, emphasizing Seth's name without his title. "You were just thanking me for my hospitality, and now you blatantly disrespect me in front of my guests?"

The chatter that had been surrounding us only moments before turned to silence as several pairs of eyes began staring at the situation unfolding before them. My jaw tightened as I realized just how badly this could go if I didn't accept the Emperor's invitation. I quickly looked to Seth, offering a tight smile before I turned to Emperor Andrew. "Forgive him; he only just got me back from the rebels and he's coveted every moment with me since," I said, smiling to the crowd.

The Emperor laughed and patted Seth on the back. "Who could blame you for that?" He said, looking at the crowd who laughed along with him. "If I were you, I don't think we would have even made it to tonight's feast. We'd both lose all sense of time after all the things I'd do to her," he said, licking his lips as his eyes roamed my body.

I swallowed my repulsion and squeezed Seth's hand, urging him not to do or say anything to put our plan in jeopardy. The Emperor's crude humor did nothing to ease my anxieties about being alone with him, but I couldn't think about that. I incessantly reminded myself of the bigger picture. I had to remember Opal, Iridia, and the countless others who had died fighting against this country.

"Shall we go now? I wouldn't want to miss too much of the feast," I said with as much charm as I could.

The Emperor smiled and offered his arm to me, which I accepted. I began following him out of the crowd, but I couldn't help but look back at Seth. When my eyes met his, he tried his best to offer me a comforting smile, but the worry and sadness that filled his expression did nothing to quiet down the alarms that my body had set off within me.

I was led into a private lift and stood awkwardly beside the Emperor as we were taken up to the very top floor. "Not many have the privilege of seeing the very top of the Crystal Tower," he told me as he pressed a code into a large door. "This is my observatory. I cherish my time alone up here. In fact, even Marie has only stepped foot up here a handful of times."

My mouth dropped as he finally opened the large door. The roof of the room was made completely out of glass and the walls were too. It was as if we were floating hundreds of feet up in the air. I looked up to see the night sky. I couldn't see as many stars as I had in Mendacia due to all the lights in the city, but it was beautiful nonetheless. "I've never seen anything like this," I said to myself, still looking up.

I tensed when I felt Emperor Andrew's cold hands on my shoulders. "Not many have," he said in a low voice. "You can come up here any time you'd like, Siv."

I pulled away from his touch but smiled. "That's a very nice offer."

"It's an offer that no one else has ever received," he said sternly, looking offended that I had distanced myself.

"Thank you," I answered quietly. I was becoming increasingly uncomfortable as he continued to move closer, and I did my best to keep my face void of the turmoil I felt inside. I cursed myself for thinking this was a smart idea as his hand found its way to my sleeved arm, and he began rubbing up and down.

The Emperor smiled as he looked me over. "All I ask in return for the hospitality that I have shown you and that boy of yours is that you come when I call on you. That's fair, don't you think?" He asked me. "You could have a very comfortable life here if you wish. There's no need for you to ever return to Saleda."

My brows knitted together as I tried to process what he was asking of me. "I'm not sure I understand. What would you call on me for? How would Seth and I rule over Saleda from here?" I asked although I was unsure I wanted him to answer.

He laughed loudly before he effortlessly picked me up and carried me to the sofa that looked out over the city underneath the observatory. He sat me on his lap and my eyes remained glued on the view in front of me, trying to avoid his gaze. "Your innocence intrigues me. You see, my sweet Siv, I am a man of many needs," he said in a husky voice. "*You* have quickly become one of those needs." His hands began massaging my thighs, making me tense. "As for Seth, he has just been a means to an end. We both know you've been putting on a false display of affection for the boy. Any man could see that. Do you really think our Sacred heir would be from him? He barely has any Vaegarian blood running through his veins." The Emperor laughed as if what he had just divulged was common sense, and I was silly for not seeing it sooner.

"If he is not to be the father, then who would?" I reluctantly asked the vile man.

His smile faded, and his expression turned hungry. "Me, of course." The hair on my arms stood straight up as his grip on my waist tightened, and he pulled me tighter to his chest. "Marie doesn't know this part of the plan quite yet, but she will fall in line eventually. She always does."

I looked frantically around the room for an exit, but I had to remind myself there was nowhere to go. I needed a code for the private lift, and even if I were to somehow get through, what would happen? I would put everything at risk. I loudly swallowed as I accepted my fate at that moment. I told myself I could get through whatever was to come as long as I kept the bigger picture in mind. I would see Jude and Mia soon. There would never be a sacred heir, and no child of mine would ever be related to these people. I would bring this Dynasty down one way or another.

The Emperor slowly pulled my hair away from my neck and I felt tears running down my face as he began softly kissing my skin. "This will only hurt for a second," he whispered and a sharp pain in my neck spread throughout my entire body, and I realized that he had cut me with a small blade from his coat pocket. I struggled against him and tried my hardest to get away from him, but he tore his mouth from me, and his grip became unbearably tight. "Relax, darling. I'm not going to hurt you. I've just been dying for a little taste of your Nativus blood," he whispered before his teeth once again bit down on my flesh.

I started to sob at that point, and the top of my white gown became damp with both my tears as well as my blood that was running down my neck and chest. "Stop! Please!" I begged him, but he only laughed at my feeble attempts to escape his grasp.

Emperor Andrew finally pulled his mouth from me, and he moaned loudly. "You have no idea how magnificent you taste." He slid his tongue from my chest and up to my neck, savoring every last drop of blood on my skin. "You will have me wrapped around your finger in no time, my sweet little Queen."

I felt disgusted as his hands began to fondle my body, and I once again tried to distance myself from his grip, but I had become weak from how much blood he had taken from me. I could do nothing as I sat against him. I was powerless at that moment, and my mind began to shut down. My body didn't feel like my own any longer; I forced myself to believe that it wasn't me who was being assaulted. I was downstairs with Seth, drinking wine and pretending to laugh at jokes. I had never followed this man into the observatory. I had never had my own blood stolen from me by him, and he wasn't currently touching me.

"As much as I hate to ruin this moment, we should get going. I would hate for my lovely Siv to miss the feast that is being thrown in her honor," The Emperor said as he lifted me up from his lap and turned me around to look at him. He cursed under his breath when he saw that my white gown had been stained crimson at the very top. "Not much we can do about it now," he said, shrugging. "It would be wise to avoid my wife's gaze. She doesn't fancy the idea of another woman having my eye."

My limbs felt so weak as I followed him out the door and into the private lift and my mind was still in a fog. I stared straight ahead as we passed floor after floor. I refused to look at the Emperor beside me. I wanted to pretend that nothing had happened. I wanted to forget about everything.

I squeezed my eyes shut as I felt his cold grip on my shoulder. "It's okay to admit you liked it," he whispered.

CHAPTER 27

I felt sick as the lift door finally opened, and I didn't wait for him to escort me back into the Grand Hall. I hastily walked toward the sounds of music and laughter despite feeling as if I was going to faint. When I entered the room, I rushed through the crowd, desperately trying to find Seth. I felt eyes staring into me and my bloodied dress as I pushed my way through the Vaegarians when I finally spotted Seth's short blonde hair and white jacket. A wave of relief came over me as I made my way to him, and my arms wrapped around him the moment I got close enough.

Seth turned around and looked me up and down. Apprehension clouded his expression before anger transformed his face as he saw the blood soaking my dress. He pulled me against him and held me tightly. I didn't care that we were in a room full of Vaegarians and that they were all fixated on the scene unfolding before them. I was in desperate need of comfort, and I had found it in Seth's embrace. The tears had never stopped streaming down my face, and I sobbed into Seth's chest as he continued to hold me.

"I'm going to kill him," Seth growled quietly. "I don't care if I die in the process. He is going to pay for this."

For whatever reason, his words had finally brought me back to reality, and I pulled myself from him. "We will get our chance," I told Seth and wiped away the tears that covered my face.

"This is my fault. I knew he was up to no good. I shouldn't have let you leave with him."

I shook my head. "It's no one's fault but his, and he will have to answer for it before the night is over," I said, cringing at the thought of the Emperor's cold hands touching me. "But for now, we have to pretend as if everything is fine. I have to pretend like everything is fine," I said, more to myself than him.

Seth nodded just as the servants at each corner of the Grand Hall began ringing a bell and everyone turned toward the Crystal Thrones in the back of the room. Bile began to rise from my stomach as I looked upon the man who had just violated me, and almost as if he could sense my gaze, he smirked at me.

"Thank you all for being here and celebrating such a rare and special occasion with us here at the Crystal Tower," the Emperor began, still looking at me.

I broke eye contact with him and tugged on Seth's cuff. "Be ready to go," I whispered to him.

"As you all know, we have a very special guest here with us tonight, but we aren't only celebrating her. No, we are celebrating the union between her and my great-great-grandson, King Seth, and the life that they will create together. The life that will give this Dynasty more power than we have ever known," Emperor Andrew announced, causing the crowd to cheer. I tried my best not to roll my eyes at the lies he spewed now that I knew he had planned to dispose of his own flesh and blood at his earliest convenience and use me to fulfill his plan to take over all of Lorus.

"Our patience and our diligent planning have finally paid off as we stand in the midst of the child in the prophecy, the Giver of Life!" He shouted, and once again, the crowds cheered loudly. "So now, let us all acknowledge and honor the womb of our little Queen by raising our chalices. To the Giver of Life!"

The crowd all raised their cups and repeated after the Emperor. "*To the Giver of Life!*"

As they brought their cups to their lips and sipped on the blood of those they had slayed, each of their eyes was closed and Seth and I quickly began to sneak toward the hallway with the portraits. When we arrived, I slipped my hand behind the portrait of Edmond. I felt a small envelope and smiled.

"Got it," I told Seth.

I handed him the key and tried my best to keep up with him as we sprinted to the stairwell.

Seth turned and looked at me with an expression filled with worry. "Siv, are you okay?"

I nodded but almost lost my footing as we descended. "He just took so much," I said, rubbing my sore neck that still had not stopped bleeding.

He took one more look at me before he shook his head and lifted me into his arms.

"Seth, no. I'm fine. This is going to slow us down too much," I whispered into his ear from behind.

"Just catch your breath first. Your face is almost as pale as theirs, and we're going to really be slowed down if you pass out," he said, running down the steps. "Something tells me this would have been a lot easier if we weren't wearing formal evening wear."

It was almost funny as I took a second to look at the both of us. The long train to my white wedding gown flowed behind us as he hurried down the stairwell with me on his back. I would have laughed if it weren't for the seriousness of our situation and how so many things had already gone wrong.

Seth came to an abrupt stop, and I looked up from his shoulder to see a small servant staring wide-eyed at him. Seth put both arms up and tried to tell her that we had gotten lost, but I recognized her. She was the servant that had escorted me to my chambers earlier. She was one of the servants that I was sure Sir Vincent had been doing experiments on.

I clumsily hopped down from Seth's grasp. "Lise?" I asked.

Her eyes fell on me and then to my neck. She stared at the fresh wound for a while before she looked back into my eyes. "Who did that to you?" She asked me.

My hand instinctively rubbed my sore neck, and I flinched as I answered her. "The Emperor."

She looked in between Seth and me for a brief moment, seemingly trying to make a decision about something before she nodded toward us. "The dungeon is this way," she said, leading us down the stairwell. "I wouldn't stay long, though. Anyone who goes down there never comes back up. Besides Sir Vincent." I winced at the mention of that awful man but nodded.

Seth's green eyes flickered with unease as he glanced at me.

"We can trust her," I told him.

Lise led us to the door and paused in front of it. "She lifted up the hem of her gray uniform and took out a blade. "A large man with a scar across his face told me to give this to the Queen of Saleda," she told me as she placed the dagger into my hands. "He told me to tell you to do whatever it takes to make it outside and that he'll be waiting for you."

I smiled as I clutched the familiar Krig blade in my hands. I knew Jude was there and now I had all the more reason to continue on with this plan. "Thank you," I told Lise, pulling her frail body in for a hug.

"Are you really the child from the prophecy?" She asked quietly.

I let her go from my embrace but kept my hands on her shoulders. "I am," I told her.

She smiled. "Kill them all," she told me.

Seth stepped closer to us and placed a hand on my shoulder. "Siv, we have to go."

Lise scurried up the stairs as we opened the door to the dungeon. Nothing could have prepared me for what we saw. When I had thought about this dungeon before, I thought it would look similar to the cells we had underneath the palace in Mendacia. I thought the walls and floors would consist of stone, and there would be bars lining each cell down a long and narrow hallway. I thought the pungent smells of human waste and blood would fill our nostrils as we made our way toward the back. Instead, bright fluorescent lighting, like I had never seen before, lit up the entire area, and it smelled like cleaning solvents and chemicals. Both the floor and walls consisted of white tile and each space was separated, not by bars, but by thin curtains.

Most of the thin cots in each space were empty but as we made our way toward the back, a consistent beeping could be heard. Seth and I both looked at one another with confusion before he pulled back one of the curtains. I gasped as I stared at the woman on the cot. Her head had been shaved, and tubes and needles were attached to both of her arms, and when I pulled back the next curtain over, there was another woman in the same condition.

"We need to get them all out of here," I told Seth as I began pulling the needles from her arms. "What are they doing to them? How many do you think are down here?" I began to ask him as I frantically looked at all of the curtains around me. They didn't look as if they were the pregnant servants Sir Vincent had been testing on, but they did look extremely unwell.

Seth pulled me from the woman. "Maybe this is where their blood supply comes from, I'm not sure. We can't stop for anything, though, remember? We're already running behind, and to be quite honest, I'm surprised no one has come down here looking for us yet. They have to have noticed our absence from the feast by now. We have to pull the levers and get out of here!"

I shook my head and looked back at the woman on the cot. "Seth, we can't leave them! Look at what they've done to her! How can we believe that we are any better than these people if we just leave them here to die."

Seth ran his hands through his neat hair, messing it up. "Fine. You get them, and I'll pull the levers. I have no idea what is going to happen once I do, though. Hopefully, they can walk on their own because we need to be quick if we're going to get out of here alive."

I nodded, continuing to pull the needles from the woman's arm, and I jumped back when she sat straight up and began screaming. I placed my hand over her mouth in an attempt to quiet her. "It's okay! It's okay! I'm here to help you."

The woman turned toward me, and when I saw her eyes, I pulled my hand from her mouth and began stepping away from her. Her eyes were entirely black. There was no iris or pupil, just blackness. She smiled slightly before she opened her mouth, revealing a split tongue and sharpened teeth.

"What did they do to you?" I whispered as I continued to back away from her.

The woman sprang from the cot and jumped on top of me, pinning me down to the floor. I used all the strength I had to keep her sharpened teeth from tearing at my face, but I was still so weak and could feel my arms begin to shake. I realized that I must have dropped the dagger as I fell, and I began to panic as I searched my surroundings. I finally spotted it about an arms-length away from me on the white tile floor. I knew I was out of options, so I turned to the side and braced myself as her sharpened teeth began to clamp down on my shoulder. I screamed in agony as I reached for the dagger and stabbed the woman's back with as much force as I could muster up.

I cursed as I pushed her limp body off myself. I flinched as my fingers grazed over my shoulder. I could feel the mangled pieces of flesh and muscle underneath the warmth of the blood that flowed from the wound. Ripping the rest of the sleeve from my white satin gown, I tied the material tightly around my shoulder. My eyes squeezed shut, and I cursed again when I realized there would be no saving Sir Vincent's victims down here. I screamed loudly from both the physical pain as well as frustration that overwhelmed my body. There were no words to describe the amount of hatred and wrath I felt toward the Emperor, Empress, and all those who supported them. Adrenaline pushed me to stand up, and I forced my legs into a jog toward the end of the vile dungeon.

When I finally reached the back wall, Seth was nowhere to be found. The familiar feeling of dread seeped into my veins as I began calling his name, but there was no response. I chewed on my bottom lip as I tried to figure out what to do. We had already lost so much time, and I needed to pull the levers before I could make it outside of the tower, but I couldn't leave Seth wherever he had gone.

I loudly groaned as I ran from the back wall in search of him, but came to a halt when I saw Seth's polished black shoes peeking out from underneath one of the white curtains blocking off a small space. I gripped my dagger tightly and took a deep breath before I ripped the curtain back. The space was empty except for Seth's unconscious body. I crouched down beside him, examining his head where a large bruise had already begun to form. He was still breathing, which brought me some relief, but it didn't last long. I called on every last bit of strength that I had left in my drained body and pulled his body to the back of the room with me. I knew that we were not alone. I couldn't be sure if it was a Vaegarian or one of the monsters they had created that had done this to Seth, but I really did not want to find out.

I set him down gently and placed Jude's dagger beside him so I had both of my hands-free to pull the levers. My hand had barely touched the first one when the sound of someone clicking their tongue pulled my attention, and I turned to see Sir Vincent. "You didn't think this would be easy, did you?" He slowly prowled toward me with a slight grin on his otherwise emotionless face. "The Emperor and Empress have guards searching for you all over the tower, but I find you down here in my *locked* research facility? You've had help from the inside, no doubt." I stumbled backward until I felt the handle of the levers pressing into my back. "And you've killed one of my test subjects. Do you have any idea how much hard work you let go to waste by doing that?"

My heart pounded against my chest. "What have you done to them?" I asked with a shaky voice.

Sir Vincent grinned as he looked around at the several curtained spaces, most of which contained his *test subjects*. "This Dynasty is known for its superior technology in weaponry, but thanks to my commitment to science, I have created the best weapon yet," he began telling me with confidence. "I have finally found a use for Saledians, other than being a source of eternal life for my people, of course. When I am finished with my work, these subjects will be a part of an entire army of biologically-engineered soldiers. They have no needs, no wants, and they will never disobey an order. They will have one purpose: to kill off anyone who refuses to bow down to the Emperor and Empress." Sir Vincent's eyes grazed my shoulder. "It looks like you've already had a taste of what they can do to a person."

Revulsion replaced the panic that I had felt only moments before, and I scowled at the twisted man standing in front of me. "You are sick," I spat at him. "They are not your subjects! They are people with family and friends. Their lives meant something before you made them into these monstrosities!" I screamed.

He laughed loudly and stepped closer to me. "*Saledian* lives mean nothing to me. They are the vermin of Lorus. If it weren't for Emperor Andrew's fixation with you and his wife's obsession with your precious womb, I would have killed you already. But unfortunately, they've ordered that you be delivered back to them alive." Sir Vincent lunged for me, but I dodged his grip, which irritated him even further. "Do not make this more difficult than it has to be!" He yelled, charging at me again.

I tried to avoid him, but he gripped the long locks of hair that Opal's girls had sewn into my own shorter strands. Pain emanated from my scalp as he dragged me along toward the front of the dungeon. I screamed from both agony and frustration as I tried to strike him with my fists, and he laughed in amusement at my weak attempts. "You are no different from them. You always fight despite knowing that you are weak and defenseless against my kind. It's quite humiliating, no?"

He continued to drag me by my hair as I did everything I could to break free. I kicked and clawed at the ground repeatedly until my body had nothing left to give. I closed my eyes and silently apologized to everyone I had failed as Sir Vincent lugged my limp body closer and closer to the door.

Despair and hopelessness had enveloped me when suddenly all of the lights flickered off before turning back on slightly dimmer. Sir Vincent came to a stop and loosened his grip on my hair, causing my head to fall on the cold tiled floor. He cursed under his breath as he quickly turned toward the back of the room. "You stupid boy!" He yelled. And I turned my head to see that Seth was jogging toward us, and I instantly knew he had pulled the levers.

"I was going to let you live! I was going to let the Emperor and Empress decide your fate since you're their blood. But now, *now* you are going to die!" Sir Vincent yelled as Seth effortlessly grabbed the Krig blade from his belt and skillfully pierced the scientist's chest before he had a chance to even react. Sir Vincent gasped, and I looked up to see the blade sticking out of his chest. He looked down and pulled the blade from his flesh. "You have no idea what you've done," he choked, blood streaming from his mouth. "My mind cannot be replaced. You have doomed this Dynasty and your family along with it." Sir Vincent told Seth as he struggled to breathe. He clutched at his chest as he bled out, and within seconds, he lay lifeless on the floor beside me.

"That was easy enough," Seth said as he picked up the Krig blade from the floor and handed it to me. "Hold onto this."

CHAPTER 28

With a heavy limp, Seth wasted no time as he somehow picked me up despite his own injuries and carried me out of the dungeon. He remained silent as he struggled to climb the steps in the narrow stairwell, and I allowed myself that time to process everything that had just happened. It was hard to accept that we didn't have the time, knowledge, or numbers to save Sir Vincent's victims. If we were to win this battle we had to continue without them, and despite the pain it caused me, I knew nothing could be done. I also knew that I was in shock, and I reminded myself that I couldn't let my mind shut down this time. Tonight was only just beginning, and I couldn't afford to fall apart like I had during the battle in the palace. Despite my weakened state, I needed to stay sharp.

After a few minutes, I looked up at Seth and squeezed his shoulder. "Thank you," I told him. "If it weren't for you, everything would have been lost."

Seth's gaze remained straight ahead. "I owe you for all of the pain I've caused, and I'm going to need you to live a long life in order for me to pay off my debt."

I chuckled at his response, and I motioned him to let me down. "I can walk from here," I told him. "Sir Vincent said there are guards all over the tower looking for us. I'm not sure what will be waiting for us when we open that door, but we'll have to get to the back of the first floor. That's our only way outside."

Seth nodded but then frowned as he took in my appearance. "Siv, can you even run?" He asked me with a doubtful tone. "I don't even know how you're still standing."

I wanted to fake a smile and reassure him that I'd be fine, but I had to remain realistic. My body had just received one beating after another tonight, and to make matters worse, I was already weakened by the amount of blood the Emperor had stolen from me. I flinched as I thought of his touch but shook the memory away. "Honestly, I don't know. But we really don't have a choice. Saleda's only chance depends on us getting outside of this tower, and I will put everything I have left into making that happen. I will crawl if I have to."

He looked me up and down again and seemed to hesitate before returning his focus to my eyes. "Saleda's only chance depends on *you* getting outside of this tower. Not me."

I shook my head. "Seth, no. I need you. I couldn't have done any of this without your help. Saleda needs you just as much as it needs me," I pleaded with him.

Seth smiled slightly as he gently set me down on the cold stone steps, but his green eyes were filled with regret. "You and I both know that's not true, Siv. I've done more harm than good." He started to climb the last few stairs before reaching the door, and just before he opened it, he turned back to me. "Thank you for never giving up on me," he told me as I tried my best to stand and rush after him. "I'm going to pay my debt in full tonight, and you're going to make it out that door."

"Seth, stop!" I screamed after him.

He opened the door slightly. "I love you, Siv," he said softly before sliding out the door.

I collapsed as I finally reached the steps right before the door. I squeezed my eyes shut while I covered my mouth with my hands. I could do nothing but listen to the loud shouts and screams on the other side for several minutes until there was nothing but silence.

I slowly opened the door and peeked outside. There were several Vaegarian guards lying lifeless on the ground. I didn't have to witness what happened to know that Seth had taken down several guards before they had finally subdued him. He had offered himself up as a distraction so that I could make it outside the tower. Seth had always been talented with a sword, but he could have never won against all of them, and he had to have known that. I found myself hoping that they had killed him when I saw the bright red stains that were spread across the floor and down the hall. I didn't want to think about what they would do to him if they kept him alive. Some things were worse than death.

I shook my head of those thoughts and peered around to see only one Vaegarian standing guard on the first floor. I knew there was only a matter of time before more guards were sent down here to replace those Seth had killed, and I inhaled deeply before stepping out and silently closing the door behind me. My body ached as I slowly walked toward the door at the back of the room.

"Stop right there!" The guard yelled and began to run toward me.

I turned around to face him, holding Jude's Krig dagger behind my back. I smiled as he neared me, knowing his orders must be to keep me alive, or he would have struck me down already. "As you can see, I've been involved in quite a bit tonight and I only wish to be escorted back to the Emperor and Empress. I never wanted to escape; I was taken against my will," I told him in a sweet and gentle tone.

The guard surveyed me and seemed to believe that I was in distress, thanks to my condition. "Follow me. I'll get you to safety, and we can call a medic to tend to your wounds," he said with his hand outstretched.

I looked over his uniform and realized the only bit of skin that wasn't concealed by his armor was his face and neck. I knew I'd have to get closer to him in order for my blade to make contact. So I took his hand, still gripping my dagger behind my back, and used my weakened state to my advantage. I let my knees give out underneath me and looked up at him with an embarrassed expression, letting a few tears fall. "I don't think I can walk any further," I cried.

The guard looked down at me with a brief look of annoyance before he bent down to pick me up. I waited until his face was close before I buried my dagger deep into his flesh. He didn't have time to scream before I tore the blade from his neck and fell to the floor along with him. I wasted no time and forced my body up, clumsily making my way to the back door of the tower.

I ignored the shock I felt creeping up on me from killing the guard and pulled on the handle of the door. I took a deep breath of the crisp outside air just as I felt an agonizing pain spread throughout my entire body. I fell to my knees on the cold, hard ground, barely a foot outside of the Crystal Tower, and looked down to see a spear had torn straight through my abdomen. I looked back to see that Empress Marie had been the one to throw it.

She watched me collapse with a look of horror clouding her features before she ran to me and assessed the damage she had caused. "No, No!" She screamed, holding my stomach firmly with both of her hands. "I didn't mean to! I just wanted to stop you!" She cried, and I watched as blood spread throughout the white satin material of my torn gown.

The metallic taste of blood flooded my mouth as I smiled up at the distressed Empress. She looked down at me and furrowed her brows with confusion just as I summoned the last of my strength and thrust the dagger deep into her side. She fell beside me and shrieked as her porcelain skin had become wrinkled and transparent. Her once copper hair had turned white and thinned dramatically. I waited until her screams became quiet moans and then nothing at all before I finally let my head rest on the cold ground beneath me, and I started to close my eyes until I heard a familiar voice screaming behind me.

Within seconds, Mia had run to me and pulled my body into her lap as he assessed my injuries. I felt her hands shaking as she applied pressure to my bleeding stomach. "You're going to be okay. We'll get a healer to help you. It's fine, you'll heal, and you'll be okay," she repeated over and over, trying to convince herself of his words more than me.

Billy arrived shortly after my sister and paused when she saw us. I watched her as she took in my condition, and I knew it wasn't good when she showed no urgency to find a healer for me. She crouched beside Mia, placing her hand on her shoulder, and said nothing as she stared at the gaping hole in my abdomen.

Mia shook Billy's hand off and turned toward her, still keeping her unsteady hands on my wound. "Go get help!" She screamed at her. "Why are you just sitting here, Nabilla? Go get someone!" She screamed again.

Billy didn't move; she just looked at my sister with genuine sympathy and shook her head. "It's too much, Mia. She won't be able to come back from this. Her power isn't strong enough to heal herself yet and she didn't train enough to come back from this," she told her quietly, trying her best and failing to keep me from hearing her.

Mia's focus stayed on Billy until realization dawned on her face and she turned back to me with tears running down the black war paint on her face. At that moment, I knew that I was dying. My chest felt heavy as I thought of leaving Jude, my sister, my friends, and my people behind. A tear escaped my eyes. I knew this was going to be goodbye. But despite all of that, I wasn't afraid. I thought that perhaps *this* was my fate. This was how I would fulfill my destiny. Maybe my death meant the Vaegary Dynasty would never get their hands on a sacred heir, and their plan to conquer Saleda and my people would fail. They would never acquire the type of power they needed in order to do so.

I smiled up at her and placed my hand on top of hers as she cried. "It's okay," I told her, ignoring the blood that filled my mouth as I spoke. "I'm not scared," I reassured her before looking behind her. "Where's Jude? He said he'd be here?" I croaked, afraid that I wouldn't get the chance to say goodbye to him.

Mia looked back to Billy before shaking her head. "Siv, I don't know. He never came back from the tower. We thought he was with you," she answered, sending panic down my spine. "He's okay, though," she backtracked upon seeing the frightened expression on my gaunt face. "He's Jude. He's probably altered his plan without telling anyone so that he can claim hero status as always," she joked, attempting to laugh but failing miserably as the look of pure misery clouded her hazel eyes.

I nodded as I remembered telling him about the Saledian servants and convincing myself he had figured out a way to free them in the meantime. I couldn't ignore the pain of not seeing him before I drifted off into nothingness, but the relief I felt from thinking of the freedom the servants would have helped settle me.

"Siv, please. You have to try to heal yourself. Please, Siv," Mia begged when she noticed me losing consciousness. "This wasn't supposed to happen to you! I was supposed to protect you!" She screamed as she continued to push down on my stomach. My eyes became too heavy, and I didn't have the strength to keep them open, but Mia began to shake me awake. "No, no, no. Stay with me. Keep your eyes open," she pleaded.

I tried to open them, but my body wouldn't cooperate. So, with my eyes closed, I tightened my grip on Mia's hand for the last time. "Finish what we started, Mia. Tell Jude that I love him and tell him to fight for me," I whispered, my voice cracking from the blood that filled my mouth and throat. "I love you."

The agonizing pain that engulfed my entire body was the first thing to go; the warm metallic taste in my mouth became bland, and then the coppery smell of my own blood was lifted. The sound of my sister's cries faded until peaceful silence filled my ears, and then there was nothing. The constant nagging of grief and anguish no longer filled my heart. All of the worries and pressure that had been a weight on my shoulders were suddenly lifted, and the pain that had been inflicted on me that evening was erased from my memory. I was finally free. I was dead.

CHAPTER 29

The peace that had come over me as I lay lifeless on the bare ground didn't last long and gave way to a type of wrath I had never felt before. I screamed in agony as a burning sensation spread throughout my veins. It felt as if my entire body was in flames. The only relief from the burning throughout my body was the memory of the Empress's lifeless body next to me. I couldn't help but smile at the image of her decrepit corpse.

The blackness that filled my vision was replaced by white, and I quickly realized that my body had been covered with some sort of sheet. I ripped the thin fabric from my body, and my hands instinctively raced to the wounds on my neck and shoulder. Although I could feel my skin slightly raised from scarring, I was no longer bleeding. I then looked down to my stomach. A hole in the center of my gown, as well as the scarlet stains on the once-white fabric, was the only evidence of the life-ending injury I had received. Despite the stiffness of my joints and the burning sensation that I still wasn't quite sure about, my body was completely healed. I had done it. I had actually brought myself back from the dead.

I soon remembered my last words to Mia, and the overwhelming sense of finding Jude eclipsed everything else at that moment. When I forced myself up from the cold floor, I didn't recognize my surroundings. Instead of the Crystal Tower being feet away from me, I was surrounded by water. I had been moved onto one of the ships that had transported the rebellion to the Vaegarian Dynasty. I must have been gone for much longer than I had previously thought.

I could see the flames from the fires in the distance and realized that the attack must have begun, but I knew it would take me some time to get back to the Crystal Tower. I did my best to quickly stretch my stiff limbs and exited the large wooden ship. Once I had left the dock, I took off running toward the echoes of explosions. I had lost my shoes at some point in the night, and the sloshing sound of my bare feet sinking into wet mud as I ran became overridden by the sounds of battle. The closer I got, the more my surroundings became littered with mangled and disfigured bodies, most likely caught up in the explosions.

I felt a surge of energy running through my veins, and despite having no idea what I was doing, I placed my bare hands on the mud below me, and the intense sensation of power flowed out of me and into the marred bodies that belonged to rebellion. I waited a moment before I opened my eyes, but when I did, I couldn't believe that it had actually worked. Slowly, and one by one, each rebel soldier began to wake, and their once badly injured bodies were now scarred over. Their leather armor was still stained with their fresh blood, but they were healed altogether. I stood and began running further into battle.

The sounds of movement behind me forced me to turn around, and I couldn't stop the grin that grew on my face as I witnessed the newly healed soldiers pacing behind me. Every mile, I'd stop and heal more fallen rebels, leaving the few dead Vaegarian bodies behind. By the time we had arrived at the center of the battle, I had hundreds of soldiers behind me.

The fighting gradually drew to a halt as more and more began to notice our presence. I ignored their stares, scanning the crowds of warriors for Jude. After a few minutes of searching, Florian rustled his way through the frozen bodies of both the rebellion and the Vaegarians, who still gawked at me.

"Siv?" He asked, slowly approaching me. "I, I thought you were, I thought you were dead," he said as astonishment took over his dirty face.

"I was," I answered him.

Florian finally raced to me and threw his hands around me. "How is that possible?" He cried. "I don't even care. I'm just, nothing would have been the same, Siv."

I hugged him back, but only one thing remained on my mind. "Where's Jude?"

He let go of me and stepped back, his gaze turning toward the blood-stained ground. "He," he paused, trying to find the right words. "He was taken after he made contact with you, Siv."

My chest tightened with alarm. "Where is he, Florian?" I repeated.

Florian looked up at the tower before quickly looking away. "He's gone, Siv."

I followed where his gaze had landed on the Crystal Tower a moment before, and my knees buckled, forcing me to the ground, which was made up of mud and blood. Although it was hard to see at first due to the height of the tower, I made out a large charred body that hung from the balcony of the observatory. Without question, I knew the body belonged to my Jude. I had trouble allowing air to travel through my lungs as my eyes stayed glued on the blackened and burnt remains of Jude. They had desecrated his body, and I knew any hope of bringing him back was lost.

Before I knew what I was doing, I began walking toward the tower, but Florian pulled me back. "What are you doing?" He shouted. "Siv, you have to think straight. To reenter the tower means certain death."

I turned back toward him. "I'm already dead," I answered as I began to turn back around toward the tower.

With every step that I took toward the Crystal Tower, my heart felt as though it got harder and harder, and by the time I walked through those glass doors, I knew something was different inside of me. Something was terribly wrong.

"No one told me that you had become a Krig whore," the chilling sound of the Emperor's voice echoed from the grand staircase that was littered with both Vaegarian and rebel soldiers. "That's no matter. You won't even remember his name by the time we get done with you." He said as he leisurely made his way down the crystal steps, not even glancing at the dead he stepped over.

Ice ran through my veins as I stared at the man I knew to be responsible for Jude's death. I had nothing to say to him. I only wanted to cause him as much pain as he had caused me.

Emperor Andrew laughed at my stillness. "You really did me a favor when you killed my wife," he admitted without emotion. "Our marriage had become fruitless many years ago, and it had been my plan all along to make you mine. I just hadn't thought of a way to kill Marie and take you as my own without anyone realizing what I had done, but you solved that problem for me. Didn't you?"

"I wouldn't plan on anything past this moment if I were you," I seethed.

He laughed again, only this time it was much louder. "Have you forgotten that these walls contain enough ettacao to render your power useless? Besides, you and I both know that you don't have it in you to kill me. Power or not. " He said, turning around and motioning toward the bodies scattered behind him.

"You couldn't save them, you couldn't save your savage beau, and you can't save yourself. Surrender, Siv. Surrender, and I might just let the rest of your friends live long enough to see you become the Empress of Vaegary."

"Would you gamble your life based on that belief?" I asked, glaring at him. I could feel the burning sensation of fire spreading throughout my veins as my anger ignited something deep within me. I had no control over my mind, body, or the power that started to take over. All I felt was the rage that had swallowed me whole the moment I saw Jude's lifeless body hanging from the observatory.

The Emperor's look of amusement vanished, and his face became blank as he looked down at me. "It's time to grow up, Siv." He told me, slowly closing the space between us. "I knew who and what that man was. I don't doubt that you loved the savage, but it's time to see the bigger picture here, my little Queen. He would have gotten you nowhere. What could he have offered you that I could not? He has no land, his title is worth nothing, and he may hold power among his people, but their numbers are minuscule compared to mine. I can offer you the world, Siv. I can hand Lorus over to you on a silver platter. What is love when there is power to be had?"

I felt my hands ball into fists at my side as I listened to him. The anger that surged through me only moments before was now intense hatred and fury. My body began to heat, and my pulse got faster and faster as he inched closer and closer to me.

"Take my hand, Siv. Anything and everything you have ever wanted, I will make sure you will have it," the Emperor told me as he reached for my fisted hand. "I want you. I want to take you as my wife, my Empress, and I want to be the father of the heir that will one day rule all of Lorus."

I allowed him to take my hand. "You must ask for a ceasefire and allow the rebels to leave this land unharmed," I told him as I motioned toward the entry of the tower. "Your guards won't take orders from me. It has to be you."

All of the sounds of the battle raging in front of the tower had been silenced. Both rebel fighters and Vaegarian guards had come to a halt at the sight of my hand in the Emperor's as we walked outside. I turned from Andrew, my hand still in his own as I took in the looks of hurt, anger, and disappointment in the faces of the rebels who had been fighting only moments before, especially those who were Krig. They most likely believed that I was about to disrespect the death of their Chief by leaving them all behind and betraying them with the Emperor.

Emperor Andrew grabbed my other hand and kissed the back of them, for all to see. "Our little Queen has finally come to her senses and has agreed to a union with both me and my country. There will be a ceasefire immediately. This war has ended. Saledians and Krigs alike will leave our land, and no harm will come to them."

I couldn't help the look of disdain that covered my face as I peered back at him, but just as he began to pull me back in the direction of the Crystal Tower, I allowed for all of the hatred, anger, sorrow, and spite inside of me to surge throughout my body and exit through the palm of my hand that the Emperor gripped. To say that I had complete control over my body at that moment would be a lie, but I allowed it to happen nevertheless.

His cold eyes looked up at me as his veins became visible, and they turned black, spreading throughout his entire body. His screams of agony were like music to my ears, and his grip became tight and almost painful as he began to plead for his life. I couldn't help but laugh at the patheticness of his weakened state as he finally dropped to his knees, and seconds later, his body tumbled over, and his grip on my hand fell with him. I had killed him with nothing more than my touch, and yet I felt nothing. Grief and fury rested within me, but I was numb as I looked at each of the Vaegarian soldiers around me.

The look of fear consumed each of their faces as a small smirk formed on my own, and I slowly crouched to the ground, resting my hands on the blood-stained mood beneath me. One by one, each of the soldiers fell to the ground with the same fate as their Emperor. I was consumed in my own wrath and let out a loud cry as power ran from my hands and throughout the vast lands of the Vaegarian Dynasty. Within a few minutes, stillness filled the air, and the cries of Vaegarian misery and pain could no longer be heard. When I opened my eyes, bodies upon bodies of Vaegarian soldiers lay lifeless in the mud.

My body succumbed to the exhaustion tugging at my bones, and I slumped over in the mud. I wasn't sure how long I had been sitting there before the sounds of footsteps sloshing toward me forced me to look up.

"What have you done?" My sister quietly asked as she looked around at the numerous dead Vaegarians.

I used my muddy hand to wipe away the tears that had just started flowing from my red-brimmed eyes. "They killed him, Mia."

My sister avoided my eyes as she continued to look at our surroundings before shaking her head. "You're no different than them now," she whispered loud enough for me to hear. "You're a murderer." Mia took one last look at me. "This isn't what we came here for! You didn't just kill the guards, Siv."

I gathered every last bit of strength I had left to stand. "What do you mean?" I asked her.

Without turning back to me, she shook her head. "Siv, there were innocent Vaegarian servants and civilians that we had secured in one of the buildings outside the tower. They weren't loyal to the Emperor. They wanted freedom just as much as we did. They're all dead. You killed them." she answered before she finally turned back to look at me. "The Queen I fought for would never do this. You're no Queen of mine."

I watched as Mia wiped her face with her dirty sleeve and I wondered if it was sweat she was wiping away or tears. I had never seen her be so cold toward me, and I couldn't fathom why she would choose now to turn her back on me. The Vaegarians had deserved the fate they brought upon themselves. They have taken everything from me. There were no innocents as far as I was concerned. Jude hung from their tower as they killed my people. They dined upon the blood of kidnapped Saledians, whom they forced into servitude so that they could live a life of luxury. They had killed not only the Nativus but almost the entire Krig race as well. Why would I let them live? Why would I extend a mercy to them that they had never even thought of extending to others? If Mia believed that I was a monster for what I had done, I would let her. The sadness from her turning her back on me began to fade, and I was left with the mind-numbing grief and anger that had consumed me only minutes prior.

I watched as Billy and Florian followed my sister out of the battle that took place in front of the Crystal Tower when I noticed Marco making his way out from behind several other rebel soldiers. He sheathed his sword as he walked toward me. "You had every right to end them," he growled.

His support surprised me, but I was in no mood to thank him. He was right; I deserved vengeance. Jude's death would not go unpunished, and their retribution was served by no one's hands but my own. I would not be made to feel guilty for that.

CHAPTER 30

The thing about Willows is that when they do break, they could always be reborn. So when Mia, Billy, and Florian had all left the Vaegarian Dynasty before the sun rose the next day, my heart didn't break for their absence. It fueled me. They, along with others, may have seen my actions as murder and no longer saw me as a sister, friend, or leader, but I did what I had to do, regardless of how they saw my actions or me. I did not regret it.

Only a handful of rebel soldiers accompanied them back to Saleda. I was surprised to see the loyalty toward me that existed within the rebellion, but I was grateful to every single one of them. The Krig warriors still viewed me as Queen, and they vowed to stay here as long as I did. Although I was indebted to them and their service, it was still painful to look upon them. They each resembled Jude in their own unique way, and it was a constant reminder of what I had lost. It was a constant reminder of why I had killed as many Vaegarians as I could.

Marco and many other rebel soldiers had cleared out a few remaining Vaegarians who had been protected by the ettacao that repelled my abilities in the tower. They were now being held in makeshift cells where the battle had taken place the day prior. Marco had also found Seth barely clinging on to life. When he told me of the news, he was still unaware of the friendship we had regained between the two of us, so he was unsure of the reaction I would have to the news. Confusion etched into the creases on his face when I excitedly requested for him to take me to him and promptly healed him using the abilities that I had still not mastered.

The irony of having Seth be one who had chosen to stand by my side after the war was not lost on me. If you had asked who my companions would be after everything, I would have answered Jude and Mia without a second thought, and yet here I was with Jude's cousin and my ex-fiance, whom I had extremely conflicting feelings about not long ago. Despite his flaws, and he had many, Seth had proven to be a loyal friend to me, and I was thankful to have him here.

Jude's charred body had been retrieved from the observatory after several Krig warriors had kicked in the locked door. The body was unrecognizable, but the absence of any sign of him being alive was enough confirmation that it was him. I didn't want to hold out hope for something that I knew to be impossible.

We had performed a traditional Krigsman death ceremony that included burning the rest of his body while they sang songs in their language and performed synchronized dances as his remains became one with the earth. It was truly beautiful, but I had a hard time appreciating it as the hurt from his absence filled every cavity of my heart. It was difficult keeping my mind focused on the path ahead of me rather than the road I had traveled before the war had taken everything away from me, but I kept reminding myself of the promises I had made Jude. The promises to rebuild his country, to give back the power that had been stolen from his people.

The laughter and pure happiness that exuded from the once enslaved Saledians that now danced and walked freely among us was yet another reminder of what the sacrifices I had made had given these people. I would do everything I could to not let my grief get in the way of that. To them, I was their hero, regardless of how I saw myself or how my sister saw me now.

I sat on the edge of the cliff that overlooked the never-ending sea leading back to the Kingdom of Saleda. I tried to push back the feelings of yearning for Jude to be sitting beside me and the grief that threatened to unleash the tears I had been fighting back, but the anger that was never too far away had inched itself back into my heart, replacing the sorrow.

The prophecy had been right, after all.

However, if the child's heart bleeds, they will release death and destruction upon the world.

I wasn't sure if it was my death that had released death and destruction or when my heart broke after seeing Jude's lifeless body hanging from the tower, but one thing was clear. I was not the same Siv who relied on others for protection or comfort. I was no longer naive and I would no longer allow others to take advantage of me or take my right to choose away.

Although most of the Vaegarians involved in this war and the death of Jude and many others were either dead or imprisoned, some had escaped. Emperor Andrew and Empress Marie's court, who had not only allowed them to carry out their atrocities but assisted them, had all somehow fled without being discovered. Edward, who had helped Jude enter the tower and seemingly helped with the plan that got him killed, was nowhere to be found either. Before I could try and rebuild the Krig Empire or protect the civilians of Saleda, I would find the remaining Vaegarians and I would make sure they would never harm anyone again.

Peace was no longer my goal. Revenge was.